C

A KIND OF MUSIC

BLUE

HOTEL PARIS

A KIND OF MUSIC

BITE ON THIS

'Bite on this,' Mavis said, and gave Adeline a half-moon of leather on a string that tied around the wrist: her own invention, she said. Adeline knelt, legs wide, arms thrown over the edge of the double bed, the top of her belly pressing into it. Mavis had rolled back the rug and put down newspaper topped with clean sheeting. Same on the bed. Bleach in the washing water. Cleanliness. Keep visitors away. She had boiled everything sterile, scrubbed her hands three times. 'Bite,' she said, 'not long now.'

The second baby was supposed to come easier, but this little bugger had started off facing out. To bring it round, Mavis had made Adeline crawl up and down the tiled passageway on her hands and knees, time after time, then stand and lean on the end of the bed. Two days. Very little rest. But be grateful it isn't a breech. And be grateful she isn't at York Road: a filthy place, and half the mothers there come out in coffins. And no high-and-mighty doctor charging you the earth. Mavis cost fifteen shillings, however long it took.

Adeline groaned, bit down hard, and when the worst had passed, she spat the leather thing out and a bit of one of her back teeth went with it. She didn't care.

'On your side on the bed, if you don't want to tear,' Mavis said.

'No,' Adeline told her as the pain obliterated all remaining thought, and forced a grunt out between her clenched teeth.

Spit oozed out over the leather thing and ran down her chin, but Mavis got her up on the bed before the next one. A good thing. Her legs were shaking so much she might have sat on it.

'I'll be damned!' Mavis said, minutes later. The cord wound three times round the baby's neck – no wonder he was slow to emerge. She slipped her finger under one of the fleshy loops and tugged it free.

Male, unremarkable, Mavis wrote on the record. Father, Albert Edward Miles, lathe operator. Mother, Adeline Miles. They didn't have a boy's name picked, so Mavis recommended Harry: 'Can be a Henry or a Harold. Works for a king, a ditch-digger or anything in between. Everyone likes a Harry.' Albert's grandfather had been the Henry sort so he was happy with that; Adeline was too tired to care.

Albert took a spade and buried the afterbirth in the square of yard out back, near the outhouse. Put in a tomato plant on top of that, Mavis advised him, though there was not enough light there for anything but the toughest weeds to grow. She brewed tea and waited two hours in case of bleeding and then he paid her the balance owing and a shilling tip for a good job done.

Adeline's baby sister Josephine, seven years younger, was married, too. When Adeline turned weepy and couldn't pull herself back together she came over, got her out of bed and brought her downstairs to sit in the small back room, its windows fogged with the steam from soup-bones boiling.

'Come now, let's count your blessings,' she said. And there were plenty. Adeline was alive, hardly torn, full of milk. She had a healthy baby, despite the business with the cord, so thank goodness Mavis knew her business . . . She had a roof over her head and a younger sister who'd taken her first, George – almost four now – off her hands, and three more sisters who might do the same. A good crop of aunts. One uncle. Still had her mother. She had all that luck, and more. Good food. A husband in skilled work, who didn't drink to excess – a fair, decent man who never hit her and never would.

It was a blessing to have any kind of husband, Josephine pointed out; the war had swallowed so many of them up. She and Adeline the only two sisters married out of five. Adeline and Albert were *both* fortunate: he to have been spared the trenches, she to be the one he selected, despite that she was twenty-seven and rather quiet. She could add, multiply and divide in her head. She spelled well, and wrote neatly, worked hard, showed no signs of religion, gave herself no airs, did not crimp her hair, or spend her time romancing. Albert Edward appreciated all that, and told her so.

It was the first time anyone had ever expressed an opinion about who Adeline was, so she didn't disagree. He talked too much for her comfort, but that was a small thing. He wanted a better kind of life and studied how to get it. He was in favour of *rational choice*. Far better, he said, to have one or two children with full stomachs than six wraiths in one bedroom, half fed, always sick, and most of them ending up in tiny graves. Don't you agree, Adeline? Of course it made sense, though at the same time, wasn't it wrong to go against nature? Wrong, certainly, to talk so much about it? *We must understand each other*, he said. Was that what men and women did? Josephine's Will never asked her opinion. Hardly spoke.

And surely it was better to have your children live, and grow up to work in an office or even teach. *Yes.* But she wished he would spare her the details of the means they'd use to limit their family's size. And did they have to be so strict on the number? Education was the key, and knowledge, power. *Yes.* Also, Albert said, there was strength in the understanding of numbers. Compound interest, especially. They saved every week. Though in respect of Harry, numbers had let them down.

'I don't understand what went wrong,' he said when they realised she was expecting. 'I've been very careful.' He had everything written in a penny notebook: her monthlies, when he'd let himself go. 'Day eight. Well before your egg would be released,' he said, bringing their doings in the darkness of the bedroom right there onto the kitchen table, where they surely did not belong; still, the egg part put her in mind of chickens, and she laughed.

'Well, I didn't *mean* to be laying.' Truth was, they'd done the same as the Catholics did. Plenty of them seemed to be making mistakes too. Perhaps some things couldn't be controlled, and maybe it was better that way, but she didn't say any of that because she had married him, for better or for worse.

'We've money saved. But as for the future – '

The future was what made Adeline weep, though for the life of her she couldn't say why.

'Cheer up now, dear,' Albert said, while she was still weepy and good for nothing. They sat in the room off the kitchen, finishing up the shepherd's pie Josie had brought. 'I promise you won't have to go through it again.'

And hearing that, Adeline, so very lucky as she knew she was, wept even harder, right into the food she was lucky to have.

'So how's he going to make sure of that?' Josephine asked when Albert had gone to stand on the back step for his smoke. 'Is he going to wear a "raincoat" in bed, now?' Josie giggled and Adeline coloured right up.

'We tried one of those,' she whispered, leaned close. 'Smelled like matches. Awful.' She was too shy to mention the nasty look of the thing, The Paragon Sheath it was called, washed and powdered, in its box. Cost two and six. Surely, Albert had said, this was a thing that could be, would be, must be improved upon?

'I don't know what he's planning, and I don't want to. I hope he don't send me to that clinic that's opened up, I'd die.'

'Will doesn't go in for any of that. Best just use a bit of self-control and take what comes.'

Harry woke. He had a very persistent cry, would not be lulled. So she gathered him up, fed him, and wept some more.

Stop it, stop it, she told herself, rubbing her sleeve over her face. Count your darn blessings: Alive, healthy baby. Good milk. Helpful sisters. Mum to mind him when I go back to work. Kitchen, sitting room, running water, convenience out back, rent paid on the dot. Food. Good husband. Better life.

'I wish you didn't tell your sister such intimate things,' Albert told her when he came into bed. He spoke very low because Harry lay between them.

'Oh, but I've got to talk to someone,' she said, 'or I'll go off my rocker like cousin Nellie did.'

'Maybe it could be someone more discreet,' Albert said. And there again was luck: another man might have forbidden it outright, or struck her, or both.

But what would they do now in bed? Make sure to pull the kettle off before it boiled every single time? Stuff herself with some stinking sponge? Would he just leave her alone? No chance of a daughter, ever? Too much care and calculation surely took the pleasure out of things, the surprise out of life.

It helped to talk, to talk to someone not so rational and reasonable as Albert. And it was better to talk to Harry than to talk to empty air. To count the blessings aloud, numbering them, as she unpinned his nappy, scooped out and emptied its liner, chucked the stinking things into the enamel bucket, wiped him clean and fit him up with fresh muslin and towelling.

'So we're both lucky buggers,' she concluded, pushing the pin through the layers. 'One day, I'll stop blubbering like this, and that'll be better still. You're a good listener. You'll be good to your wife. You'll know what she wants.' The blue-grey eyes fastened on her face. He had a thoughtful expression, she decided. Understanding. Didn't judge. And so, while she could have left him asleep in his box when she popped out for ten minutes, she carried him with her to the shops, telling him on the way how she would cook a bit of beef, and then, when they got there, how no, it was too dear and they'd have neck of mutton instead. She set him on the table while she cooked, on the floor while she did the washing and hung it out. She told him exactly what she was doing even though he could see for himself.

At the end of the fortnight Josephine brought George back. He seemed taller and thinner. 'Eating us out of house and home,' she said. 'Al was too damn right about keeping a family small! Besides, I've been throwing up. Must be expecting again.'

'Now, if your brother doesn't behave,' Adeline told Harry, 'if he's rough or forgets you, or does the slightest wrong thing, scream. I know you will. And George, if you watch him well, then soon you'll get to feed him a rusk, and I'll buy you a string of liquorice.'

Two strong boys. George, Albert's favourite; Harry, hers. These were likely all the children she would have. Her luck.

Count your blessings, Adeline reminded herself many nights, awake, in the small bedroom with its two bedside tables and small closet, her body longing for something she had no words for. *Two healthy boys. Rent paid. A decent man.* She clenched her teeth, and a memory flooded her mouth, of leather, of how she kept the sound of the birth pains inside.

Harry had a window seat at the front of the classroom. Morning sun fell across his desk, picking out its fine coating of chalk dust, the marks of his fingers. Stray tendrils of Virginia creeper, a deep scarlet, framed the wooden sash window, the top arch of which was made from four pieces, the careful joints just visible through white paint. He could see the railway lines running to Clapham Junction, the sports fields, fence, trees and buildings beyond. To his right sat Gorsely, behind him, Fitzgerald. He had a close-up view of the new teacher, Mr Whitehorse: of the gravelly texture of his skin and the jagged white line that ran from his cheekbone to the corner of his lip.

'Miles,' Whitehorse said as he marked Harry present, 'do you know what your name signifies?'

'A measure of distance, sir?'

The class tittered. They did not yet know what to expect.

'Where's your Latin?' Whitehorse continued. '*Mīles, mīlitis*: a foot soldier.'

Whitehorse, tall, gaunt and stooping, asymmetrical in almost every respect, was already known as Dark. He straightened his back somewhat, and looked slowly around the class. It took them a moment to realise that only one eye, the left, moved. 'Since we are talking of war,' he continued, 'I'll take the opportunity to let you all know that the rumour is correct. I wear a glass eye. I lost my real eye in what is called the Great

15

War.' He indicated his right eye, in case they were not sure. Beneath it, the white scar. 'Lost is a *euphemism*, from the Greek. Who knows what that is?'

No one replied. He did not explain, but continued: 'Shrapnel impaled my eye, and the nerve behind. Pain seared through me. I passed out, then woke still in agony on my back in the mud . . . Yet I was lucky. We should remember that one hundred and seventy men from this school died during those four years, including a former headmaster and both of his sons. They were of course very brave. However, I sincerely hope you all avoid such a fate.' He inhaled sharply, looked around the room. The boys at their desks sat perfectly still.

'The guns are silent now,' Whitehorse continued, softly, 'and in this class we shall study verse of various kinds. The poetry of love, the poetry of the land, and the poetry of the soul. I hope to avoid the poetry of war. We shall take verses apart and put them back together again, speak them, write them; you will learn poetry so that you have it in you forever, beating like a second heart . . . I wonder, what was the last poem you read and liked? Armstrong? Godwin? Bowles?'

The silence became unbearable and Harry raised his hand.

'I liked "The Lady of Shalott", sir,' he said.

Whitehorse stiffened, fixed him with his single, seeing, sky-blue eye, and then a second later, turned his head so that the unseeing one appeared to look as well.

'Miles, I must ask, did you also enjoy "The Charge of the Light Brigade"? One of the most dishonest poems ever to be written:

Theirs not to make reply,
Theirs not to reason why,
Theirs but to do and die.
Into the valley of Death
Rode the six hundred.'

Transfixed, Harry shook his head. Whitehorse leaned closer towards him. The white of his real eye was veined red, but that of his glass eye was pure, somewhat bluish white.

'Yet you'll admit they're similar? Content: death. Form: a relentless rhythm and an equally relentless rhyme: Lie, rye, sky, by, loom, room, bloom, plume. Is that your taste, then?'

He knew he must say something, thought of the Lady, half sick of shadows. How she left the web, left the loom, made three paces through the room, and looked out at the world. The mirror crack'd from side to side. That was what he liked.

'What did the Lady do wrong, sir, to get the curse laid on her?' he asked. Snorts of laughter erupted behind him, inexplicable to a sisterless boy. Whitehorse let out a long breath, his shoulders relaxing as he did so.

'A good question, Miles,' he said. 'Though I can't answer it.'

It was Harry's second year at the school. He'd been awarded a scholarship to cover most of the fees. They had bought the uniform second-hand: cap, boater and blazer with *Pour Bien Desirer* and the portcullis sewn in gold on the breast pocket. Each evening his mother sponged and pressed the uniform while he slept, and each morning she rose early to pack lunches for him and his father and brother. Then it was a half an hour's walk between two worlds.

His father had accompanied him the first day. It was straight all the way once they reached Earlsfield Road; as the hill picked up, the shops thinned out and the terraces grew progressively bigger, until they detached themselves from each other at the top, where they sported stained glass, carved gables, and attic rooms for the maids. The road ran close to the railway, past Spencer Park, where the roof of the Royal Victoria Patriotic Building became visible above the trees, and on to the Roundhouse and Battersea Rise. The school gates, right next to the railway line, were unassuming. But through them you could see a gatehouse and a tree-lined path. The school had an ancient charter and had moved out from the city fifty years ago into a steep, red-brick building with a tower, arched windows and a courtyard, a warren of a place surrounded by gardens and huge, perfect playing fields.

A sixty-pounder from the Great War, given in recognition of the school's sacrifice, was parked in the grounds in front of the main entrance. The day began with prayers in the dark wooden chapel, and the Officers' Training Corps was all but obligatory. Boys had the use of a library and a swimming pool and ate their lunches at long tables in a room flooded with light; they learned Latin, calculus and physics, literature, modern languages, mathematics, rugby and rowing.

'You'll not get this chance again. Pay attention and speak up, but be polite,' Harry's father said at the gate. His hand glanced heavily from his son's shoulder, as if to push him on and in, then he strode away, already late for his job at the United Metal Works.

Albert Miles had started out on the lathe, moved up to setting the machines. He knew his numbers, enjoyed reckoning and brought it to every aspect of his life – even laid out his allotment garden with exact measurements and calculated yields in advance. From their early years he'd drilled both sons in mental arithmetic. At Harry's age, his older brother, George, was a natural whose lightning calculations became a party piece. But George was also drawn to roaming the commons, shooting neighbours' cats with his pellet gun, and begging rides on motorbikes. He didn't *apply* himself.

Harry did not have the same gift, but found a kind of satisfaction in numbers. They were a means to an end. He excelled in the London County Council Scholarship Exam because he badly wanted to and it was clear to him that what they were looking for was obedience to the task, to the given facts and rules. You must take the time to understand exactly what was required, write the calculation in neat, well-aligned columns without errors, then state the correct answer in a well-constructed sentence free of spelling or punctuation mistakes: They travelled seven thousand miles in six months. They consumed fifteen apples per family per week. The journey lasted four days, three hours and ten minutes. Answers must be underlined, using a ruler. No smudging.

Parsing sentences started out in a similar vein, but the bare sense that arose from the relationship of one part to another was only the beginning of what the words might say to you, of where the thread of meaning might lead. Harry half hated and half loved words, held them in a kind of squeamish fascination because of their very slipperiness, because they could take you anywhere at all, including somewhere you did not wish to go, and because his father trusted only facts – and, despite the lack of application, preferred George: George this, George that, George the other, who had now talked his way into a half-decent job in the Gramophone Works and was in everyone's good books again.

'Writing out the poet's words, you retrace the path of his thoughts with your hand,' Whitehorse informed the class. They copied the third part of 'The Lady of Shalott' into their notebooks, then used coloured pencils to underline the rhymes and half rhymes, and to indicate the stressed and unstressed syllables with a pattern of crosses and dashes. Meanwhile, Whitehorse speculated aloud: perhaps the curse was connected with art, and what it was to be an artist. The Lady of Shalott could only experience the world through the mirror, and express it in her work at the loom. She could not weave and love – she could not be fully of the world, yet yearned to be, and that was why she must die . . .

Whitehorse paced back and forth in front of the blackboard, his dusty gown billowing out behind him. He stopped, faced them, and lurched towards the impossible questions they could all sense were on the way. Must art involve some kind of sacrifice? Did it compete with human affections? Wentworth? Proctor? The room froze. He continued around it, studying each boy. The living eye, Harry noticed, swam with complicated feeling, while the glass one merely gleamed.

'I really don't know, sir,' he said quietly, when his turn came. And then, for several minutes, they worked in silence until the bell rang.

'Art, of course, is part of what I shall call the poetry of the soul, and that is an excellent place for us to begin . . . ' *Whyte's Treasury of Verse in English*, bound in red and embossed in gold, lay on his desk, and Whitehorse bent over it, flicking through its whisper-thin pages. Beyond their classroom, the school was all movement. 'Blake . . . later. Read "The Windhover", page 402,' Whitehorse announced as they fled, through Mr Barker's and Mr Chamberlain's rooms to the courtyard stairs.

'He has a wooden leg, too. And one of his balls is shot off!' Smart said, as they plunged down the rickety iron stairway. The son of the school bursar, he often had inside information. 'The man's shell-shocked to all hell. Flies off the handle. Battersea Grammar let him go. When Old Denton kicked the bucket in the holidays, they had to act fast and he comes cheap.' They crossed the courtyard as fast as they could without running. 'But really, it's all your fault, soldier-boy,' Smart told him as they pushed through the double doors. Harry shrugged, grinned.

'What does your name signify?' said Teddy Davis, exaggerating Whitehorse's crisp enunciation and booming tone.

'My friend at Battersea says Dark goes wild if you quote that bit from Brooke about a foreign field.' Smart was a very solid boy, and now he moved closer to Harry, so that their arms and shoulders collided: the hint of a threat.

'So do it, Harry,' Smart continued, as they approached the chemistry lab. His voice slowed, quietened: 'Unless you're too scared. Give us some effing fireworks, and we'll forgive you for putting us through the *lady's curse.*'

'No,' Harry said simply, pushing past him into the gassy tang of the lab. 'Do it yourself, if that's what you want.'

Not that he actually liked Whitehorse. But he disliked Smart, knew how this could go, and wouldn't turn on an underdog; his instincts went the other way. He was thirteen, constantly hungry, growing so fast that his shins hurt in bed at night. He was starting to notice girls, to feel the power they secretly wielded. He understood that men had a duty to provide, and that he would have to work hard, but because of the school it was possible that he might give orders or sit at a desk and so earn more for his efforts. Who and what would he become? His knowledge of the ways of the world expanded with every breath he took – but even so he could not know that a new war would begin in just six years' time. He, despite his adolescent cynicism, despite being in love, would have to be part of it. Reginald Smart and Teddy Davis would die before they reached twenty-two, and the older Davis, Alexander, would leave his left leg and a good part of his mind in Italy.

Whitehorse soon earned other nicknames: Whitearse, and Workhorse. By Christmas, they had transcribed, analysed and memorised over thirty poems of the soul. They returned in January to rugby fields a foot deep in snow of purest, almost purple white, and criss-crossed with fox and bird tracks. The railway line had been cleared, and as Whitehorse welcomed

them back and declared that their new subject would be 'the poetry of the land and the sea', a long, dark train threaded itself through the surrounding whiteness, belching steam as it headed for the junction.

The room was so cold that they could see their breath. Carson, stammering, delivered John Clare's 'Emmonsail's Heath in Winter', page 201, and then Wright sniffed relentlessly through all ten pages of 'January'. No one, said Whitehorse at the end of it, would deny the shorter poem – its 'crimpled' leaves and 'oddling crow', the sheer liveliness and pleasure in it. But the endless rhyming couplets of 'January', he thought, would teach them something about the ear's need for variation, though there were still jewels to be found, and certainly a feeling lingered in the poem's wake – how would they describe that feeling?

'Sad,' Harry said.

'Sir,' Smart asked – he seemed to have grown a head taller in the past few months and looked too big for his desk – 'sir, it says here that Clare was in an *asylum*!'

True, Whitehorse admitted: a crisis. Nervous collapse. From memory, he quoted 'I Am', which was not in the book. It described the poet's desperate state of mind: *The vast shipwreck of my life's esteems* was, Whitehorse said, a masterful phrase. 'Feeling,' he continued, 'is one of the things poets do for us. As we saw last term, they travel to the farthest reaches of the soul's possibilities, and record the journey, something of as great a value to those who have not made the same journey, as it is to those who have. Intense emotion, Smart, may seem like madness to those who do not share it.'

Davis glared back at him from the desk next to Smart, whose heavy features gathered into a fleshy knot.

Withering and keen, John Clare had called winter. The cast-iron radiator beneath the window was barely warm, but

Harry sat close enough to press his left leg against it, absorbing all its heat. He had come to enjoy the poetry class more than anything except for games. He liked chemistry too, and there was a similarity: explosions, transformations. You never knew where the lesson would go, what would happen, how you might feel, what you might discover or be forced, suddenly, to think about.

Another train passed, its whistle hooting mournfully, like some huge mechanical owl. The railway, Whitehorse told them, had changed everything. It ran along what had once been a field's edge and the boundary of a mediaeval estate, and set the boundaries of the school's current property. Just forty years ago the streets they walked to come to school had been open fields. The old landscape and the people who had tended it persisted in the names of places and streets: Lavender Hill. Southfields. Earlsfield. Osiers Road. And the rural life of Northamptonshire that John Clare had depicted so lovingly over a century ago was changing even as he wrote, and that, surely was why the poem seemed to ache with nostalgia, a word derived from Greek words for pain and a longing for home . . . Harry, looking out at the snow, thought suddenly of his father, in summertime, bringing home, along with the usual vegetables, a bunch of red and purple dahlias that he'd grown on their allotment by the cemetery. The way his mother's face opened up as she set them in the jar.

They considered 'The Lake Isle of Innisfree', page 405, and 'Composed upon Westminster Bridge', page 399.

Humankind, Whitehorse said, should not be separated from the natural world. A pastoral vision was something they carried inside them, in what Yeats had called *the deep heart's core*, and it was part of the poet's task to keep that vision alive.

Old fart's bore, someone wrote on a scrap of paper. The back of the class shook with laughter, but Harry screwed the note up and shoved it into his inkwell then had to surreptitiously dry his fingers on his trouser leg when Whitehorse invited him to read.

It was the last poem in the book, page 539, on the left side: four verses, twelve lines in all. Harry ran his eyes over it, drew breath.

It was hot, and a train stopped unexpectedly. That was all: the name of the place, a man coughing. Heat, haycocks, plants and birds: it was a poem in which nothing happened. And yet as he read, the words remade the room. There was a silence when he finished, in which he at least felt the heat and heard the birds.

'What did you think of it?' Whitehorse asked.

He'd noticed that the sentences either stopped before the lines' ends, or ran over them, so that you did not so much notice the rhymes, which in any case came only alternately, and in the final stanza seemed somehow to relax. He'd noticed that, and more, too much to say.

'Different, sir,' he said.

Whitehorse gave an almost imperceptible nod, then switched his attention to the class in general, swivelling his head this way and that in that slightly exaggerated way of his to which they were all now oblivious. 'This writer, I believe, will turn out to be one of the twentieth century's most important poets,' he said.

'But sir!' Davis spoke without raising his hand. 'I beg to differ, sir. I much prefer Rupert Brooke, "The Old Vicarage, Grantchester", page 520. It brings tears to my eyes, sir.'

'And,' Smart chimed in, 'what about "The Soldier", sir, page 526. "Some corner of a foreign field / That is forever England." That's very fine, wouldn't you agree, sir?'

Harry did not quite know why his heart thudded so hard in his chest. Whitehorse, his fingers tented on his oak desk, looked down at them for a long moment. Then up.

'I am glad you like something, Smart,' he said. 'You and Davis will each take three pages to compare and contrast "The Old Vicarage, Grantchester", with "Lob", also by Edward Thomas: two very different poems about our country. By next Tuesday.'

He continued, his voice tightening: 'As it happens, I once ate a very good supper with Thomas and Brooke, in Gloucestershire. And not long after that, we were all overseas. Brooke died en route, and Thomas's heart was stopped by a shell in Arras. But what men endured before their deaths matters more, and if you seek to understand war, avoid platitudes. Read Sassoon. Read Owen, read especially 'Dulce et Decorum Est':

Bent double, like old beggars under sacks,
Knock-kneed, coughing like hags, we cursed through sludge,
Till on the haunting flares we turned our backs,
And towards our distant rest began to trudge –

'No, it's not in our book. And it was not my plan to recite it today, but you, Davis and you, Smart, have raised the matter, perhaps intentionally – and I find myself unable to stop. And perhaps war can be construed as a place, a hellish one. One that it is far better to read about than to visit. One that should be described honestly, especially to young men. And so I'll continue, even though it may be unwise:

Men marched asleep. Many had lost their boots,
But limped on, blood-shod. All went lame; all blind;
Drunk with fatigue; deaf even to the hoots
Of gas-shells dropping softly behind.

Gas! GAS! Quick, boys! – An ecstasy of fumbling
Fitting the clumsy helmets just in time,
But someone still was yelling out and stumbling

And flound'ring like a man in fire or lime,
Dim through the misty panes and thick green light,
As under a green sea, I saw him drowning.

In all my dreams before my helpless sight,
He plunges at me, guttering, choking, drowning.'

Whitehorse's voice was harsh. The lines came in gasps. He struggled for his breath as if he too had been gassed.

Standing before the class, he screwed his eyes shut as he continued, his hands on the desk, his arms rigid:

'If in some smothering dreams, you too could pace
Behind the wagon that we flung him in
And watch the white eyes writhing in his face,
His hanging face, like a devil's sick of sin;
If you could hear, at every jolt, the blood
Come gargling from the froth-corrupted lungs,
Obscene as cancer, bitter as the cud
Of vile, incurable sores on innocent tongues, –
My friend, you would not tell with such high zest
To children ardent for some desperate glory,
The old Lie: *Dulce et decorum est*
Pro patria mori.'

No one breathed.

'We'll stop there,' Whitehorse said, opening his eyes just before the bell rang. Harry, the last to leave the room, turned at the door and looked back. But he dared not ask whether Whitehorse was all right.

'I'm not writing any blasted essay for any bloody lunatic teacher. If he's still raving fifteen years after the end of the frigging war, the man must be a grade one coward!'

'You're not in a position to know that, Smart,' Harry said, not thinking, and Smart's fist crashed into his cheek, knocked him back into the cloakroom wall, his head narrowly missing the coat hooks.

'What position are you in, then?' Smart asked. Harry launched himself forwards and Smart crashed into the floor, his head clipping the corner of a bench on the way down. Blood gushed from the wound; as they watched, his eyelids fluttered, then closed. His heart racing, Harry pressed a scarf onto the wound while Gorsely ran to fetch Nurse. The rest of the group vanished. When Nurse came, Harry rushed to the toilet and heaved.

Dr Devine, the First Master, did not care who began it or why. 'I see you have a scholarship. Well, ask yourself, do I deserve to be here?'

The strap bit, ten strokes, inflaming every nerve in his hand, flooding his entire body with the effort of bearing the pain. The thing that mattered most was not to wet yourself and it was better to tell your parents before the note came in the post. Besides, he had a black eye.

'If you want to leave, say so. We put up ten shillings for that uniform,' his father told him before silence settled over the supper table like snow. Directly across, George, whose constant sparring had taught him how to fight, caught Harry's eye and winked.

Suppose I had to? Harry asked himself later, sleepless in the dark. Suppose I killed someone? *Thou shalt not*, the Bible said. Yet soldiers must. And according to Whitehorse, his name meant soldier. The last war had ended not long before he was born. His father's occupation had saved him from service, but there were two uncles he'd met only in pre-embarkation photographs, and another who came back seemingly intact, but a few years later emigrated to Canada, and lost touch. There was 'Sarge' Hedges, a man with only half a right arm, who worked at the station paper shop, deftly pushing things across the counter with his 'right hook' and counting change with his left. There were tramps, who knocked on doors to offer themselves for work, then later in the day hung around the Sailor Prince and the Halfway House hoping someone would buy them a drink. Many of them had been in the war. The more you looked, the more you saw: those who limped, did not stand straight, stood too straight, who kept a stump hidden from view. And now there was Whitehorse, who, the very next day, apologised for talking to them about the war; who, when Smart reappeared with a thick bandage around his head, made no mention of the essays and did not make the class read Thomas's long poem, even though it was in the book. Instead they read 'Sea-Fever' and 'Cargoes', then week-by-week and place-by-place moved towards Easter, when daffodils bloomed on the commons, and birds dipped past the windows, bearing twigs in their beaks.

In the third term, Whitehorse spoke about love: it was wrong, he said, to think of this topic as beyond their reach. Love was the only thing, in the end, that mattered. It came in many forms. It flowed between man and woman, between mother and child, between brothers, sisters and comrades, between friends and associates of all kinds. Love was affection, chivalry, yearning, compassion, sacrifice, admiration, companionship, desire. It was sometimes romantic, sometimes sexual, sometimes platonic; it was sometimes reciprocated and sometimes not, it was simple and complicated at the same time. Its expression demanded the use of assonance, dissonance, the patterning of syllables and stress, caesurae, metre, rhyme; it expressed itself in ballads, sonnets, blank verse, in countless songs.

Form, he had often said, was a vessel that contained, carried, but also embodied thought and feeling. It was paradoxical that love, a wild thing, had often been expressed in the stricter, more intricate verse forms. Their study of the poetry of love would begin with Shakespeare's sonnets. He took some time to explain: the proposition, the development, the volta or turn, the rhyme schemes and metres favoured by Petrarchan sonneteers, how Shakespeare had moved to three quatrains and a couplet, as opposed to an octave and a sestet, and had shifted the volta to the very end, to ring out forcefully in the couplet there.

Whyte's *Treasury* included fifteen out of the hundred and fifty-four, almost enough for one each to study and present to the class. The sixteenth member of the class could take a sonnet by Elizabeth Barrett Browning, a woman writer quite as good as any man. Questions?

'Sir,' Davis' voice broke awkwardly between one word and the next, 'what is meant here by a youth?'

'A young man,' Whitehorse told him. 'Quite possibly, some say, the Earl of Pembroke, a patron of the arts at the time.'

'I don't understand. Why was Shakespeare writing love poems to, to – '

Impossible to know, Whitehorse said. Other sonnets in the sequence were addressed to a Dark Lady, and historians also loved to speculate as to her identity. Shakespeare was an actor and a dramatist, used to adopting a persona, to taking on roles. He would prefer them not to get caught up in the specifics of the person addressed, but to consider the sentiments expressed and the literary context, against which Shakespeare was perhaps rebelling. Later, they'd move on to Andrew Marvell, John Donne, Shelley . . .

'I bet they were all nances. I bet he's bent himself. Stands to reason. He shouldn't make us read crap like this,' Davis protested.

'Too difficult?' Harry asked, as he passed him on the stairs, knowing he was pushing it, wanting to.

He read Sonnet 116 that same evening, sitting on the back step. He noticed the image of the ship, the many iterations of what love was not, puzzled over *the remover to remove*. He was excited by the poem's extremity. It seemed to him that choosing to make a commitment even to the edge of doom would in some way that he could not begin to explain enlarge a person. 'If this be error and upon me proved, / I never writ, nor no man ever loved': the drama of these adamant words thrilled him to the point that when he spoke them aloud, as if they were his, hairs rose on his arms. But how, in that room, with Smart two desks away, could he say any of this?

He never did.

'Boys,' Whitehorse told them towards the end of the next class, after a lengthy discussion of sonnets twelve, the clock, and eighteen, the summer's day, 'Boys, I have to let you know that I am not prepared to modify my curriculum in response to ill-considered parental opinions, and so must leave you unexpectedly.' His one-eyed gaze lingered momentarily on Davis and Smart. 'A pity. The First Master will take this class until the end of term. And I thank you for your kind attention. I believe we have learned something together this year, and now I must wish you all goodbye, Godspeed, and good luck.'

The class chorused their goodbyes and clattered out of the room, but Harry sat on by his window in a pool of spring sunshine, unable to leave, to move at all.

'Miles,' Whitehorse said, 'come here.' So he rose, took a few steps and stood, acutely aware of gravity, next to the oak desk.

'You have an ear for verse. I would have put you forward for the Reader's Prize, but under the circumstances I've not been asked to nominate. So – ' Whitehorse reached down for his briefcase, extracted a slim volume, bound in blue cloth. 'I hope you will enjoy Thomas's collected poems.' Harry gulped for air, unable to staunch the tears.

'Sorry, sir!'

Whitehorse put a hand on his shoulder, and left it there.

'Why should you be sorry?' he said. 'It's good to feel things. Though the day must go on. Here – ' He offered a tobacco-smelling handkerchief, and steered Harry towards the door that led to the outer stairs.

'Will you find another teaching post?' Harry asked, as they began the descent.

'Don't trouble yourself. Something will turn up,' Whitehorse said. 'Do you know Shelgate Road?' he asked conversationally. 'About half a mile, Clapham way? Thomas grew up there, at number sixty-one. Walked the same streets as you when he was a boy.'

What did he mean by connecting them in that way? Harry wondered then, and periodically afterwards – concluding only in middle age that his teacher had very likely meant no more than to be friendly and matter-of-fact.

A brief handshake at the bottom of the staircase, and then they parted. Harry never saw the man again. But he kept the book: *To Harold Miles, for outstanding work. With all good wishes, David Stanley Whitehorse*, his teacher had written on the flyleaf in the careful copperplate he had learned long before the war, when he was himself a boy.

Across the hallway, the librarian had decorated the Ladies' Reading Room with vases of tulips and ferns, but the chairs there were hard and the tables wobbled when you leaned on them. Evelyn preferred the other room, where the panelling was in oak and the light fell softly from the gallery above, and everything exuded an aura of solidity and permanence.

She had started *Rebecca* only to see whether it was worth carrying home. Now she found it hard to put down, despite the fact that she was more than half irritated with the girl telling the story, who did not stand up for herself and constantly complained to the reader, even about her own good fortune. This girl was living in Monte Carlo, of all places – a seaside resort that Evelyn could only imagine, its white buildings clustered around the foothills of a mountain, and the surrounding sea an intense ultramarine, the colour of longing itself . . . Yachts jostled in the marina, and along the front were grand hotels, casinos, theatres, cafés with orchestras and awnings, marble pavements, palm trees. The vehicles were spotless, the women elegant, the men clad in cream linen suits. Jazz orchestras played all the latest dances. There were no headlines about Hitler and Mussolini, no long speeches, or ominous warnings on the radio – absolutely nothing to worry about. This nameless girl, blind to her own luck, had been hired as companion to an older woman (hardly heavy work!) and was staying with her in a hotel called the Côte d'Azur. She'd met a rich, sophisticated older man who (heaven knew why!) was showing interest in her: you would think she might enjoy at least some of this? But no. *I am glad it cannot happen twice, the fever of first love*, the nameless girl wrote, complaining again, *for it is a fever, and a burden, too, whatever the poets may say.*

Why should love be a fever and a burden? Evelyn looked up, momentarily meeting the hungry eyes of the tweedy-looking man opposite her. She turned slightly to avoid his gaze. Why not exciting, or satisfying? And why should anyone believe a woman who did everything wrong, who, clearly desperate for attention, had no sense of her own dignity and put up with rudeness and bad behaviour? In this she reminded Evelyn of her mother, who allowed all and sundry – including Evelyn, but especially Evelyn's father – to take advantage of her. She forgave him repeatedly, gave him money to waste, new starts, last chances; to Evelyn, she said, *I can't help it, sweetheart, I've made my bed, but I hope you choose better than I have.* Could you do worse than a man who forgets to hand over his wages, and has to have his soiled trousers pulled off him when he comes home singing in the middle of the night? A man who stinks of drink, urine, and menthol, and wants you to sit on his knee while he tells you that you are his favourite girl? Who coughs right over the dinner table? And if this is what love does, if it turns you into a fool and a drudge to be used and trampled on, then she would have absolutely nothing to do with it, nothing at all.

Still avoiding the man's gaze, yet aware of it, she returned to the book. Despite its heroine's faults, the story had something to it. What did Maxim de Winter see in the girl? Was it her very brokenness, her weakness, her stupidity that attracted him? There were men like that: tyrannical, bullying types, and Evelyn planned to avoid them, too.

There was no hurry to be married. On the other hand, it got you away from home. Perhaps she would stay single, and live on her own in a flat, though it might be lonely and was hard to imagine. Clearly the unlikely pair in the book *had* ended up together. Something terrible had happened but they were still being waited on hand and foot, albeit in lesser hotels; naturally she wanted to know what momentous thing had occurred, so she read on, skipping some of the girl's ramblings and putting aside thoughts of her mother, who would have supper ready for half past six. Evelyn was not expected to help. Her mother worked until four, charring, then came home and *did for herself*, an expression that made Evelyn want to run screaming from the house. I'm used to it, dear, her mother said, I *like* to spoil you.

So Evelyn read on, perfectly poised in her chair, her bag by her feet, her elbows on the desk, taking care not to crumple the light jacket she wore. At the end of the sixth chapter, in which Maxim de Winter delivered his boorish marriage pro-posal, hunger ambushed her. She closed the book and made her way down the flights of red marble steps to the terrazzo floor and out through the reference library, which she liked for its coat of arms with the golden bees, and the clock and the curved glass ceiling that made it seem like a railway station – as if everyone studying in that room, their heads wearily bent over school or trade text books was actually going somewhere else: Monte Carlo, perhaps.

Traffic choked Lavender Hill. A collision between a cyclist and a motorcar had brought his tram to a standstill and Harry, already late, half ran towards the library. He normally used the main entrance but that day, for no better reason than to get away from the main road a moment sooner, he turned into Altenburg Gardens and arrived at the reference library entrance just as Evelyn, leaving the double doors to swing shut behind her, stepped out. She paused for a moment at the top of the three semicircular steps, framed by the white stone and the carved motto above, *non mihi, non tibi, sed nobis,* which later he would translate for her: *not for me, not for you, but for us.* Intended in the civic sense, he would jokingly explain.

She had the type of figure he liked best: full, yet not heavy. She held herself straight and proud despite carrying several books pressed close to her body with one arm, and a small leather bag in the other. Her hair, an intense brown, softly waved, fell to her shoulders. It set off a clear complexion, framed large, dark eyes and subtly rouged lips – not a rosebud, but the opening flower itself. She took the steps as if they belonged absolutely to her, as, suddenly, did he: was it his gaze, the sheer intensity of the attraction he felt, that made her drop one of her books at the bottom of the steps, or did she stumble slightly on the rougher brickwork there? In any case a book slid free and landed splayed open halfway between the two of them and he stopped and bent to pick it up, noting its author, du Maurier. He brushed the bright yellow jacket clean with his sleeve.

'Is it good?' he asked as he handed it to her. He heard his own voice as from a distance.

'I'll find out when I read it,' she told him. 'Thank you.'

'I'd be very interested to hear your view.' He did not move aside but occupied the space in front of her, ostensibly ignoring yet acutely aware of a man in a tweed jacket who had also just left the library. Harry knew, just knew, that he'd been following her. Who wouldn't? 'Harry Miles,' he said, stepping closer to Evelyn and making the situation clear. 'May I carry those for you?'

She shrugged, but told him her name, Evelyn Hill, and handed the books over, managing to suggest by a certain coolness in the way she thanked him that absolutely no obligation would be incurred: that indeed, she was doing him a favour, which she was. South, she told him when he asked which way she was going, in the direction of Magdalen Road. So they continued down Altenburg Gardens, the tweedy man left behind, and Harry's thirst for *New Writing*, de rigueur for someone who felt at times that he might one day write, completely forgotten. It would be months before he read anything modern again.

He noticed neat, summery shoes, the faint sheen of her stockings. Her walk was brisk, but stately at the same time. *Magnificent*, he thought, caught up in a great tide of longing that seemed almost as if it must come from outside of him. Her heels sang out on the pavement. His whole body was aware of her every step. It was, in a way, preposterous.

'Do you read much?' he managed to ask.

'It depends on my mood,' she said, and feeling as if everything would indeed depend on that, he forced himself to look away from her towards the houses on their left: massive, classically inspired, stone-built, with wide, studded front doors. Split into flats, though, he noted. On the right were smaller, neat, three-storeyed terraces, with flowers in their front gardens and window boxes: this was the kind of street where a few years ago each house might have had a maid, or two. But now the area was changing, as money moved ever further out. The city was in a state of flux, subdividing, thickening, expanding – Cobbett's Great Wen becoming greater still.

'Were you coming from work?' he asked, and learned that she had just started working for a West End solicitor, reception and correspondence; she could write shorthand, type at seventy words a minute and speak a little French. She had never been to France, but would like to go there, especially to Paris. Like him, she preferred the Battersea library to the one nearer to home.

How come they had not met before? Yet now they had, and that was the thing. He told her, as they skirted the south end of Clapham Common, where, behind the trees to their left, the emplacements for anti-aircraft guns had already been installed, that it had at one point been suggested to him that he try for a university scholarship. His school had pushed the idea, and every year more students succeeded. But frankly, he said, he was sick of being a scholarship boy. He couldn't settle to the idea of studying any more, couldn't quite imagine what it would lead to. And even with a scholarship there would be incidental expenses.

The other part of it was that he couldn't hold his tongue; more and more he found, just as his brother had, that he didn't care for routine or being told what to do, and those two things increasingly seemed to be what education was about. The classes, the rowing and rugby, the obligatory parading around in a uniform and being yelled at after school: what they were after, in the end, was obedience. So he had taken a job as laboratory assistant for Chalfont and Klyne because at least you were *paid* for doing what you were told.

At the school leaving-day ceremony Dr Devine shook his hand and told him that *So long as free public libraries exist, no one need let his mind atrophy.* He'd scoffed, at the time. But since then he'd begun to make the effort. Books, after all, were expensive. He mainly read poetry.

'And in any case,' he told Evelyn, 'it seems that everyone's studies will be interrupted before long. Shall we cross here?' He offered his arm, and briefly she rested her hand on it. There was no traffic and the narrow terraced streets were in deep shade now, though it was still warm. Voices wafted through open sash windows and open front doors hung with strips of fabric. Behind these, the narrow corridors would be dark. Two rooms twelve foot square, a galley kitchen, stairs up. Outside conveniences.

'So long as Chamberlain doesn't still think he can stop them by *talking*,' Evelyn said. '*Everyone* saw this coming but him.' For a moment, he was startled by her vehemence.

'We'll surely go in now,' he said, aware of the euphemism, the familiar dishonesty that hovered over this kind of conversation. *Going in* meant that they would fight with tanks, heavy artillery, bombs and bayonets. Many would die. Just as before men went *over the top*, so now they would *go in*. Though when? How much longer would they continue in limbo, obsessively following the news? It was like being becalmed or enchanted. Hypnotised. Part of him was impatient for war to start, yet just as large a part secretly hoped it would still somehow be avoided. He could sympathise with Chamberlain for trying to do just that, but Hitler was not someone with whom you could make an agreement.

'Everyone understands now that Hitler has to be stopped,' he said.

'An utter brigand,' Evelyn said. 'And what on earth are the Italians thinking of?' There was a certain drama to the way she expressed herself, and this was very different to the measured way things were discussed in his own house, or had been at school, for that matter. It was very attractive, he found, the way her feelings coloured her words, and how very certain of her opinions she was. She brimmed over with life.

'I'm not twenty until next year,' he told her. The houses they walked past still huddled close, but now some of them had tiled paths and panels of stained glass in their doors. Here and there a rose or a hydrangea had been planted out front ... Millions will die, Harry thought. Because *We'll go in* meant troop ships, torpedoes, landings, marches, gunfire, tanks, air raids, bombs, corpses, grief, devastation. Even so, despite whatever he might have said before, and despite understanding that all over again the old men were sending the young out to die, he would have to take part, and for the first time, at that moment, walking next to Evelyn, he truly knew it. And at the same time, none of what was happening – not even Hitler's army in Czechoslovakia, his tearing up of the Naval Agreement, not the tanks rolling across Europe, not the submarines prowling the seas – none of it seemed fully real in comparison with this moment, now: Evelyn beside him, her dark, complicated eyes ablaze. The sky, turning between day and dusk, ached with longing.

'When we go in,' he told her, 'doubtless I'll volunteer.'

'In a way, I envy you,' she replied; Harry shrugged, not wanting to say that although yes, it did seem different to last time, no one really had any choice, nor to observe how different were the lives of women and men. He did not wish to spoil their walk. He wanted them to continue, side by side, sharing in the same warm and lavish air, air the temperature of skin, lively and caressing. The breeze touched his face, and then hers, then rustled through the leaves of the young lime trees planted hopefully at regular intervals on each side of Salcott Road. It gathered strength, blew on towards the expanses of Wandsworth Common ahead of them.

'They do say it'll be over in a year,' she said. He moved her book over to his other side.

'Meanwhile,' he said, 'a wonderful evening,' and she smiled back at him.

They took the tree-lined path along the edge of the common. 'Imagine living in one of those!' she said, nodding at the grand Victorian villas set far back from the road, surrounded by large, well-tended gardens. 'Imagine looking out of your big bay windows on all of this.' It seemed a sweet, intimate thing to say and he wished they were not already halfway to Magdalen Road, turning in now towards the little bridge over the railway tracks. They paused there to look up and down the lines, then continued past an elm tree full of chattering starlings. They walked easily together despite the rough grass; he offered his arm again and she took it. Her skirt blew against his legs.

At the top of Magdalen the ghost of a moon began to rise and lights showed downstairs in some of the new houses with their big square bays. Behind and below these was the new accommodation the borough council had built on what used to be fields: newly paved streets of fixed-rent maisonettes, where a few children chased about and kicked balls. No trees had been planted yet and everything was stark and bare. On the other side of the road the cemetery was locked. Like him, she had sometimes played there as a child. It was in deep shade now, and all the marble angels, carved lilies, granite crosses and cypress trees sank into the approaching night.

'Let me take you right home,' he said. 'I live down this way, too.' Perhaps, he thought later, she was disappointed to discover that he came from an almost identical narrow, treeless, terraced street? Though to his mind, you had to start somewhere. It was only a beginning, an inspiration, even. Neither her accent nor her diction fitted the streets she came from; she had modelled them after those of the announcers on the radio, teachers, actors in the films and now, her superiors in the solicitor's office, just as he had learned to do with his teachers at school. Like him, she spoke to suit her company and situation. A girl like her would need him to be ambitious, more so than he had been so far. Even as he realised this, he committed to it.

At the bottom of the hill and in sight of the commercial clutter of Garratt Lane was the smaller library they both spurned, then the railway bridge, the tramways, pubs and shops, all shuttered now. They turned left into the terraces, and crossed what remained of a river that now ran dirty, foam-flecked and almost silently between smooth concrete banks.

It must be very unlikely, he said, as they reached the end of her road, but did she have any free time on the weekend?

Not this weekend, she told him, but possibly the one after.

She insisted he leave her at the corner. She would be in the library at the same time next week, she said, as he handed back her books. She walked from lamp to lamp then bent to unlatch a low gate. Two more steps, and she vanished.

'I was beginning to worry!' her mother called out. 'But I waited. Hurry, now. Your father's home.'

The house smelled of mutton stew. Evelyn hung her jacket in the tiny cupboard under the stairs, then looked in on the galley kitchen, where her mother stood by the sink draining overcooked potatoes in a flurry of steam. 'Sorry. But you know I can look after myself. I got lost in a book, then a man from the library walked me home . . . '

'Here,' her mother said, handing her a soup plate brim full of the stew, 'This is for your father.'

'Hello, princess,' he said, as she carried it in, then coughed into his hand. The table was the folding kind, and they kept it pushed up against the wall that divided the kitchen from the back room. As ever, he sat propped against the wall; he was about half gone, she noted from the looseness of his face and the too-careful way he spoke. There was an empty glass in front of him. His eyes held her as she approached. They were large and glistening, the irises a mixture of deep greens and browns and gold, irresistible, her mother said. It had been remarked many times that Evelyn had her father's eyes.

She said nothing, put the plate down between his cutlery.

'Not talking to me?' he asked.

'I hope you have an appetite tonight,' she said, though he never did, and the waste infuriated her. He studied what he had been served, the meat in its brown gravy studded with orange carrots, the two dumplings marooned next to the edge of the plate. Evelyn and her mother busied themselves with separating the soft meat from the bones, and spooned up the rich, salty juices. There was near-silence for a while, just the clinking of cutlery and their breath blown out to cool the food.

'Not hungry, Ted?' her mother asked. 'Try a little.'

'No,' he said, pushing the chair back and pressing on the table's edge to help himself stand. 'Not now. I need to rest.' He turned away to cough on his sleeve. There was not a hint of thanks, Evelyn observed. She and her mother, eating more slowly now that their plates were all but empty, listened to his heavy but uneven progress up the stairs, the drag of the bedroom door.

'Who brought you home, then?' her mother asked.

'From round here, it turns out. I liked him,' Evelyn said.

'I worry you'll rush into something just because there's a war coming,' her mother told her. 'Take your time. Don't settle, because you might well meet someone through your work. A widower, say.'

But Evelyn was not at all drawn to older men, and didn't like to be advised: if her mother had been encouraging about Harry, she might have begun to dislike him. As it was, she pointed out that he was a rower, had a good build and clear blue eyes, and seemed to be in work.

'Which is more than can be said for some. I'm not rushing, and I am perfectly capable of making up my own mind,' she added, carrying her dish to the sink and leaving it there.

'Will you take your father a glass of milk?'

'I'd rather not,' she said.

If Harry called for her Saturday week, she decided later, lying in bed with *Rebecca* propped up on her knees and a layer of cold cream on her face, she would go walking with him . . . And if she ever married into a country estate such as Manderley, her first move would be to send Mrs Danvers packing and make the place her own: its many floors and sea views, its morning room, the antique writing desk, and outside, the beds of crimson rhododendrons. She wanted to have a garden one day, and a gardener too.

Harry could neither bear to go home, nor to be inside. He strode back the way they had walked, up towards the higher ground of the commons, where he could see the whole of the sky. The waning moon, enormous now, hung low, brushing the tops of the trees. It drew all the water in the world towards it, and he could feel that subtle, ethereal gravity in his flesh – he and everything in the universe were united in a yearning he could hardly bear, yet at the same time he wanted it to continue, to grow, to overwhelm him. His heart raced, his lungs were hungry for air. He rehearsed the walk over and over in his mind so that he would not forget it. He imagined Evelyn at her window, breathing in the same breeze that he felt on his skin, how it joined them to each other and to all that it touched and he felt, inside of him and out, the sheer loveliness of the world . . . Evelyn, Evelyn! The sound of the word, the feeling of it in his mouth was almost a kiss. He did not sleep that night, or the next. All the week following he could not think, and made mistakes at work. He tried, during these warm, restless nights, to write her a sonnet. Any kind of verse. A letter, even. But despite or because of the intensity of his feelings, it was impossible. He could barely read. It was as if he had lost all access to language.

She wore a blue dress, fitted, with a belt, and she liked the idea of Wimbledon Common and tea afterwards. Her shoes would be fine.

Rebecca had turned out well, she told him. The last part especially: from the point when the boat containing Rebecca's body was discovered until the end. The best character was Mrs

Danvers, a complete madwoman infatuated with the dead first wife, who tried to get the girl to commit suicide and almost succeeded, too, though Rebecca herself of course was the truly evil one who made De Winter's choice of a second wife somewhat more understandable. The part that Evelyn didn't like was that the house, Manderley, was set on fire and destroyed by Mrs Danvers as she left, so that the girl who told the story never got to properly live there and run the place: no wonder she was so miserable. At least that was explained.

Dreams of the fire had kept her awake half the night. It was ridiculous, just a story, but she felt as if it had happened to her, or as if it might.

'Do you think they'll bomb us?' she asked.

It was best not to worry, he said. Though it was hard not to with the commons being excavated for shelters and studded with anti-aircraft guns, and parts set aside for allotments. Even without a declaration of war, troops and equipment were on the move and training camps had sprung up; there was no final word, and yet no escaping what was to come.

'We must make the best of the summer,' he told her. She sat on his jacket, he on the grass. He watched her close her eyes and tilt her face to the sun.

They met almost every week at the library. On the weekends they wandered over the commons or rode the bus to the city centre and walked in the grand London parks, where brass bands played in the afternoons, and swans and ducks languidly circled pea-soup lakes. They saw *Les Sylphides* and *The Tempest*; they wandered riverside paths, caught trains out of town and followed paths and country lanes. Emerging from shady woods, they glimpsed old manor houses, saw new brick villas and old cottages in knapped flint and thatch.

They brought books with them but Harry rarely opened his. He preferred to watch Evelyn, to see her absorb what she read, to wonder at the smooth, shadowed skin of her eyelids, her long lashes, the way her mouth softened as the story took hold. He liked to watch her eat, too. As if aware of the austerity ahead, they ate their fill: picnics, pub lunches, fancy high teas, fish and chips, steak and kidney pies, hunks of cheese, strawberries and cream, chocolates, cherries, plums – and then, the most perfectly ripe peach, which he halved with his penknife and a twist of his wrist, dripping its juice onto a brown bag. He waited as long as he possibly could before he leaned forward to taste the salty sweetness of Evelyn's lips, and she did not pull away.

What did he know of her, other than that for months she had driven all else out of his head? He knew that she was bitterly ashamed of her father, a drunkard with a hacking, tubercular cough. She could walk for hours without tiring. She had an appetite for the better things, quick judgement, a very strong will, a dislike of doubt or ambiguity, and a way of making her words count. Her opinions and feelings stormed through her. She warmed to appreciation. She would let him touch the side of her breasts, her knee, but absolutely nothing between there and her waist. Once, she had allowed herself to fall asleep with her head on his chest.

On the second of September, when finally the radio told them the news, he remembered how his one-eyed English teacher, Whitehorse, had warned them, over and over again, about what war meant, and his skin tightened as he remembered it; his heart lurched in his chest. But even so, he took the pen, and signed his name.

Evelyn said she was proud.

He went north to train. It was the coldest winter for sixty years.

In the blackout, the moon and stars shone far more brightly and there was an eerie kind of beauty to the city at night. It was like living in a photograph. Also, sounds seemed more acute. Voices, laughter, footsteps. On moonless nights, the darkness was thick, substantial. People passed on the street without being able to see each other's faces, and all their other senses strained towards the approaching stranger.

'I'm absolutely, completely sure how I feel,' he told her on his first leave, 'but of course I can wait. I wouldn't want you to say yes to me because of the war. Or no, for that matter. I wish we could keep the war out of our thinking.'

Yet the war was all there was. They breathed it like air.

'If he doesn't like you taking your time, then that will tell you something. Are you *in love*?' Evelyn's mother asked, and Evelyn did not know how to answer, except that she had missed the walks, his face, his eyes looking steadily at her; his attention to her comfort and well-being, the feeling of her own value, a deep acknowledgement of that. On her part, there was no suffering, no feverishness, no lovesickness, thank goodness – but her heart lifted when she saw him emerge from the train and stride towards her on the platform at King's Cross. His bearing was confident, and she could see that people responded to him with respect.

He said that his life was all about doing what he was told and getting others to do the same, but at least you could see the point of it with soldiering, and the others were good men.

They went out every evening of the leave and then suddenly they were saying goodbye in each other's arms, their frozen breath fogging the air around their faces.

'I think of you every night,' he wrote, 'perhaps more than I should. Please consider what I asked. There is talk of us moving on. I'm keen to go, except that I would be further from you.' Evelyn kept the letters in her top drawer. Her father had been in hospital but was home again, coughing his guts out in the big bedroom next to hers. She felt it would be better for him to die sooner rather than later, though thinking this way made her cry and clench her fists at the same time, and she knew she must never say it.

In any case, the German armies pushed on, and a house was nothing. It could be blown up, flattened, burned down. Generals made mistakes. An army could be forced to retreat – after Dunkirk came the shock of the French surrender. The story had changed: it was not a good one, and all they had was their new leader's words, his idea of a finest hour that could be bought with blood, toil, sweat and tears. Bombs and burning planes dropped from the sky. The city erupted in flames. Evelyn lived amidst the wail of sirens, the whistles and screams of falling bombs, the thud and rumble of explosions, the groans and shudderings of collapsing masonry. Fire engines and sandbags. Gas masks. Broken glass. Silver barrage balloons dotted the sky. Wire mesh was fixed to the bus windows, so you looked out as if from inside a cage. Impossible to predict how long a journey would take. Sometimes it took her two hours to get home from work. When the alarm sounded, she and her mother and her father fumbled to the shelters, and emerged, after sleepless nights, to heaped rubble where once whole buildings used to be. The smell of burning, the terrible endless dust: it was frightening, but more than that, it made her angry. Sometimes her racing heart woke her in the double darkness of her room and she could not sleep for hours, even if it was perfectly quiet outside.

'I am constantly busy,' he wrote, 'and at the same time, all I do is dream of you.' He might be posted next week, or the next year; he had no idea. 'My life seems easy by comparison with yours: a cosy billet, some men to shout at, three meals a day,' he wrote. 'My love, get yourself out of the city, find some war or land work if need be.'

There were cousins in Wiltshire with whom she and her parents could stay, but they would not put up with any drinking from her father. Even when he was taken into the hospital again her mother insisted on remaining in the city so she could visit him. Evelyn felt she had to stay, too.

'We won't be driven out,' she wrote.

It was only going to get worse, he told her. 'Please,' he wrote, 'protect yourself.'

There was talk that it might come to a land battle on home ground. She slept with an iron poker under the bed.

Harry's next leave came in October. The sirens sounded every night, but they went out to the matinee of the film of *Rebecca* with Joan Fontaine and Laurence Olivier: it was good, even though the house and gardens were not quite the way she had imagined them and the story still ended with it all burning down. And, for some reason, they had changed the part just before the end so that the new wife did not go with De Winter to the doctor in London . . . They were almost home and still debating the rationale for this when the sirens wailed and they had to run to the Underground.

Deep beneath the streets, the platform shook as the bombs struck closer and closer to where they lay, small, packed so close you could smell the next person's soap, or lack of it. A man with a sketchbook stood by the exit, then moved among them, drawing: a war artist, he said. Two hours passed. It was quiet for five or ten minutes so that they began to relax and then a thundering blow shocked them and a piece of the tunnel came down and gouged a man's face. Pebbly dust clattered down and then, after a sharp cracking sound, darkness engulfed them.

'No! Please!' Evelyn called out. As people fumbled for their torches, Harry shifted and lay over Evelyn, propping up his weight on his elbows and knees: it would hardly help if the ceiling fell on them, yet he could feel it calmed her. Both of them, truth be told. He felt her breath on his face. *Sshh*, he told her. She was shaking. His lips by her ear, he began to recite poetry he'd learned in school, instinctively choosing simple things with a rhyme and a steady rhythm, words that painted a clear picture in your mind: Walter de la Mare, Shelley: *The fountains mingle with the river* . . .

Could this be why they had been taught it? Did old Whitehorse set them to learn so much by heart because he suspected that it might come to exactly this kind of hell, bodies pressed close in a dark place, the words pouring out of him like an incantation, or a reminder at least of what they must struggle to reclaim? His childhood was now a half forgotten dream, something that had happened in another country since destroyed. But the words were in his head and he continued. Eventually, her breathing grew steadier beneath him and when the lights came on she blinked and smiled. Coughing, he shifted on to his side. The worst of the dust had settled, coating everyone and making them look like statues or ghouls.

They emerged dry-mouthed into a cold, wet morning. A hundred yards down the street, the cinema was gone. There was a choking smell of burned brick and wood mixed with leaked gas but the rising sun gilded the puddles and the wetness of everything, and drove up curls of mist.

It took half an hour to get home. Evelyn's mother and the house were safe, but the road was littered with debris, roof tiles, broken tables and even a broken bed right in the road. A house at the far end had been reduced to rubble. Two elderly brothers, Edward and Alan Jones, eccentric and rarely seen, had died there.

'Chin up, and count your blessings,' the warden said. 'Balham took it. One went right through the road and down a ventilation shaft. The tunnels are flooded and they're still counting the dead.' Harry checked on his parents then came back and pitched in with the clearing-up, working until it was dark.

Only the next day, they were at the station where sooty glass burned a tarnished gold in weak afternoon sun, and streams of soldiers surged to and from the platforms, their footsteps and banter echoing in the chill air, the rattle of the rails and the hisses and chugging of engines waiting, arriving and departing a constant reminder of the temporariness of everything.

Harry and Evelyn stood at the end of their platform, a little apart from the rush, their hands clasped together inside the pocket of his greatcoat. She did not want him to go, and the words sprang from her mouth:

'About your question. You know I've been spoiled rotten,' she said. 'I can't cook. Really, not even boil an egg.' The Army was feeding him rather well for now, he said, and pulled her to him.

Yes, she told him. And minutes later, the whistle blew, and he had to run for his train, leaving her there, all of a sudden and without intending it, *engaged.* Her lips tender, her left cheek aflame from rubbing against his coat, she burst into tears. Part of her wanted to turn and stride away, but at the same time, she could not. The last few doors slammed. Another whistle sounded, followed by a few shouts, and then a tight hissing sound as pressure mounted and mounted until the pistons moved and the engine chugged and pulled the train slowly out of the station; bit by bit it accelerated, and then, suddenly, was gone.

WATER, WATER, EVERYWHERE

He had been half frightened, when they stood before the registrar in Reading, that marriage would make things ordinary, but so far the reverse had been true. They'd been married a year and a half; their one-night honeymoon upstairs in the pub had been followed by islands of cohabitation in an ocean of separation, but to his mind, when they were together, it was better every time.

That last night they'd had to keep from waking Lillian and could not bear the squeal of the bedsprings a second time. They'd made use of a kitchen chair, set against the wall, with a cushion on it. She half sat astride him and teased him by not giving him what he asked for, or not for long. Her breasts in his face and hands. An exquisite suffering. Unable to drift off afterwards they lay awake talking. Banking arrangements. Her impossible mother. How she must get out of London. That night on the bowling green. *Frenchman's Creek*, which Harry thought was mostly trash yet managed to say something important at the same time. He tried to explain and couldn't, gave up and rubbed her back between the shoulder blades.

They dozed and got up at five. It was a short walk to the bus stop. She pushed Lillian in the pram, the landlady's boy carted the trunk in a wheelbarrow, and Harry had two bags to carry. Naturally they were both tired, and they were weary of saying goodbye, too. It was something they had done often over the past two years. A longer and far more dangerous separation lay ahead, but it was hard to remember that, since the shape of it was so very familiar, a ritual almost: the shared journey to the depot or station, a wait until one of them, usually him, boarded the train or bus or truck, and then the stab of loss as the vehicle pulled him away, leaving her to decide whether to wait and watch, or wave and turn away. Normally the sadness afterwards was sweetened by reliving the night or days before, and by looking forward to the next leave. This time, though, there was no destination, just *Overseas*, and no estimate as to the duration of his absence. He was about to enter another world, one they had seen on the newsreels but never touched or smelled.

Even so, birds sang in the garden hedges. Mrs Williams had packed him a sandwich and Evelyn had successfully made him a small cake. It would go stale if he didn't eat it soon, she'd told him, and he had replied that there was little chance of that.

The High Street swarmed with uniformed men and officers. Brick buildings and stone pavement amplified and sharpened their shouts and the clatter of their boots and equipment. Wives and other civilians stood marooned on the periphery. Buses filled the air with the stink of diesel.

Evelyn followed him, the pram juddering on the flagstones. Lillian moaned, woke. Her face convulsed; she gasped, wailed. The bus was almost full. The trunk had to be wrestled into the storage locker below. 'What you got in here?' the driver complained. Harry paid the boy off then covered Evelyn's hand with his and leaned in for the last kiss, gentle, but enough to make him want her all over again. He pulled her tight and close, let go, then bent into the noise and stink that was his daughter.

'Goodbye, minx,' he said. Her face glistened crimson with frustration: she was not at her most appealing, he thought, but was expressing, in her way, the absolute essence of the occasion.

He knew Evelyn was trying not to cry.

'Look, don't wait. Go back to Mrs Williams and sort Lily out. Just remember I love you both.'

She jiggled the pram.

There was part of him that thought it could not be happening.

'Write!' she reminded him as he climbed on board. He wiped the window with his sleeve. She stared up at him, her forehead puckered, her lips drawn into a smile. She stood very straight, in her blue pre-war dress and the cardigan her aunt had knitted for her. A minute or two passed, and then the engine rumbled into gear. Fighting the appalling constriction in his chest and gut, he smiled and returned her wave as the bus pulled away.

It could be that was the last they would see of each other. There was no way to know.

And now he was at sea.

The cabin was a hellhole – a windowless, fume-filled space close to the engines and twenty degrees hotter than outside. Beneath grey paint you could see the mouldings and panelling, and the embossed lion: Cunard. Also painted grey was the brass button you pushed to call for service, disconnected, of course. The space was designed for two (budget travellers, he supposed) and accommodated five: himself, Royle, Hunter, and Thomson on bunks, plus, on the floor, McKenzie, an engineer who had somehow got hold of a camp bed which filled the entire free space. Other obstacles included three tin trunks and a couple of suitcases sticking out from under the beds, a washstand (cold fresh water for two separate hours daily), a dressing table, and a single set of drawers. There was a porthole, permanently blacked out and too small to admit a significant amount of air even if it had not been fixed about an inch ajar, and also two electric fans that did nothing but pick at the edges of his paper.

It was strange to write knowing it would be weeks until the letter left the ship, let alone arrived at its destination. The throb of the engines vibrated in the board he was leaning on, and transmitted itself to his knees, arm, neck and head. Sweat oozed from his hands; he had to write with a pencil to avoid smears. It would be cooler on deck but the entire population of the ship was milling around up there.

30 July 1942

Darling, it would be a fine thing to travel this way in peacetime, with a band playing in the lounge, to go for walks arm in arm on the top deck at night looking at the moonlit waves, and then to bed, but not to sleep, absolutely not to sleep. Idleness makes the longing worse. I can't help it. You are the sweetest wife and the most adorable mistress any man ever had. I am so glad that you can be wicked, too. However much I think of you, and however delicious that can be, it is in the end not the real thing and brings me back to the unwelcome fact I have left behind me the best wife a man ever had and an extraordinary little daughter.

We embarked at about six o'clock. It was a lovely morning and this helped to make up for the miserable journey. It was exciting at first to be on board. I stayed on deck to see the banks of the river (excuse my vagueness, but were I to name it, the censor would black it out) sliding away slowly behind us; the ship still as steady as a rock and the sea quite calm & our little escort of seagulls in pursuit. I prepared myself for an emotional upheaval, a sentimental orgy as I saw the last of home go away. This was not leaving Great Britain, it was being dragged away & my heart rebelled at such violence . . . And then far stronger than all these was the feeling within me that turned all others to nothing: I had already left home when I left you in the high street. I shall always remember you standing looking half unafraid, half frightened, hardly realising, I suspect, that it was indeed the end. Half of me died as I got on that bus (it was the wrong bus too). How quick and how small an ending to all our goodbyes.

Routine so far includes Boat Stations twice a day (parading in Mae Wests), and Captain's Inspection. Both these things keep everybody standing about for hours. When one is not standing about one can either lounge and read or lounge and drink, or lounge and sleep. In any case, it allows one to brood so I try as much as possible to keep moving and stop worrying.

The men are having a very poor time. They are overcrowded down below and sweltering in their hessian hammocks inches below the ceiling in the same place as they eat their miserable food. I deplore the distinction, but I am also very glad to have my pip.

There were five thousand of them on board, all ranks, all nationalities, army, air force, navy, medics, nurses, even a group of musicians out to entertain the troops.

'A ship of fools!' Harry told Royle.

As for the sea, he'd not done more than paddle in it before. How endless it was, how boring and fascinating at the same time. He studied the gathering swells and the patterns on the water's surface, and farther out, the colours and the shifting appearance of the horizon. It wrapped you round. At night it became another thing entirely, secretive, half seen, full of subtle sounds, and after that came the sunrise, the slow lightening, then the flood of gold. It was so vast and absolute that he found it hard to believe in the existence of submarines.

4 August

The nurses mostly act like queens, being such a minority, though none of them would attract attention in other circumstances. I don't think much of them, but then I have you to remember and I do more of that than is good for me. Perhaps because we saw so much of each other in the last few weeks, neither of us could quite believe that we were parting, and it made saying goodbye somewhat easier. But now it is real and appalling to think of us becoming farther and farther apart day by day. I shall love you however far or long I am away. I shall think of nothing but –

But there was Royle, in his PE kit, tall, already tanned, racket in hand.

'Miles! Still writing your darned love letter? Must be an effing book by now! Come on! Deck tennis! You're needed.' Deck tennis was inane and, bar the net slung across the so-called 'court', *nothing* to do with tennis itself – no rackets, not even a ball involved, just hard rubber rings called quoits – but it was good policy to seize upon any opportunity to exercise, and to play it was a privilege, since three of the courts were taken up with lifeboats and only officers could use the fourth. He signed the letter, and slipped it in an envelope.

They emerged to a muggy white sky, a deck radiating heat. He and Royle drew Anderson and Cowley respectively. 'Let's flatten them,' Royle said.

His first serve was, Harry had to admit, spectacular: the quoit rose steadily past the net and over Cowley's arms, then plummeted down just inside the line. Catching the things was the devil and having one thump into your neck worse still. So he started off strong, and he didn't want to lose it even though Anderson, not a bad chap really, came back hard. You bastard, you smug pile of nothing, he said to himself, good shot, so what: I'll do better. And he'd be lying if he didn't admit that he was aware, too, of the gaggle of nurses watching from the upper deck, of their oohs and aahs, the occasional burst of applause or twitter of feminine laughter: the quoits wobbled through the air and more or less turned corners. You had to run hard, fling yourself up, manage not to fall. They won the first set 4-2, lost the next 5-1.

'Got you on the run now,' Anderson called out, half joking, just that bit too cocky.

'What? Boot's on the other foot!'

The women liked the banter, cheered.

'We'd better turn this around,' Harry said to Royle. They were both dripping and he could feel his face starting to burn. They lost the first game, and it was Royle's misses that did it: the man had a good serve but was exhausted and always tried to run when half the time he didn't need to; Anderson saw it, and was sending his shots accordingly. But Harry had a feel for the throws: could give the thing a flick at the end to get some twist into it, make it land just out of reach.

'I'm covering your back,' he told Royle, giving the man a break until his wind came back, and that way they limped through the game, and eventually, agonisingly, won the set and then the match, to protracted applause. They stood by the drains and tipped buckets of seawater over each other before they went below.

8 August

You can't go for a long walk, but today the sea was deep Mediterranean blue and the breeze saved the day from being unbearably hot. I now make it my routine to do exercises at about ten and have a refreshing bath afterwards. The baths are all seawater. Difficult to get a lather even with the special shaving soap but very refreshing – and always available! In the sea at night are queer phosphorescent flashes. At such moments my longing for you becomes an ache. I am conscious of nothing but you and me and the barrier between us. Nothing I can think of would be too much to give to be lying down beside you tonight.

10 August

About noon today we sighted land and it was obvious we were making for it. I didn't feel unduly excited, because I knew I wasn't going ashore. I couldn't anticipate what the country would look like but I was surprised when I saw that the hills were green. Even so, they didn't look like English hills, the vegetation was obviously different and the quaint buildings that cling on to the hillside would never be seen in England. The sand of the shore is a deep red colour. There are many rather odd-looking boats with a sail that appears to be the wrong way up. Now's the time to put on the mosquito ointment. Nice to see that there is no blackout on shore and strings of lights are reflected in the water, and for the first time we are allowed to smoke on deck after dark.

This is the place from where my letters go to you my darling, so I have a friendly feeling for it. I have been told it could be a month and a half before post goes again.

14 August

Water, water, everywhere. An incredible sea this morning. I was late for breakfast through marvelling at it. As smooth as Lillian's bottom. Well, at least as smooth as any lake or pond I have seen. And such a deep blue. When the breeze blew, the only effect was to produce a very fine matt finish. The ship cut through it and it folded back like icing from a cake. It seemed sacrilege for the boat to do this.

The new cabin is not quite so noisy and has only four in it. We are wearing our tropical uniforms. A new routine has begun, with four hours of work a day, drilling and teaching men how to use and maintain the Bren gun and other such things, often things we have learned just five minutes before. We do PE every morning and play deck tennis whenever possible. Royle and I are not often beaten and hope to rank in the championship. There is a swimming pool on the top deck but it's blocked off and full of stores. I lean over the rail, gaze at the water rushing by and dream of jumping in, but they would leave me behind and then court-martial me in absentia. And I suppose there might be sharks.

There was still endless time to read. He could, as he had intended, have tried again to write something more than a letter, some verses about the longing he felt and the blessings and perils of depending so much on memories. But his efforts so far had frustrated him. He could have continued with Auden's *Another Time*, but despite admiring some of the later poems enormously – to the point of outright jealousy – he wanted something less immediately connected to the war and so he carried Charles Morgan's novel *Sparkenbroke* to a cool and semi-private spot in the shade of a lifeboat on the upper deck.

The story, set between an English country estate and Italy, dealt with the relationship between an intense, Byronesque poet, Sparkenbroke, who owned the manor house, and a woman, Mary, engaged to Peter, a decent but dull man.

There were long passages detailing Sparkenbroke's thoughts about poetry and myth, quotations of his own and other poets' verses on art, death and transcendence – all very interesting. Sparkenbroke wrote to Mary at length on the same topics. Their discussions and letters were very much a seduction. Harry liked the book, though he liked the ideas more than the fiction. He carped at the way Sparkenbroke and Mary seemed to have nothing else to do but debate the purposes of art, the nature of ecstasy and other finer points of life. He warmed to the heroine less than he had to the woman in Morgan's previous book,

The Fountain. From the name on, there was something blank and flat about this girl, he thought. She asked questions, and received the answers. In some way she was there only as a foil for Sparkenbroke, there to incite and then absorb his torrents of words . . . Whereas, Harry thought, his eyes finally parting company with the page, one of the things he loved about Evelyn was her fierce pride, her willingness to argue even when the facts were against her, to interrupt, to refuse, to insist –

Startled to hear an actual woman's voice, he looked up and saw two of them approaching. They were dressed in an odd kind of tropical get-up: knee-length shorts pretty much like his, with shirts and caps to match. The taller, fairer one asked him for a light, and he sprang to his feet and searched for his lighter. She had fine arched eyebrows, large grey eyes, a small mouth.

'You look rather familiar,' he said to her, the book at his feet, its pages flapping in the breeze.

'You were probably listening to us last night,' she said, and ran her fingers along the keys of an imaginary piano. 'And we watched *you* and your friend win again yesterday afternoon. Well done! Thank you, Lieutenant.'

'Harry Miles,' he said.

'Cicely Osborne,' she told him, 'and this is my friend Charlotte Barber. You probably saw her at the concert, too.'

He cupped the flame in his hand and the two women leaned in. They put their elbows on the railing and looked out to sea while they smoked, and so as not to be rude, he did the same. He did remember them – particularly Cicely, in a silver dress, sitting straight-backed at the piano. Charlotte had been one of the dancers. The whole thing had been far better than he expected.

'Thank you for the entertainment,' he told Cicely. 'Lovely to hear that tune from *Les Sylphides*. I saw it in London, with my wife.'

'But aren't you far too young to be married?' she replied and he felt himself colour. She turned quickly back to look at the sea; Charlotte leaned towards him and said, 'Just a little joke,' and smiled as she did so, and he found himself asking politely where they had been before this assignment and what they felt about being at sea. Charlotte angled her head towards Cicely.

'Charlotte's been all over, but it's my first trip. I get to play the piano where there is one, or else I sing . . . In a way it's almost boring,' she said, looking him in the face. It was her turn to colour a little. Despite her boldness, she was, he realised, very shy. 'All the same, I wish it would never stop.'

'I know what you mean,' he told her, and he did, but he couldn't think of a thing more to say, and bent to retrieve his book to stop the flapping noise of the windblown pages. Cicely threw her cigarette over the side.

'We interrupted your reading, and I need to get out of the sun.' She held out her hand, and he shook it, then watched her walk back the way they had come.

'Cicely's just hideously nervous with people,' Charlotte told him before he too could escape. 'Especially men. She's perfectly fine on a stage, but in the real world, she needs to get her confidence up. So I told her: you just need a little practice with a gentlemanly type.'

'Excuse me?' he asked. She smiled back at him. She was older than her friend. Her lips were rouged, he noticed, just a little redder than they would naturally be. It was rather well done.

'In times like these,' she said, 'it's best to live for the moment, don't you think? *Carpe diem*, make hay, all that. Very nice to meet you, Lieutenant Miles.'

Then they were both gone and he was alone with his book. He found the passage he had been reading, but couldn't re-engage with it. He had the distracting feeling that he too was inside a story, one of the two women's making. And had he upset the half-shy girl? What was he supposed to do?

'I was held captive by two lady musicians. I think the younger one's after me,' he told Royle. 'Or maybe both.'

'Well, aren't you lucky!' Royle said. 'Which reminds me, I've been meaning to ask . . . What's the difference between a thrill and a shock?

'No idea.'

'Nine months!' Royle guffawed. 'But you'll be God knows where by then.'

'I'm not interested, Royle.'

'Why the hell not? Your lovely wife is many leagues away.' It was getting on over three thousand miles, Harry thought, as the crow flies. Though they'd travelled farther than that, and would travel thousands more miles only to end up nearer home than they now were. At Freetown they had been told, as they already knew, that they were set for Egypt, via the Cape.

Practice on a gentlemanly type! It was a bit of a liberty but he could see that a sensitive, good-looking girl from a well-to-do background, as Cicely seemed to be, might well feel the heat on a ship full of soldiers and want to take control of the situation. He could also see that a certain kind of woman, wilful, and very independent and artistic, such as Charlotte seemed to be, might enjoy some new freedoms in wartime. Another man, he thought, might well take advantage of the situation, but he *wasn't* interested in Cicely, other than in the general human way . . . Though it was only honest to admit that he might well have been, if he was not already lucky enough to be a married man. Which Royle was not. The nurses were a different matter: they'd surely overcome their embarrassment, and seemed the opposite of shy. They were used to being in charge of their patients and had each other for backup. *Bitches in heat*, Royle had called them, though none of them were after him. The whole thing was foolishness.

20 August

Day and night are now exactly the same length. It is actually a little cooler due to breezes from the south. I have been feeling rather strange but it is hard to determine the exact cause, perhaps the sea itself and the sheer amount of time aboard. We are still busy. The other evening, a woman on the piano played some music from *Sylphides* – however much I try to shut them out, these bittersweet memories track me down.

I read poetry for distraction at night, and try and, as ever, fail to write it, but sometimes quite suddenly I see you & me together on the grass. You are lying on your back with your eyes closed and a lovely tumble of hair twisted in the grass and of course it's a good memory but at the same time you know it is not the real thing.

August 22

Such a day! A gale blew in from the south and pushed up waves that tossed even this stable tub about. Like a Disney cartoon to see people pawing the air to get along; to see people unconsciously let go of the rail they were holding and be hurled across the deck; to come round a corner and have so much air blown into your body that you are left gasping until the wind pushes you back to where you came from.

Three of us stood at the forepart of B-deck on the port side and watched the waves splashing against the bows. The sun behind us was rainbowed up in the shower of spray that each wave caused. Some waves are bigger than others & when a big wave coincided with a downward plunge of the bows the shower was sent high up to where we stood & we had to duck behind the rail. We thoroughly enjoyed being children until we were too cold and too wet to do so any longer. A large fish – about 5ft – with bony fins and a blunt nose was thrown right out of the water.

Even in a storm, the albatrosses weave in and out of the waves: huge mysterious birds, far more graceful than gulls. They glide down the troughs of the waves but never get caught in them. You can't but ask yourself, who could ever kill one? But it's a silly question because men do far worse things.

He ran into Cicely again in the aftermath of the storm. She was on the upper deck, clinging to the rail and retching. He thought it better to slip by unnoticed, and not long after that, they stopped for two weeks in Durban to wait for their next convoy, and he saw her in the town on the last afternoon. He had been camped near the racecourse and had been taking advantage of local hospitality and of the buses – no charge for service personnel – to get a sense of the place. He had embarked again that morning but had afternoon leave and so he slipped into the Royal Hotel hoping for a quiet drink. It didn't disappoint: tiled floors, rattan furniture, ceiling fans and palm trees, very elegantly done. He glimpsed Cicely in the tea lounge sitting with Captain Chesterton (a bit of a boor in his estimation), Charlotte, and a South African naval officer. She had taken her hat off and her hair, set in rolls around her face, caught the light. She sat straight but at the same time loosely, as if, he thought, she were on stage again at the piano and about to play. The reach of the keyboard and the long fingers rippling over it were a mystery to him; if you wanted to learn the piano you needed to possess one, and no one he knew did. Music lessons. A big house. Plucky, to throw herself into this . . . From a distance she seemed happy enough, in her nervous way, and he was not sure whether he should join them, but when she caught his eye and beckoned him over, he was surprisingly glad of it. An extra chair immediately materialised, and despite wanting beer he agreed to a cup of tea.

'Lieutenant Miles has excellent musical taste,' Cicely told Chesterton, and then turned to smile at Harry.

'Not really, sir,' he said. 'But I do think these ladies do a wonderful job.'

'We're thinking of going to the jazz matinee at the Royal,' Charlotte said.

'Bit of a busman's holiday?' Harry suggested. 'Though it sounds suitably sophisticated. On the subject of my taste, I'll admit I went to the cinema yesterday afternoon, saw *Dumbo*, and thoroughly enjoyed it.'

'I went last week. Some of the songs are lovely!' Cicely said. Who had she been with, Harry wondered. No one at this table, at any rate.

It was pretty clear from their lack of conversational response that Chesterton and the South African, Birk, would rather see the back of him, but on the other hand, Cicely and Charlotte were keen to keep him there. As they prepared to leave, Charlotte, arm in arm with Birk, suggested that Harry join them for the matinee.

'Please,' Cicely said, reaching out to touch his arm. 'The more the merrier.' Her smile was tight, her expression, he felt, suddenly close to entreaty. Hadn't he made things clear? He clearly remembered using the word *wife*, and her joking about him being too young to be married. Perhaps he was imagining it. The truth was he had things to organise on board, given their departure in the morning, but he did like her, and there was no harm in it, surely, so he agreed to walk to the theatre with them on his way to the docks. He knew well enough not to offer his arm to either of the ladies when superior officers were present, but clearly Cicely did not think the same way, because, at the end of the fuss and muddle of their preparations to leave the bar, and in clear view of Chesterton, she slipped her arm through his. He ended up with her on his right side, Chesterton on the other.

He guessed that she would prefer the shade, and she agreed.

The streets were crowded, but the temperature was perfect, with a breeze rustling through the palms planted in front of Victorian brick and stone buildings, which looked almost British, yet at the same time sun-kissed and exotic. Cicely, her long fingers resting on his sleeve, nodded and smiled.

Not a bad city at all, Chesterton agreed. He found it very well organised. The blacks, Harry had noticed, did all the hard work. Whenever there was digging or shifting to be done, there they were – unlikely, he thought, to be so impressed with the organisation.

'It's been good to be on land,' he said. To be able to walk, to turn a street corner and see something unexpected – and also to see women, not just nurses, but women who lived here, wearing dresses, going about their everyday lives, and children too – he had enjoyed all that.

'Unfortunately,' Chesterton continued, 'where we are headed will be far less pleasant.'

'Afraid so . . . Are you travelling with us, or staying here?' he asked Cicely.

'We're going to Cairo, but not until next week. Two shows here first. We sail on different ships from here on,' she said. 'Are you sure you won't come with us this afternoon?'

At the theatre, he waited with the women while Birk and Chesterton bought tickets. Part of him did want after all to join them, to spend his last night on land on a velvet-covered seat beside Cicely, shielding her somewhat from Chesterton's attentions, whether that annoyed the man or not; he felt quite strongly that she wanted it, that she had, for some reason, taken a shine to him. But at the same time, he resisted the complications – suppose, for example, there was a goodbye kiss at the end of the evening – an expectation of one, or the actual thing. He knew it would be hard to resist and also that he wouldn't take such a thing lightly; he was afraid when he thought of it. Cicely was so utterly different to Evelyn.

'I do hope you understand, that under the circumstances, I won't . . . I hope the concert doesn't disappoint you, and that the new ship is at least no worse than ours was,' he said, taking in the smooth planes of her face, her glistening lips, the curious, vulnerable eyes looking back at him. 'It's been a very great pleasure to meet you.' He offered his hand.

'Yes,' she said, taking it briefly in both of hers, which were surprisingly cool, and seemed to stroke rather than hold, 'I do expect that's best, Lieutenant Miles.'

'Harry,' he told her.

'Good luck, Harry,' she said, and then when the others returned, he said some more casual goodbyes, and left.

So it was not true to say that he had not been interested in her, and admitting this was disturbing. And also, this parting reminded him of more important goodbyes and made him feel his distance from home. On board the *Rajala* that night, he avoided the cabin and stayed on deck. There was no moon, and the city's blackout was thorough; he looked out over the undulating darkness of the sea and allowed his thoughts to wander.

He liked being married, and not just the bed part of it. There was something surprising about the dailiness of life together, the way you came to understand each other better in all ways, to see the more hidden parts of a personality . . . But if he had not found Evelyn, or supposing she had turned him down, or if he had been another kind of man, then he might have fallen for Cicely. And in that case, it could have gone many ways. They might have embarked on a brief romance that no one at home need ever know about, ending with a few tears here in Durban. These things often happened in a war, of course, though perhaps that was a good reason to avoid them. Or, it could have started out that way, but become an ongoing complication, with its own stream of letters, the possibility of future meetings and partings, and even of something that lasted beyond the war, if they both lived through it . . . It was shocking to realise how all the other stories that a life might become were there, waiting, jostling at your elbow, even when you had made a clear choice. But it was over with and by now, he told himself, she would be free of Chesterton and, hopefully, asleep.

They sailed the next morning. Everyone who was free flocked to the port side. Perla Gibson, an opera singer, had come to the pier to serenade them. Apparently she sang to every ship as it arrived and departed, but due to his responsibilities as a baggage officer he had missed her on their way in; now, not expecting very much of the event, he joined the crush at the rail and stared down at a distant but discernibly dumpy middle-aged woman dressed in a white frock and a red straw hat, a megaphone clutched in her right hand. It did not seem promising.

She raised her free arm and brought the megaphone to her lips. Without preamble she began to sing, her voice powerful and surprisingly pure. It took him a moment to recognise the song as 'I'll Be Seeing You'.

So sentimental! Such an obvious choice that to begin with he resisted it, even as men standing by him began to sing along, some sincere, some in parody, all of them muddying the sound. But by the end he was all but weeping as he stared down at the singer, who now seemed both absurd and brave, both ordinary and magnificent. As she flung out the last line the deck vibrated and the engines roared below. Amidst shouts and applause and the mournful hooting of its whistle, the vast ship began to pull away. The figure on the dock bowed, raised the megaphone and began again, her voice now staunch and less emotional: 'There'll Always Be an England'. She waved with her free hand as she sang on, the ship second by second leaving her behind.

22 Sept

I had had no idea that leaving Durban would stir me up so much. And then, two days later, we had an alarm – the sighting of a suspicious vessel – and had to rush to Action Stations. There was considerable chaos as men, not only sleeping but also lulled into a near-coma by weeks of doing nothing much (I include myself here), woke to the idea of an emergency. Crew positioned themselves to lower the lifeboats. We rushed to our positions on deck, Bren guns at the ready, though there was at that point no possible use for a small weapon with a five-hundred-yard range. We waited like statues, sweating, our hearts galloping in our chests. I remember wondering whether those maintaining this ship's guns had done as good a job as I did when it was my responsibility on the last. There were no further orders. We held our positions as the sun rose, yellow and pink, and the ship and its convoy steamed on, almost as if bewitched. It grew gradually lighter and then word came down that it had just been a fishing boat. Breakfast tasted delicious when we eventually got to it.

After this, the war seems more real, even though it is still some weeks away for me. The journey is less like an adventure or a peculiar dream. At any point, the enemy could materialise. Sooner or later, he will. It could be at sea, but the chances are that I will be behind one set of guns, firing across the sand and rock while he fires other guns back. The other thing, darling, is that the war wants me to be another man. It requires me to be very methodical and obedient as much as it requires overcoming fear and inhibition, and this is something I will do for a necessary cause, but I am not drawn to it as a way of life in the way that some men seem to be, and actively dislike it. The war, because of its deadly mechanical nature, makes me crave love even more.

Of course it's true that without the war I might never have seen the southern stars or the albatrosses. I might never have come to feel the pull of the sea, or been brought to tears by a fat lady singing on the pier, or any number of extraordinary things that may lie ahead of me. I might never have understood how between one moment and the next a new chapter in life can end, or begin. Bear with my rambling, darling. These feelings and understandings (for which I have not yet paid by doing what I have been sent to do) are in their way wonderful, but I would surrender them – and far more – to be able to hear your voice, smell your hair, to run my hand down your back and press your body close to mine.

Cicely and the thoughts she had provoked were, he felt, included in the comment about chapters beginning and ending, and besides, it was already in the past. They had crossed the equator again and now sailed steadily north towards Suez, Cairo and the Delta. Before long, the voyage itself would be forgotten. He would live, plagued by flies, in an ocean of sand, hot all day and freezing at night.

They trained in the desert for almost a month. Just before they went into action, Harry was given afternoon leave in Cairo and bought for Evelyn, in a small shop owned by an ancient woman who spoke only French, a pair of twenty-denier silk stockings. He tucked the slim packet inside his shirt and then joined a group of slightly tipsy officers on the patio of the Shepheard's Hotel. Chesterton leaned in and asked, 'Did you hear about Cicely Osborne?' At first, Harry assumed that she was in the city, performing in one of the clubs or theatres. He wondered should he go and hear her, and thought that yes, he would. 'She was on the *Macedonia*,' Chesterton continued, leaning in closer. 'One of three casualties. Drowned. Awful business. The ship limped back to port, but before that some fool had the women loaded onto a lifeboat that promptly capsized. They've kept it rather quiet. I just heard today.'

Chesterton locked eyes with him for a moment.

'Nice girl. I was planning on keeping in touch,' he said, then shrugged and tipped back his whisky and soda.

Harry lay sleepless in his tent that night. He remembered Cicely's hands holding his, her odd persistence in singling him out. He felt terrible for saying no to her. Part of him wished he had not. And yet what sense did that make? It would have made things worse. For him. But for her?

At least they were moving on, he thought, as light began to seep through the canvas. Soon there would be no time to think this way.

For a long minute, Evelyn had no idea where they were, or of the time of day. The bedding was heavy. Lillian breathed next to her, and somewhere outside a distant dog yelped, then fell silent. Nothing else. She sat up in utter darkness, but as her vision adjusted she could see that light oozed in around the edge of the blackout covering a small, sunken window. The ceiling sloped. Then she remembered Mrs Saunders, a short, wiry woman with a harried, windblown look, who had warned her last night about hitting her head in the low side of the attic room, and also about the wooden staircase as they came up: 'It's worn slippery. Mind you wear clean shoes, or slippers with a good sole on them,' she'd said, 'not stockings or socks, and watch out for the little one. We won't be responsible for any accidents.'

Mrs Saunders had also shown Evelyn the chamber pot under the bed. She'd not used it and hoped never to do so, but now she badly needed to go. She fumbled to the window and pulled back the blackout, revealing a view of rolling country cut up into fields. She shoved her feet into her walking shoes and slipped her winter coat – lucky she had thought to bring it – over her nightdress. Lillian seemed deep in her sleep, but all the same Evelyn latched the door behind her so that there was no danger of her somehow rolling out of bed, then out of the door and down the stairs.

The landing and the next flight of stairs were carpeted. In the hall, a rug and a grandfather clock gearing up to strike: ten o'clock. No one in. She found the kitchen – dishes piled by the sink, an uneven, stone-flagged floor that needed a sweep – and then the passage at the back that led to a large pantry and a room with two more sinks, huge square things, and some drying racks. Beyond these, she came at last to the lavatory that had been built on at the back of the house. You had to step outside to get to the plank door of the WC, which was, thank heavens, unoccupied. An elderberry bush obscured the tiny window. Torn newspaper hung on a nail, just like home.

Each breath plumed briefly, and then vanished. Wasn't it supposed to be spring? It was bright, though, and there were tiny leaves on the bushes.

I got away, she thought. I got away. She'll be sorry now.

Letters arrived at intervals, in bundles and out of sequence, and hers were even slower to reach Harry than his were to reach her. Now, on top of that, his would be forwarded, delaying them yet further. At first, when nothing came to the farm for ten days, she had to remind herself that this did not mean bad news, because that came quickly, or so she'd been told.

She'd brought his last with her, and reread it often.

Thank you for letters 65 and 58. I love reading them, and knowing what you did many weeks ago, but whatever you write I have sadness and longing & always I want to join with you in those wonderful ordinary things. What can I write to you in return? I can't say what we are doing or where we are, except that you can follow it on the newsreels and it is hard and dirty work. It boils down to sand, more sand, even more sand, flies, and shooting. Some places have somewhat less sand, perhaps rock instead of sand, or even some trees and flowers, plus mosquitoes along with the flies, but we are never far from sand. Here there is some grass that almost covers it, and few trees, but we are about to move again. Hopefully somewhere better . . . If you feel like risking a parcel, our needs are cigarettes, tobacco and soap.

But these are dull enough subjects, which slip from my mind when I think of you. What I should write to you about are the thousand memory-torn longings that are the you that lives with me. Always in adversity or when I feel so little a part of the life around me – and this is often – that all men and things are enemies, my mind shuts out the present and I can spend timeless hours with my head safe-pillowed between your arm & breast. I see you do again countless things that you did so long ago. I can feel the still coldness of December nights on the heather when you restrained my hot lover's abandon. So vividly, the soft pressure of your breasts, the tautened touch of your thighs while your lips passed the silent message that was hearts' conversation. But the present is even harder afterwards.

I love you. Only love's madness could give hope in life's morbid sanity. Forgive me, my love, I am very tired and half mad.

Yet when new letters did finally reach the farm, they were thin things in comparison: brief, hasty scrawls that did not compare with what he had written earlier. Of course, he had been in action for weeks. He was exhausted. It was important to remain positive.

At the back of the fenced garden where Mrs Saunders grew herbs and flowers, a gate led onto a track that skirted a field dotted with sheep and then joined the back road to Bourton. The walk, on a narrow lane that meandered along, never too steep, took just over an hour, and Evelyn liked to keep up a good pace, even when pushing the pram. Foxgloves, buttercups, vetch and cow parsley sprouted in the ditch. Her letter to Harry was tucked under the covers by Lillian's feet. *So here I still am*, it began, though since he seemed not to have received anything she had written since her move to the farm, she could not imagine him knowing what that meant.

What would he think when he finally realised where she was? He wanted them out of London, but she knew he'd rather she didn't work, or that she found something *better*. He'd dislike the idea of her with a bucket of gritty potatoes to peel, or cleaning out the greasy oven, or wringing other people's wash: it was not on a par with working for Wilson & Wilson, who had let her go the moment she married. It was, basically, charring, the kind of work that her mother did, and since she didn't like it herself she hadn't yet given Harry a real sense of the situation, saying, rather, that she had applied not exactly as a land girl, and she and Mrs Saunders had 'come to an arrangement'.

She'd prefer to be making shells or guns: excellent pay, but full-time, often with involuntary overtime. She was loath to hand Lillian over to someone all day, *especially* if it was to her mother, who never stopped pointing out in backhanded ways how badly timed this baby was, or suggesting that they should have waited to marry, and that she was just asking for trouble and grief . . . *Believe me, I am not!* It had been awful, going back home after the weeks alone with Harry.

'I don't want to be told what you think about my choices in life every two hours. And I don't need your advice about Lillian. That's what the nurse at the clinic is for. The one thing I *do* want is for the house to be safe and hygienic.'

'What are you on about? I keep things very clean!'

'I'm not talking about dirt, I'm talking about *germs*. Every time he coughs! You can't see them, but he's spraying the air with bacteria that could infect us as well.'

'Well leave, then, if it's not up to your bloody standards!' her mother had told her, and then wept and said she didn't mean it, how very much she loved Evelyn and Lillian and just wanted the best for them both.

'How am I supposed to believe you?' Evelyn said, though actually, she knew it was the truth. What she really meant was, *What good is any of that if you won't do what I need? Why won't you put me and Lillian first?*

So she had left, and already, she could see that hygiene here was no better than at home, and quite possibly even worse, given the animals and the enormous amounts of manure standing around in piles. In that respect, there was little or no improvement. But at least here in the country you got safety, fresh air and good food, and no one here was suggesting that when Lillian fretted at night she should slip brandy into her milk. All in all, the farm seemed to offer a calmer and more prosperous kind of life, as well as distance from her parents.

'Isn't that so, Lily,' she said, stopping a moment and leaning into the pram. Lillian tended to be pale, but today her cheeks were rosy; Evelyn kissed each of them, unbuttoned Lillian's cardigan, then pushed the pram hood down so that she could see the trees and the sky. She picked a buttercup and gave it to Lillian to hold: *yellow.* One day soon the answering echo would come and she was eager for it. She was always pointing things out and naming them: *tree, sky, bee, bird, Mummy*; she loved the feeling of her daughter's eyes on her face, the way she studied her lips as she spoke or sang – though today those eyes, very bright, seemed to stare beyond Evelyn at the sky. *Blue,* Evelyn said, smiling, *blue.*

For half a mile or so, pale stone walls ran along the edges of fields now beginning to colour with new crops, and then came a part of the walk where the trees touched and knit themselves together above their heads, creating a tunnel of greens. After this, the trees thinned, allowing a view of lambs playing on the higher fields; she stopped, took Lillian out to see them, watched her frown in concentration, felt her body tense. *It won't be long,* Evelyn had written to Harry, *before she is answering me back.*

They passed a wrought-iron gate, always closed, that she imagined led to some stately pile. Few people used the back road, though occasionally a horse and cart or a cyclist rattled past. There was a postbox on the main road near the farm, but in Bourton she could buy stamps and hand her letter over personally. There were shops, a library, people milling about, trains. And on the way, she could think her thoughts and sing to Lillian. It was the best part of the day, and really, once you got outside, the whole arrangement was not too bad at all, and so there she still was.

It was not her fault that she could not cook.

Mrs Saunders had not listened when she told her so. Hard potatoes. Not enough gravy. Coordinating the different elements of the meal for so many people was new, and beyond her. She'd turned it into a story for Harry, but at the time it had been mortifying. 'I'm sorry, but I'm more used to typing,' she had explained the next morning.

'Not much call for that here,' Mrs Saunders replied, passing her the peeler. 'Didn't your mother show you? If you can't cook, you'll have to prep and clean and that way I can help the girls outside. Cheer up, now. You're doing your bit, away from the smoke and bombs. And,' she added, 'don't worry yourself about waste. We feed our peelings straight to the pigs.'

Two egg-sized potatoes for a woman and four for a man. Counting the Saunders, various old men and a spattering of land girls, there could be ten or more eating at the big table in the kitchen. Potatoes featured in *every* meal, enough to put you off the darned things for life. But there were plenty of fresh eggs.

All in all the arrangement was fair.

She only partly envied the land girls. They lived in huts close to the road and got to go around in a band and have a laugh together, but were out in the weather and the mud all day, driving tractors in the rain, digging, cleaning out the barns, and growing mannish biceps. They smoked and drank. None of them was married; some were surprisingly well-to-do. All of them loved Lillian, and she could leave her with them for an hour or so if she had to wash and set her hair, and they had insisted that she should join them when the Americans from Toddington came in cars and trucks to take them out. She'd put on her good dress and squeezed into the car. The dance was in the village hall where they watched the newsreels; a band and a singer soon had everyone joining in, and it *was* fun, though she was an anomaly: 'Your husband at the front, then? Bet he can't wait to get home.' The Americans were well-built and had lovely teeth, but if you danced, you had to deal with their wandering hands. And because she didn't drink more than half a glass of cider, while everyone else got soused, she was very aware of the smell. They probably thought she was stuck-up.

And maybe I am, she'd written to Harry.

So it's not perfect here, but it is very picturesque. I'll keep looking for something better, but meanwhile this keeps Mum from driving me wild. She still doesn't see what I'm getting at . . . Not to speak of him, who has never thought of other people in his entire life. He acts as if there was nothing the matter at all, except he's too weak to work or pick up his own shoes.

I'm glad to have Lillian away from all that. I'm sorry I can't send you many books. Charing Cross Road is out of reach and there is nothing much locally, but I found a biography of Edward Thomas, and will send that with some soap and tea. The village he wrote about is not far from here.

We have your photo on the dresser in our attic room. I hope you stay safe, and are soon out of that terrible desert. I can hardly bear to watch the newsreel, Harry, though I do, in case you are in it. I know this is how it has to be for now. Our girl now has ten teeth. She is nearly walking . . .

The post office was built of the creamy yellow local stone: pretty as you approached, but gloomy inside. She wiped the stamp on the sponge provided, pressed it on, and slipped the letter across the counter. She always made a point of handing her post to Mrs Mathieson in person so as to be sure of catching the last collection.

'How's it over at the Saunders'?'

'Good, thank you. Not quite so busy as last week.'

'And your mother in London?'

'Pretty well.'

'No letter for her? How she must miss you and the baby. And your husband in Tunisia, still? From what they say, we're pushing those devils to the edge.' Mrs Mathieson, small, silver-haired, touched Evelyn's hand. 'Everything will be all right, dear, and I think a letter went out to you today.'

For some reason, tears sprang to Evelyn's eyes.

She stopped by the river, sat on the bench with Lily on her lap. The poor thing's hair was stuck to her scalp with sweat, her face very red; Evelyn removed the little yellow cardigan, and blew down the back of her daughter's neck. She broke the crust she had in her pocket in half and mimed how to throw it to the ducks; when Lily tried, her first attempt landed on the grass and she wailed in disappointment. Even so, the ducks chuntered closer.

They moved right to the water's edge for the second attempt, watched the birds jostle and squabble. A man with an eyepatch who had been sitting on the other bench strode over and remarked on the fine weather. She felt compelled to reply since he had seen her feed the ducks, technically a prohibited waste of food – but of course he then wanted to know what she was doing this evening.

'If it's any of your business,' she said, 'I'm looking forward to bathing my baby then reading a letter from my husband.'

'I only asked,' he said.

'Not all there,' Evelyn told Lily once they were clear. She peered in under the pram's hood. 'What shall I sing to you? You're very hot, still. Are you coming down with something? Please don't.' Her hands and jaw tensed up – but it was important to remember, she reminded herself, deliberately relaxing them, these things usually turned out to be nothing much.

'I hope you've had a good afternoon,' Mrs Saunders said when they arrived back. She peered abstractedly into the pram, where Lillian lay, red-faced, damply asleep. 'But I've got to remind you about the floor. It needs washing every day, or we get ants.'

'Do you want me to do it now?'

Mrs Saunders sighed. She was wearing her cooking apron, but, Evelyn noted, her hands were filthy, especially under the nails.

'You'll be under my feet. After supper.'

'And then again in the morning?'

'Like I said, every day,' said Mrs Saunders. It was a stone floor, and looked bad whatever you did to it. To her surprise, Evelyn's eyes again pricked with tears; she stopped them in their tracks by thinking that if she and Harry ever had a house or even a flat of their own there would be proper tiles, or linoleum. Also, an electric stove and a fridge, a big window with a blind, and an immaculate stainless steel sink. It would be as clean as a hospital.

Her letter, a proper one, not just a card, lay on the shelf by the front door.

'Dinner then bath,' she told Lillian as she lifted her from the potty, but when the food was ready, Lily turned her head away from the spoon with its mush of carrot and minced meat.

Evelyn couldn't help but follow the puckered little mouth with the spoon, even though she half knew it was the wrong thing to do. A child must eat! 'For heaven's sake!' she said, when the food she'd managed to slip in came back out, spattering the tray.

'Leave her be,' Mrs Saunders butted in.

'Thank you! I do know how to look after my own child.' She went to rinse the bib under the kitchen tap and get a cloth to wipe the high chair. 'If she doesn't eat, she'll be hard to put down. Will you keep me some supper, please?'

Mrs Saunders didn't reply.

'There's sick in your hair!' she told Lillian. It was in the creases of her neck, too. The smell appalled Evelyn, almost turned her stomach. She wiped away the worst of it, filled the little tin bath, tested it with her elbow and slipped Lillian in. Her dress was soaked by the time she'd washed and dried her, emptied the bath on the herb garden and hauled Lily upstairs to the attic, where, despite the open window, all the heat of the day had accumulated. She settled Lily, stripped to her underwear, and lay on top of the bed. *Mmm, mmm ma, ma, maa*, Lily said, over and over, her tone low, but relentless. Now and then she coughed. Waves of hot air rolled through the room.

Well, Evelyn thought, as Lily's cries peaked, then gradually diminished, you'll probably be better in the morning. She allowed her eyes to close, fell instantly asleep. When she woke in darkness, Lily still slept beside her. Holding her torch in her mouth, Evelyn used a nail file to open Harry's letter.

12 April 1943

Dear Evelyn,

Thank you for 59 and 60. And thank you for sending the parcel, which needless to say, has not arrived. I live in hope, and I love to hear of you both.

I don't know which letter you mean, and certainly don't feel offhand. If I sometimes seem strange or cold, I am just low and worn out, too tired to feel anything much or just not able to write very well. We are very busy and often on the move. When we stop we can do nothing but sleep, night or day, which is my excuse for writing few letters. And there are other times when I feel angry or depressed and do not want to infect you with my misery.

It has got to the point where all emotions connected with home are of necessity remembrances. And perhaps memories become less accurate, and less full, over time. If you try remembering me now, you'll probably find the picture beginning to blur. Perhaps certain details stand out, and other things you have to reconstruct. Photographs are a great help, so please send any new ones you have! And please understand, the conditions are such that it is so difficult to really *feel* love, or anything, out here. We are hard at it and not getting much sleep so we don't – can't – feel much. So if I say, 'I love you,' it is a kind of shorthand and it really means 'I do remember that I love you.' So, shall I say rather 'I will love you'? Because I know I *will*. But does this sound too hard? And perhaps you will not love me when I return? I hope not, but suppose I don't coincide with your memory of me? I am prone to dark thoughts.

The hairs rose on Evelyn's arms as she read this, because she had been thinking, as she read, how this Harry was not exactly like the one she remembered. This man was less practical, less positive, and less affectionate . . . Exhausted or not, she had the feeling that he was writing for himself, rather than for her. She abandoned the letter, switched the torch off, lay back in the dark and deliberately remembered the brisk sounds of Harry washing and dressing in the morning. How he brought her tea, and told her she was beautiful.

She remembered that she was supposed to do the floor, and the dishes, but did not go down until four, when Lillian woke, coughing and crying. Drinking cooled boiled water sweetened with a drop of the cordial that Mrs Saunders kept in her pantry only made her worse.

'Burning up,' she told Mrs Saunders at six. 'It hurts her to cough.' Two of the land girls had something similar, Mrs Saunders commented. These things never happened in a slack period. It would pass. There was no need for a doctor.

Evelyn washed the floor as quickly as she could. Lily's eyes were pink and watered profusely. When she fell into an exhausted sleep, her face crushed into Evelyn's shoulder, Evelyn carried her upstairs. Sleep at least was a good thing. Despite the reluctance she felt, she unfolded Harry's letter again.

So I hope you understand. I know that I love you. And I know that I love Lillian, even though my memory of her is nothing like what she now is and I am sure she has no memory of me.

Yesterday morning, I had a rather nasty adventure, but don't worry – I am here to tell the tale. It was my turn in the observation post, out ahead of our infantry, which is not anyone's favourite place to be. At seven, the time when I was due to be relieved, nothing was happening. I was desperate for an end-of-shift smoke, and had no tobacco. I set off back towards the lines to cadge some. I met my replacement, Anderson, coming down, but he didn't have any either. 'Never mind,' I told him, and clapped him on the shoulder. Minutes later came a horrible thud, and that observation post, and Anderson, were blown out of existence.

She put the letter down. Yesterday morning? she thought, while I was peeling potatoes? But of course, it was not *this* yesterday. It had happened the day before the twelfth of April. Almost a month ago. And he was all right. Or had been. Where was he now?

> A grisly business. I'm pleased that in this case tobacco saved me, but terribly cut up about Anderson. Of course, there's no justice or meaning to who gets it or doesn't.

But the point is, Evelyn thought at him, you are alive! Surely it made bad things worse to think about them so much?

> I'm stuck with the memory of him walking away. Suppose I had said more? But I didn't want to keep him and leave the post unmanned, and I wanted to fill my pipe, so we both went on our ways.
>
> Ever since, when I have the time to feel anything at all, I've felt rather low, but this afternoon cheered me up because we visited a mobile bath unit. The equipment was Italian and quite good and it is lovely to feel clean again. It was the nearest thing I've had to a bath since leaving Cairo, in November. Normally I am very dirty. You would not want me near you, darling.

Well no, she would not.

A rash blossomed behind Lily's ears and under her hair.

'Measles!' Evelyn told Mrs Saunders, who was filling the oven with bread and listening to the news. I should never have come here, Evelyn thought. It was a stupid thing to do.

84

'We've all had it,' Mrs Saunders replied, as she closed the oven door. 'You don't help by fussing.'

'Fierce fighting continues north of Enfidaville,' the radio announcer told them, 'with our artillery pounding enemy positions in the hills.'

'That's your Harry,' Mrs Saunders pointed out, needlessly. The woman was even worse than her mother, who at least cared for her and for Lily, however foolish she was. Who, if she had been there, would have taken her in her arms . . . Her child and her husband, in danger. Suppose she lost one of them? Suppose Harry was shot while she stacked plates in a wooden rack? Suppose she lost both – but that kind of thinking got you nowhere. Harry had survived this far. He was a lucky man, and said so himself. She'd had measles herself as a child and made a full recovery.

The nausea she felt was only nerves, and she said nothing of any of this in the quick note she wrote to Harry, concentrating instead on how proud she was of him, how she would not complain again about his smoking, and telling him the tale of the unwashed floor. There was no point in worrying him with the measles. He had said he wanted a picture of her feeling and thinking, but suppose he had to wait weeks to hear how it turned out?

Lillian, wearing only a vest, lay limp on top of the quilt with a towel under her in case of accidents. The rash had invaded her face, neck and chest; 'Poor monkey,' Evelyn told her, dabbing her skin with a spongeful of tepid water. She sang Rockabye again and again . . . Lillian, damp, blotched, stared up at her, her hazel eyes swimming, her mouth slack. Evelyn kissed her then stood, stretched and looked out at the fields and the sky, the swallows swooping over the garden; from inside the dark attic it seemed like another planet. There was an odd sound, half gasp, half thump, from behind her and she spun around:

Lillian's arms and legs thrust stiffly out. One foot beat the towel in a rigid dance. The whites of her eyes gleamed under half-closed lids.

'Lily!'

She gathered the child up and, holding her as still but also as gently as she could, ran down the treacherous stairs. Mrs Saunders was pulling her gumboots on.

'Please get me a doctor!'

'All right,' Mrs Saunders said. 'I'll send for Bascombe. But it's you he'll charge, and you're likely wasting your money.'

Money? She would have given her life. Why had they ever come here?

When, a few minutes later, Lillian relaxed, Evelyn thought she had died, but first one eye, then the other righted itself.

The doctor arrived, on a bicycle, his bag strapped to the rack. He was dressed in a suit and, oddly, a motorcycle dispatch-rider's helmet, army-issue. He set his bag on the hall table while he wiped his shoes on the mat. 'Bascombe,' he said, offering his hand, then removed the metal helmet to reveal a mess of wiry grey hair. He handed the helmet to her; she hung it on the coat stand.

'If you had seen as many head injuries and fine men turned into cripples and cabbages as I have, you wouldn't wonder at my wearing such a thing,' he informed her. 'It's cork-lined, very hot, but the best they can do.' She burst into tears. He offered her his handkerchief. 'Somewhere to wash my hands? The sick child?' he prompted, and followed her into the kitchen and then to the sitting room where she, crying harder now, sat down on the end of the couch where Lillian dozed, and explained about the fit.

'Eleven months. The fever started yesterday. She had a fit. Her eyes rolled back! And also she suddenly seems awfully thin – '

86

Bascombe lowered himself slowly to his knees, shook the thermometer, slipped it in Lillian's armpit. She seemed to half wake; he kept his hands there, steadying it.

'I dare say the worst is over,' he said softly, 'though you were wise to send for me. Occasionally measles can affect sight or hearing and at this age, it's hard to tell. Encephalitis and meningitis are *very* rare but I want to keep an eye on her . . . 102 is still high.' He felt Lillian's neck, under her arms, his hands enormous on her tiny body, but very clean, Evelyn noted, the nails trimmed and filed.

'From London?' he asked as he worked. 'And your husband?'

'With the 8th Army, in the Artillery. In Tunisia.'

'There's nothing to be gained by worrying,' he told her as he unpinned the nappy she'd put on as a precaution, though Lillian was already pretty much potty-trained during the day. It was still dry.

'Urine?'

'Last night. Dr Bascombe, will she be all right?'

'I expect so, but she must drink . . . Little and often. A bottle, a pipette, or a teaspoon. Or let her suck a clean wet cloth. If she doesn't produce urine within the next four hours, I'll need to know . . . How do you find it here?' he asked, still kneeling in front of the sofa.

'The countryside's very pretty.'

'Have you made friends?'

She shrugged.

'Do you have family?'

'I wanted to get away from my parents,' she told him, surprising herself. 'My father is in and out of the hospital for treatments for his tuberculosis. I don't want him coughing over Lillian, and my mother telling me what a mistake I've made marrying and all that. But of course it's just as filthy here as it was at home! I'm sorry,' she said, and wiped her face with the back of her hand. The doctor shook his head, grasped the sofa arm and, with some difficulty, stood.

Lily, unbuttoned, fragile, still half delirious, stared at the ceiling.

'No one likes to lose anyone, mothers included,' Bascombe said. After a pause he added, 'Keep up with the sponging. Call if she's still dry by six, or if anything seems worse. Otherwise, I'll come by tomorrow at this time of day.'

On the face of it Bascombe had done nothing but take Lillian's temperature, but Evelyn felt a gush of gratitude and affection towards the man. He refused her offer of tea.

'What do I owe you?' she asked.

'I've been here five minutes and it's on my way home . . . I'll not charge you this time, though I would charge Lord George Whitmore if he deigned to use me, or Mrs Angela Badcock, who does so, frequently, though she is perfectly well.'

Back in the hall, she handed him the helmet, noticing as she did so the thick leather ear covers, the tang of sweat and Vitalis. He reminded her in some way of Harry, and at the same time he was, she realised when thinking about it a little later, the kind of man she'd have liked to have had for a father: an odd thought, and one she dismissed.

'Remember to rest yourself, too,' he said as he put the helmet on, then picked up his bag and left.

No one else was in. She checked Lillian again and then fetched the newspaper. *German and Italian forces continue stubborn in their resistance,* she read, *but are cut off from their supply chain and their defeat is inevitable. The Allies will not let them rest . . .* Moments later, she slept.

On his third visit, Dr Bascombe pronounced Lillian out of danger. Her appetite had returned. The pink tinge had vanished from the whites of her eyes and she sat up, happy despite the rash.

'Mrs Miles,' the doctor said, 'You know, it might be better for you to go home. Saunders keeps a very clean herd, but cows are not the best company if you're anxious about tuberculosis. And I think there's something I might be able to do for you. A friend of mine runs a residential treatment centre for patients with lung disease, and is sometimes very understanding about the fees.'

Dear Harry, she wrote at the end of the week, addressing herself to the Harry she remembered, not the brooding, rather unsettling man who had of late been writing to her.

> Dear Harry,
>
> I am still here, though only just. Lillian had the measles, but has recovered now. For a while I was worried but the doctor assures me that it is over, though she may need glasses later on. You will not catch it from a letter. The doctor was very kind. He came three times from Stow and did not charge. I hasten to add, he is an old man.
>
> I said I am still here, but not for long. Dad has been offered a paid-for convalescent place in the Lake District, starting in a fortnight's time. I told Mum I would consider returning if he accepted it, and she saw sense and put pressure on him, so, since all these stairs are an awful nuisance with a baby and also, I don't feel that Mrs Saunders, especially as regards hygiene, is a significant improvement on my mother, I plan on returning home, though only temporarily. I'm determined to find a flat.
>
> I will miss the eggs.
>
> Don't worry, London is fairly safe at the moment. So long as you have had a bath, I am sure we will soon make up for lost time.

'You're very kind,' she had told Dr Bascombe when he explained about the treatment centre in the Lake District. He wrote the name and address of her father's doctor in his notebook, tucked it in his breast pocket, and said that he would deal with it as soon as he got home. Again, he had brushed away the notion of payment.

'Thank you,' she said and they made their way to the hall.

'What for? This has been a pleasure in its way. Now, if I were a younger and more impulsive man, and not so aware of the circumstances – ' he smiled. Their eyes met, and to her surprise, Evelyn blushed. She liked him, and, old as he was, the idea of him touching her was not as repugnant as she might have thought; indeed, she wanted to be held, and without really knowing it she took half a step towards him, though he remained where he was, bent to don the bicycle clips, reached for the helmet, settled it on his head, buttoned up his jacket and took hold of his bag.

When all this was done, he held out his free hand to shake, but Evelyn instead reached up and kissed him – she aimed for the cheek, though because of the headgear her lips landed closer to his than she'd intended.

And then he was gone.

BLOODY NOTHING

Harry forced down a mouthful of the diesel-scented liquid that passed for tea and peered out from the shade of the tent into the glaring light of yet another day. It was the purest bad luck to be set up here, just north of Enfidaville at the bitter, pointless, dangerous end of it all, working on while everyone else engaged in an ecstasy of back-slapping. Heroes! The end of the war in North Africa! Not here, three miles south of the enemy's nearest position. Tucked behind the many ridges and peaks to the west and north (*djebels*, they were called), the Germans and Italians were well protected, though at the same time completely surrounded. Their situation was both brilliant and hopeless, and they must know it, yet out of pride and stubbornness – and even in defiance of orders – they refused to surrender and so he had to be here, despite the so-called victory, *mopping up*. That was the phrase. Quite a euphemism – the artillery battle here had grown even more intense since the fall of Tunis and Bizerta.

And then, yesterday, after a thunderous air raid which really should have been the end of it all, von Sponeck had, so they were told, surrendered. Though Messe still held out. Even so, Italians as well as Germans swarmed down the mountain roads, their white flags appearing though the binoculars like a flock of giant cabbage-white butterflies: a cheering sight, though at the same time, many of the guns from both enemy armies had clearly not surrendered. They fired with such intensity that for the rest of the day 230 Battery had spent as much time cowering in their holes as they did returning fire. Mid-afternoon, Harry lost his voice from shouting orders, so they wired telephone lines from the command post to the guns. The night shoot stopped just after eleven, but everyone was kept ready until one.

So his throat ached and his eyes burned and there was no way not to hate the invisible enemy for needlessly prolonging this mutual agony, and yes, it could be even worse: he could be dead, but it was *very* bad luck to be there, in the lee of a not especially protective ridge looking out at an amphitheatre of hills, behind which climbed yet other higher ridges and peaks still bristling with weaponry, as another too-hot, too-bright, unavoidable day began.

Yet here he was. He dashed the rest of the tea on the ground, dropped the enamel mug by the tent flap, and walked across to the row of guns. He made his way from one detachment to the next, doing his best to joke for a few minutes with each crew. Fortunately, his husky whisper was such that almost anything he said became mildly entertaining, the very opposite of how he felt.

'I think they're doing their best to make this a memorable trip.'

'Good breakfast then? Hope you enjoyed the delicious tea with extra dust and grit?'

'I'm sure you'll look back on this and laugh one day.'

The third detachment he treated to a quotation: '"No water but only rock, rock and no water and the sandy road . . . " Sorry! Mr Eliot. God knows where that sprang from.'

'Doesn't mention any guns, does he.'

'Seems that Hans and Giovanni just can't leave us alone,' he told the fourth, 'but it won't go on forever.'

'You sure of that, sir?' replied Alder, the number three: a wiry chap, with bright blue eyes, always cheerful and willing. He didn't seem to have a girl, but wrote long and often very funny letters to his parents; Harry, who had to censor the troop's mail, enjoyed reading them.

'This is the last day,' Harry said, 'I'm all but sure of it.' Huggins, who hardly ever wrote a letter but sang well, said that clinched it then, and he looked forward to the party.

They all laughed at that, and Harry made his way back to the command post, just thirty feet back.

How sick he was of it, of the sandbag walls, of the rough scrim-and-net tent erected over a depression scraped out behind an outcrop of rock, of the ammunition boxes they sat on. Of the world men made, and this particular bit of it.

It *would* end soon. They would go to the ball . . . But he felt no sense of imminent relief, just exhaustion, and fury.

Marsh, seated behind two telephones and wearing one set of headphones on his head and another two pairs round his neck, looked up as Harry came in. His eyes seemed to have sunk into dark pits; his cheeks were concave.

At first light, he reported, there had been a small party of surrendering Boche on the road from Takrouna, but now it was empty again. Harry remembered the Maoris who only weeks ago had taken the hilltop fortress at Takrouna – he'd been fascinated by the strange war chants heard from their nearby camp before they went into action. In that one night they lost most of their officers.

'No news,' Marsh said, 'bloody nothing.'

Like a child napping at school, Wilkinson sprawled over the improvised desk that held his maps, rules and range tables, the artillery board propped beside him.

Harry settled by his phones and checked that they were still working. Minutes stretched and swelled, more or less refused to pass; talking might have helped but they were too exhausted to attempt it. When Chesterton called in from the forward observation post everyone sat straighter, then slumped again: no orders, no information, more bloody nothing.

Though in the absence of gunfire, you did hear other things: he noted the oscillating hum of flies circling relentlessly and the rasp of other insects, the dry rustle of some small creature – a lizard or rodent – skittering over loose ground and dead leaves. From time to time, men's voices, even laughter, ahead. And in the absence of gunfire, you became aware of stray thoughts, or bits of thoughts surfacing in what had once been your mind. And you wanted to sleep . . . Harry's eyelids, indeed, the whole of his face, yearned to succumb to gravity. To keep himself alert, he took his binoculars and went to peer through the observation gap. The intense green, almost turquoise, that gave the mountains their name had been scorched by fireballs and ravaged by countless explosions, but higher still, the pale, rocky peaks still glowed, apparently pristine, tinted purplish by the distance. Lurking behind the ridges, the enemy were impossible to see. Shooting at them depended entirely on maps, aerial photographs, and the forward observers' deductions.

Harry turned back to the others.

'Maybe,' he croaked, 'they've left by the back door, or shot themselves. Maybe they're having a big fry-up of all their food supplies, just so we can't eat them. Let's hope they don't start hurling plates.'

'Plates would be fine,' Marsh replied, and then at 8.45 the radio hissed into life.

'Messe offered unconditional terms. Temporary armistice in force until 12.30. Stay ready . . . They say they are hoping we have a quiet morning.'

'About bloody time!' said Wilkinson.

After Harry had phoned it through to the guns he felt his shoulders loosen a little, though it was soon clear that while their immediate targets remained silent, someone was still firing to the north-west of them.

'It's not so very quiet,' he pointed out. 'Perhaps Giovanni's lot don't listen to his orders any more. Perhaps they're sulking, or didn't pick up the phone.'

'Or can't hear it.'

'Firing north of Saouaf,' Chesterton informed them on the radio. 'Well out of our range.' They listened for almost an hour to the intermittent crack and echo of fire, and watched a trickle of surrendering troops progress down the road. Harry's shoulders relaxed a little more. He wandered out to pee against the bush they used and was only halfway back when the obscene, moaning shriek of a rocket launcher, the thing they called a *nebelwerfer*, tore through the air. Five more followed in rapid succession. As everyone dived for cover, all six rockets exploded in open ground a few hundred yards ahead of their position.

During the few seconds' silence that followed, his heart thudding, his body ready for anything that might be asked of it, Harry hoped that what had happened was a mistake: the work of some battle-crazed Kraut gunner disobeying orders, who would be restrained, or shot. But six more rockets screamed towards them and landed much closer, their collective impacts jolting through the rock in close series. Debris and soil clattered down on the command post, followed by a soft patter of smaller pebbles and twigs.

'Oh, bugger off!' someone yelled.

'Call this a ceasefire?'

'We've taken a fucking hit!'

Harris was on the phone. 'I have to report two dead, sir.' His breath sucked in. 'Alder and Huggins. Jameson from the third has joined us.'

'We'll get them back,' Harry told him. 'Stand ready.' You could not pay attention to death during action. His ruined voice showed no new feeling, but he could have wept; maybe, he thought later, that would have been a better thing than raging as he did. Had these idiots not had enough bloody war? And where the hell was Chesterton? Everyone knew how quick and easy those rocket launchers were to move –

Six more. Logic suggested they would repeat their last shot, yet they landed well short. Who cared why? He wanted to pay them back. Normally he'd avoid thinking that way by concentrating on the technicalities, but he wanted whoever had fired that weapon dead.

Where was Chesterton?

'Maybe he didn't get a sight of the smoke. Wasn't expecting it.'

'What the hell's he for, then?'

But he came in: 'Battery gunfire target, over . . . '

'Battery gunfire target, over,' Harry repeated into his phone.

'Map reference east two seven four six owe and nine one, north five eight owe, one seven two owe . . . '

It was Djebel Tine, south-west of their last target. Harry crouched next to Wilkinson, double-checking the angle and velocity required, streaked back to his phone, whisper-shouted the numbers into its mouthpiece. He wanted them dead. They might hope for accuracy within thirty yards.

'H-E one hundred seventeen, charge two, zero fifteen degrees, angle of sight . . . Right ranging seven two five owe.'

The din, heard and felt in his entire body, the noise of wanting something gone from the earth – a missile seeking revenge – he had ordered it and now he wanted to become it. To be hot metal hurtled through the air, to explode into countless lethal pieces, to pierce, to cut, to annihilate whoever had fired from Djebel Tine and killed Alder and Huggins. He wanted to stop them for good. He wanted their particular deaths.

'Shot over!'

'Shot over!' His right leg was shaking. He gripped the phone, repeated Chesterton's corrections: 'Right five owe, fire when ready, five rounds of gunfire.' Again, the wall of noise. More adjustments. Five more rounds. A concentration, five rounds.

And after all that, nothing came back. Silence expanded in their ears. Minutes passed and then Marsh, at the radio, raised his hand, listened, and looked up.

'Messe surrendered. Cease firing. Cease firing!'

Harry hesitated, because the men who had been firing at them, if still living, were likely beyond the reach of orders. And as for Messe, who could trust –

'Cease firing!' Marsh shouted, and it was not something to whisper into a telephone so Harry grabbed the megaphone, and ran out towards the gunners. They stood ready, their backs to him. The sun was at its zenith: no shadows, just dust-coloured uniforms and dust-covered equipment blending with the ground. He hauled his broken voice out of his throat:

'Cease firing! Cease firing!' They turned towards him. He repeated the order. A cheer gathered momentum as the other detachments received their orders, and yet even at its loudest, the human noise was dwarfed by the days of cacophony that had preceded it; it seemed at first too quiet, but then Harry understood that its scale was a sign of what it was, a noise made only of voices.

'Empty guns!'

'Guns empty!'

He'd remember later how he could have knelt; could have sung, but for his throat, and could have cried, too, except there was no liquid left in him. Instead, he shook hands and back-slapped with his gunners, then returned to the command post, where the three of them stood, facing each other. 'Thank God, about time,' Marsh said.

'I don't know,' Wilkinson added, 'whether they'll want that last little lot on the record.'

It was over. It was over, and now they had to bury Alder and Huggins. Chaplain McKenzie supervised a work party to dig the temporary grave. For all of ten minutes they stood in the ruined olive grove while he talked about fellowship, sacrifice and duty. They would always be remembered, he said, and then led the singing of 'Jerusalem', during which Alder's voice was conspicuously absent. Harry just mouthed the words. And as for the remembering, he thought, it completely depended on your situation. He was glad that Chesterton was the one who would have to write to their families.

They dragged the guns through scrub and abandoned fields, and then south on a short stretch of decent road. His throat burned and tasted of blood; there was a new stretched feeling to it, as if he were about to cry, though he still did not. *Star, star, beautiful star*, some were now singing, *I'd rather have beer by far* . . . The air smelled of sweat, hot metal and exhaust. Ahead of them, two hundred Italians marched to British orders and did not seem to mind the change, along with a smaller group of Germans, still stiff and proud. Where did that get you? he thought. Soon the prisoners would take a left turn, and trudge north towards the ports.

'Who is going to feed them?' he croaked.

'I don't care if they starve,' Chesterton said.

How many had died here? But that was the past now. It was done, done, done, and the truck rumbled on, silence ringing in his ears.

Enfidaville, for months a dreaded hot spot, now seemed a rather pleasant village. It had been knocked about but retained at least the vestiges of charm. The main avenue was a row of abrupt stumps, but elegant palm trees still rustled their fronds outside the town hall and the church. Most of the white-painted buildings were in the French colonial style, their shutters and trim painted blue; others – domed, Moorish – held out a promise of calm, cool interiors. Bougainvillea tumbled over a fence. A few locals in western clothes waved flags and cheered as they passed through; already, he guessed, they were preoccupied with rebuilding their lives. It was good country, once you took the war out of it. Every part of it seemed to grow something: olives, almonds, and oranges. Where the war had not been, wildflowers bloomed in every possible colour.

'Sir, can we bloody well get something to bloody drink?' Bennet asked, but when Harry tried to answer nothing came out.

They set up in a grove of almond trees south of the village, and those who could play took turns hacking out a tune on a piano they found under a tree. They turned up some local wine, a thin red.

'We got them in Medemine, at the Mareth line, in the Wadi and at the Gabes Gap, and here, we've darn well got them for good,' Chesterton said, clapping Harry across the shoulders.

Huggins, Harry thought. Alder. Country boys. But in a war, you could not pay too much attention to death. They'd had the funeral. You kept moving on. He held the mugful of wine without drinking it, thankful no one expected him to speak. He was glad that it was over here, but would miss the sky clotted with stars in strange southern constellations and the dry, empty country breathing softly behind them for thousands of miles, the enormity of sand and rock.

The obvious thing would have been for the whole battalion to drive to the coast the next day and throw themselves into the glittering blue sea, but the plan was for an officers' review of the battlefield. They set off at 6.45 a.m. in three trucks with the major and his staff at the front and a cloud of grit and dust hovering over them all. At the far side of a tract of cactus and aloe, the road twisted up towards the craggy ridges that had hidden the enemy so well. They passed through a plantation into a zone of stunted but densely packed forest, a mixture of broad-leafed trees, cedars and junipers. They overtook a Berber shepherd and flock, and later passed a family of five walking downhill; neither did more than glance in their direction. Clusters of mud-built buildings, terracotta or washed with white, perched in unexpected folds or on hillsides that they'd been unable to see from the lower ground: it was an intricate landscape that suggested many possibilities in terms of concealment. Long before this war, its settlements had been built with defence in mind.

Engines growling, they swerved onto an even smaller, rougher road. Now they saw craters, landslides, and large areas where the vegetation had been crushed, uprooted or burned. Smoke rose from a fuel store ignited the day before. They turned again and lurched to a halt behind the other vehicles. A burnt-out truck blocked the track; behind it, the beginning of a ridge. The view down towards Enfidaville and the lowland fields and groves was vast and unimpeded. It was easy to work out where their last position had been, dug in behind the rocks and scrubby hummocks that bordered the olive groves. Beyond that, the salt marshes and then the glitter of the sea; the road to Tunis was dark with traffic, all of it moving north.

The ridge, scattered with shrapnel and debris, was narrow, and behind them, at the back of the position, the enemy had cut a deep L-shaped trench into the slope. They'd built low bunkers, tucked their guns and placements behind the ridge. Towards the end, the ground fell away into an almost sheer drop.

'Lucky we didn't need to take it,' Chesterton said.

They followed Major Hamilton to the far end of the ridge and found the rocket launcher that had killed Huggins and Alder: a big drum-like thing, its six short barrels still pointing their way.

And at first Harry was appalled to think that all their counter-fire yesterday had no useful effect, but as he came closer, he saw, about ten yards beyond, where the weapon's remote firing station would have been, a litter of rubble and fragments, and what was left of the bodies of two men, humming with flies. Beyond them, wheel tracks led to the very edge of the ridge and disappeared. Another rocket launcher, they guessed, had been dragged to the back of the position and pushed over the cliff behind them, where most, but not all, of the shells they had fired yesterday had exploded.

They stood a respectful few feet away from the bodies, one of which was without a leg, while the other lacked a face and hands. Two for two. Here, Harry thought, even if the damn murdering fools had brought it upon themselves, was equality in bad luck: to be at the bitter, unnecessary end, shooting unnecessarily from a position where most shells would fall harmlessly to either side, and yet you *still* manage to be blown to bits.

Why did the dead men move their fire once they'd hit 230 Battery? Could it be that they were only offloading their shells and actually didn't mean to strike any targets? Did they even know what they'd done? Impossible to judge.

'Good work,' Hamilton said.

Yes and no, Harry thought.

Marsh took a group to hunt for stores. Harry chose to examine the trench and bunkers. Radios and telescopes had been smashed, but clothes, billies, maps, books, cigarettes, full and empty ration cans, steel helmets, photographs and letters were strewn around. One bunker had taken a hit, but the other three were intact. His party began rooting around for knives, cameras, watches, and binoculars: the prime pickings they were entitled to commandeer before lesser ranks came the same way.

Before too long, someone discovered some schnapps.

It was just after nine, very hot, and they had at least four more such sites ahead of them. Sweating, Harry crouched amongst the litter of discarded possessions in the second bunker's shade. A pair of wire-framed glasses lay still unbroken on the floor and he picked them up. Without warning, then, he was on the brink of tears. The feeling of abandonment, of nobody being at home, affected him despite his allegiances, as did the hostility of the environment: the concrete, the rock, the dry mountains beyond. An awful emptiness lived there, or in him, or both. Eliot's words surfaced again:

Here is no water but only rock
Rock and no water and the sandy road . . .
Amongst the rock one cannot stop or think . . .

He remembered how at school, Whitehorse had read them extracts from *The Waste Land* during the first term when they discussed what he called poems of the soul. Allusive and elusive, he'd called it, rather dismissively; it was not in the anthology, and he did not require them to study it. Even so, the feeling of it stuck and Harry had read the whole thing a few years later. Parts of it seemed to have burrowed into his brain and chosen this moment in the deserted bunker to revive. Eyes closed, back against the wall, knees akimbo, his hands resting loosely on them, he mouthed the words, which emerged as little more than shaped breath:

A woman drew her long black hair out tight
And fiddled whisper music on those strings
And bats with baby faces in the violet light
Whistled, and beat their wings
And crawled head downward down a blackened wall
And upside down in air were towers

Tolling reminiscent bells, that kept the hours
And voices singing out of empty cisterns and exhausted wells.

He was in a classroom on the second floor. He was in a cathedral, with all the poets from *Whyte's Treasury of Verse in English* sitting in the pews: Shakespeare, Shelley, Blake, Hopkins, Thomas, Rossetti, Dickinson, Barrett Browning, even newcomers like Owen and Thomas. Everyone listened, and he was there, at the back, leaning on stone, whispering them over and over again. He did not care about the sense, but submitted to the rhythm and the sequence of images. It was a peculiar kind of medicine, a sort of service, even, but he began to feel a little better: still empty, but not utterly desolate.

He opened his eyes. A gust of warm air blew through the bunker, stirred up a mess of documents on the bench at the back, and drew his attention to an open box of writing paper. He wiped his fingers on his filthy shirt, picked up a sheet, and held it to the light: cream-coloured, deckle-edged, almost smooth, it was watermarked with a coronet. The same symbol and the words *Papeterie Saillat* were printed on the lid of the box. Beautiful stuff – made, doubtless, before the war. Would it be made again, after it? Hunting through the debris, he found just two envelopes.

He tucked the box of stationery under his arm, and climbed awkwardly out of the bunker. Blinded by the light, he stumbled, righted himself, and then, without turning back to look at the dead soldiers by the rocket launcher, made his way towards the others' voices.

A KIND OF MUSIC

Lily had the day off school and she and her mother wore their best frocks, both made from the same thin material – navy blue with white dots. Her glasses were in her mother's handbag because she didn't really need them out of school and she wanted to look her best. They were at Clapham Junction, on platform four, right by the stairs down, under the exit sign. He would have to come that way. They had asked the platform guard and he told them it was impossible that they would miss him if they stood right there.

They had come very early to make sure.

The platform guard passed again.

'Excuse me – are you sure,' her mother called out to him, 'are you absolutely certain that the 10.30 from Woking stops here?'

'Yes, madam. Twenty minutes until it comes in.'

'Thank you.' Lily's mother took her hand again, squeezed.

'I'm hungry,' Lily said.

'You should have eaten your breakfast.'

'I couldn't!' She'd been unable to even sit down. And now the rails made the strange, high, singing sound that came just before the throb and clatter of the train, which grew louder, then slower, then stopped with a hiss, the engine just a little further up from where they stood – but, for the third time, it was not the right train and only a handful of people got off.

A man with a briefcase paused at the top of the stairs and said, 'You must be waiting for someone important.' He said it to Lily, she was sure, and, very quickly, just in case her mother answered for her, she looked him in the eye and told him *Yes*.

Yet Harry, as his train rattled down the line through a blend of railway suburbs, patches of woodland and tangled, blackberry-covered sidings, did not feel at all important, just free: a man demobbed, thanked, let go, and now in motion between one thing and the next, on a sunny Tuesday in June. Asked, he'd have said that no one could claim to be important; that they were all pushed on by huge forces and could do very little about it except, perhaps, choose how they went. He had felt a certain specialness, some swellings of pride, even, when, after the landings, the 84th drove at walking pace through jostling crowds that lined the streets in northern France and Belgium. People had waved and laughed and wept; they threw flowers, offered glasses of beer, warm loaves of bread, bowls of fruit. Women hugged and kissed them, and in the face of such joy the trail of misery and loss and destruction that led to that moment had suddenly seemed worthwhile.

That was two years ago, and they had subsequently had to drag the new 5.5 around and do more of its nasty work. There was plenty more trouble, and another year of service once the war was over. Yes: the army had kept him under its thumb as long as it could. Even so, he had been lucky. Unlike Anderson, Alder and Huggins and others he'd known, unlike poor Cicely Osborne, unlike millions he had not known, and unlike Edward Thomas, the poet he felt he somehow knew, he had survived his war to sit now in a half-empty train carrying him towards the wife he had thus far lived with for a patchwork of weeks, and a rather serious daughter who scarcely knew him. In the year since the war ended, he had seen them just twice for a week each time. Now they were about to begin the 'deadly routine' that he had joked about and longed for: an endless series of kisses and meals and walks, the pattern of conversation, affection, and arguments. And work, of course, though he didn't like so much to think of that and what it might be.

He preferred to let his mind open itself to how it would be between the two of them now that they began what could almost be called a new marriage: real now, an everyday, actual thing instead of a frenzied week trying to make up for lost time and then a slew of letters – he'd be happy never to write another one of those. Day after day he would wake up and touch Evelyn; his words would be spoken to a breathing woman who heard them, then and there, and replied . . .

Suddenly he was remembering that poor boy – he'd looked to be about fourteen – whose wedding he'd watched in Tunisia: how he had been shoved into the tent with all the relatives chanting outside – then came out after half an hour and was surrounded by men, who pushed him back in. He'd emerged eventually with a bit of bloody cloth which sent everyone wild.

Why think of that? A shame to be so obsessed with purity, a not-very-interesting quality in the end. He was fairly sure that Evelyn had not been seduced by an American or a Canadian. He felt he was open-minded, quite modern in his outlook, yet he'd been faithful, if you discounted the kisses of the grateful liberated, and his thoughts about Cicely, and that poor woman they'd billeted with in Belgium, who'd been arrested one morning, separated from her children – collaborator or not, he'd felt very sorry for her – and then of course there were those parties with nurses, ultimately dull but impossible to miss. He'd been sex-starved, had thought all sorts of thoughts. The sight of a leg sent him wild, but at the same time, whose leg was it?

And now the train was rattling through Surbiton past the backs of well-kept houses and shops, and then past smaller houses and patches of ruin where fireweed and buddleia grew, and he was only twenty minutes away from Evelyn and Lillian, a little girl who hardly knew him. He would learn what they muttered in their sleep, the smell of their hair. Their laughter and tears: another kind of adventure entirely.

The demob suit lay folded in his suitcase on the rack opposite. The material was decent. Doubtless it would come in useful, but since both legs and sleeves needed adjustment, he'd chosen to wear his uniform on the journey home. He had it in mind that Evelyn would undo the buttons and peel it off him. It made sense that she would be the one who liberated him from it for good.

Thinking of this, of her fingers working, first at the knot of his tie, then on the gilt buttons of his jacket, the horn buttons of his shirt, and finally the buckle of his belt, he rested his head on the upholstered seat back, and let his hands lie loose on his thighs. The greens of the bushes and trees, the bright, cloud-whipped, cerulean sky hurtled past the window, and there was nothing to do but smile as the miles and the minutes passed and the distance between him and Evelyn's actual fingers, and all the rest of her, second by second, shrank. They would stay up late and lie in bed long past breakfast time; he was an extraordinarily lucky man.

Evelyn kept hold of Lillian with one hand, and thrust the other into her pocket. She was trying hard not to bite her nails: a weakness of hers. She despised herself for it, especially on such a day, yet she couldn't stop. All her worries amounted to was whether they had the right platform, and would the train be on time, and should they after all have stayed home and waited until he knocked on the door, or simply gone to meet him at the corner of the street . . . And there was lunch: the fishcakes she had made and left in the icebox. A new recipe, from the newspaper, with real cod. Parsley, potatoes, breadcrumbs, with lettuce from his parents' allotment to put next to it. It should be all right, so long as the fish was, as promised, fresh, and she would murder Mr Jeffries if it was not. In the evening, everyone would be at his mother's; she would not have to cook, just help. The dresses, at least, had turned out well, though Lillian's hair was already flying out of its braid. She licked a finger and tried to damp it down, felt her daughter stiffen.

Relax, she told herself as she took Lillian's hand again. Relax . . . and yet, and yet: alongside the recipes and the upbeat news in the papers lurked stories about soldiers who returned, apparently whole, yet seemed like different men. There were some who missed the excitement of war and couldn't function in everyday life, others who had nightmares and needed constant comfort and understanding, took to drink, or became suspicious and strict. She'd not be able to bear any of that. Then there was the adjustment to regular work, and what often turned out to be lower pay . . . All that, and then, she did wonder: since she was so used to missing Harry, and to having no one to consult, which in some ways was a loss, and in others, not – now that he was coming home for good what would it be like to live with him, day in day out? To have a marriage that you lived inside, instead of something that would resume one day? For it to be real, and go on *for ever*? And why, now, was she asking herself whether she should have told him about the Polish pilot in Torquay? It was three years ago, and in any case nothing had happened. A single kiss. It was just a mistake.

'Mummy,' Lily begged her, 'stop squeezing!'

'I'm not.'

At Wimbledon, a few carriage doors opened and slammed and a clerkish-looking man climbed into the carriage, muttered good morning, settled opposite Harry and folded his paper into reading size. I'm also lucky, Harry thought, not to be that slug of a man, pale and oblivious, bored, existing, yes, but not much more than that. Or, I am lucky to not *yet* be him . . . Having survived the war, I hope not to be ground down by the peace. I want to stay alert. To love passionately. To go beyond myself. Even, still, to write.

You could think these things, but they were hard to say.

The two men sat together, unspeaking, and the train passed well-kept houses and shops, then the bomb sites, patches of ruin, half houses laddered with half chimneys and squares of faded wallpaper that used to be people's bedrooms, open patches where weeds grew amongst the rubble – places that now would become building sites and then new houses, schools and shops. The huddled homes and close streets of the city proper lay ahead, behind, to either side, busy, intricate, familiar. They passed signal boxes and trains going the other way. Rails converged and merged, a mass of them, leading to the junction. Amidst a chorus of groans and squeals the train began to slow down.

Lily pulled free of her mother's hand and ran towards her father, ignoring Evelyn's shout. She saw him see her and put down his case, kept running, jumped. He caught her, and she had the first kiss, then they were all together on the platform with the train and the other passengers long gone, her arms around the two of them as they kissed. It looked more like eating, so she shut her eyes.

'I was already looking forward to the walk, but now it's better still,' he said as they emerged from the station tunnel into the light and noise of the street. 'What a lovely surprise! If only I could balance this case on my head I could hold both your hands!' As it was, he was arm in arm with Evelyn, and Lily was on her other side.

'Mummy can carry it,' Lily said. 'Or me.'

'It's a very nice idea, but I'm not supposed to let women carry my things.'

'Is it heavy?' Lily asked.

'Not really. But still, it's just too big for you.'

Because of crossing the street and all the people, buses and cars, it wasn't until they turned into Strathblaine Road that they noticed she was crying.

'What on earth is the matter?' her mother asked, but Lily couldn't say it aloud. She could only whisper it.

'Pardon?' her mother asked, bending low.

'*I want to hold his hand!*' she repeated.

'Remember, it was a treat just to miss school! But cheer up,' her mother said, 'I'll carry the case for a bit.' This was a thing that would not have happened on any other day. His hand was hot and big around hers, her mother's cooler on the other side.

Soon there were no houses to the left and they were by the railway line.

'That's where I went to school, look, down there,' he said. 'Through the trees, the other side of the tracks. You can just see the colour of the brick.'

'Will I go there?'

'No, it was for boys. I must say, it seems like another world,' he said, and then they were in the park, with sunlight dappling through the trees, almost home.

'It looks different,' he said. He'd last been in the flat in November, so partly it must be the change of season that gave a brighter effect, as well as making the place rather hot, but surely, he thought as he stood in the hallway, from where he could see through into the kitchen and the L-shaped living-dining room, surely there was something else? Evelyn, already in the kitchen, refused to say, and signalled to Lily to keep quiet, which she could not quite do:

'It begins with a C,' she said. He was looking at the window, and understood immediately, but pretended not to understand.

'Couch?' he asked, 'Clock? Carpet? Chairs? Ceiling? But those all look just the same . . . '

'Daddy,' she yelled, 'C-C-curtains!'

'Mrs Dickenson said I could take down those awful brown things, provided I replaced them. But you still can't get decent fabric so I had to hunt around . . . It's not too much of a pattern but a lot lighter . . . No lining, of course. I hope you like these fishcakes.'

'I like everything,' he told her, and went to wash his hands and unpack. The bottle of 4711 he put by Evelyn's side of the bed, and since the teddy bear was unwrapped, he sat it on the dining table next to one of the plates. Lily eyed it warily.

'But is it a *German* bear?' she asked, peering at the label tied around its neck, which said *Mein Name ist Hans*. Maybe he should have taken that off.

'What about thank you?' Evelyn said.

She was rather strict, he thought, though perhaps it was the best way to be.

'It was made there,' he explained. 'Probably before the war. Once that started they were too busy fighting and then rebuilding to look after their bears. And anyway, animals don't really have countries.'

Still, she hesitated.

'If you don't like it, someone else – ' Evelyn began.

'The war's over now,' he continued. 'We can all be friends again. He's a very affectionate bear, and you could always change his name . . . Aren't these fishcakes delicious? I'll finish yours if you don't want it.'

'Why don't you show Hans your bedroom?' he suggested at the end of the meal.

He followed Evelyn into the kitchen and offered to help.

'No thanks,' she said, as she always would, because it was easier to do something how you wanted it than it was to explain how you wanted it done, or be pleasant if it was done wrong.

'I'll distract you, then,' he told her, and stood right behind her at the sink. He put his hands around her waist and pulled her close. She felt him harden, press himself into her buttock. He kissed her neck, moved one hand to cup a breast while the other settled into the vee at the top of her legs and began to stroke it through the thin cloth of her dress. It was silly, though admittedly rather nice.

'I'm washing up. And Lillian will be out again any minute.'

'But I'm desperate! I want you to take this damn uniform off me. I want you to do it.' She pushed back and turned around. He grasped her buttocks and pulled her close, nudging now where he had stroked. She leaned back and ran her hands down the row of buttons; she could understand him being sick of the uniform, though she liked him in it. The regularity of the garments – the way they fitted, the tidy ranks of buttons and the belt, balanced a certain irregularity in his face, the brightness of his eyes, the way he kept his hair just a little longer than others did.

'We'll have to wait until she's asleep,' she said.

'When is that?'

'Seven o'clock. Later tonight because we're out. We'll walk over there at about four. Stop now . . . ' He would stop, she knew, and she appreciated it – though there was part of her, she sometimes felt, that would quite enjoy being overruled.

'Mum?' Lily stood at the door, watching them. 'May Daddy and I go to the park?'

That evening they sang 'For He's a Jolly Good Fellow', and his mother Adeline clasped him to her and wept: not something he could remember seeing her do before. Still holding him, she looked up, her face glistening. He felt his own eyes begin to water.

'Every day I made myself believe you'd come back. I told myself you would. And here you are. I couldn't have borne to lose you,' she said. 'I'd have gone mad, like poor Aunt Em. But, see, all's well.' She looked over at Evelyn and smiled at her before releasing him. 'Now you two can settle down,' she said. His father, just back from work, clapped him on the back and took to his chair to watch the festivities unfold. It was not much more than six months since he'd last seen them, yet both his parents and Evelyn's seemed to have aged. They were somehow less defined than they used to be, like old photographs of themselves. It was the same with what had once been his home: the front room, twelve by fourteen and wearing the same but somehow fainter paper and paint, struggled to contain even a smallish crowd: him, Evelyn, Lily, his parents, his brother George, who had not left the country during the war, but moved to the Midlands and gave the impression that he was involved in some kind of secret war work. Alternatively, it had been hinted that the secret was black marketeering . . . There was George's wife Alexandra, Evelyn's mother May and her father Edward (currently just about on his feet), Josephine and Will, and the other tenants from upstairs, Fred and Lottie, also the left side neighbours, Ernest and Margaret. The right side neighbours were new and disliked. Not everyone had a chair. Periodically, when men went out back to use the convenience, or women to the kitchen to help with the food, others took their seats. There was ice in the kitchen and beer and lemonade, and what his mother called 'a small bit of a ham', sliced very thinly, new potatoes from the allotment, some tomatoes, beetroot, lettuce, bread and margarine, and a cake made with saved rations.

Things were still very scarce. Evelyn and Lily filled plates and brought the food around.

'So what's next, Harry? What's the plot?' George was the one who asked, but it was what everyone, and especially Evelyn's mother, wanted to know. It was tempting to reply that he was planning on taking to the stage, running a brothel, writing poetry or even turning into the laziest, fattest ginger tomcat possible, say, or a frog, a hare, or a butterfly, but he reined himself in.

'No idea,' he said, and took a half slice of cake from the chipped willow-pattern plate Lily offered him, 'but something will turn up. Look at all the council houses and hospitals they say they're going to build, at all the reconstruction that needs to be done. It'd make a pleasant change to build something instead of ruining it. Mind you, I've had enough rubble, sand and dust, so I hope not have to get on my knees and lay the bricks.'

'I'm sure there's plenty looking for work,' said May.

Oh, damn you, he thought. Look at who you married! But you'll not change your mind about me, whatever I do.

'And I'm sure that's true,' he told her, smiling.

'To the future!' George cut in, raising his glass. His voice was noticeably slurred. 'Whatever it is!' No one dared, Harry noted, to ask *him* what he actually did.

Thanks, goodbyes, and promises to come round soon took a while. Everyone squeezed into the narrow hall for a last toast, and his mother came out to wave them down the street.

'Remember, whatever that lot say, it's bye-bye, not *boy-boy*, and like, not *loike*, and had, not *'ad*,' Evelyn told Lily as they turned the corner. 'Sometimes I think Mum does it on purpose to annoy me . . . '

'The least of her crimes,' Harry said.

'And your brother was awful. We've got to get away from here,' she told him. 'I can't bear it.'

He loved how clear her desires were. She was right, of course, and he said so.

At home, he sat on the chair by Lily's bed and offered to read her a story. She chose Peter Rabbit even though it was too young for her now; to make it more exciting, he changed the story to be about Peter Bear, who stole apples from Mr McGregor's apple tree and narrowly missed being shot. She reminded him that she still had the velvet rabbit he sent her from the war.

'The label says made in Manchester, but I bought him in Cairo, and it feels like a very long time ago,' he told her. 'Which of them do you want in bed with you?' She explained that she wanted both, but worried because rabbits and bears did not get along. That was so in the wild, he said, but when they were toys things were different.

Evelyn, in her dressing gown, looked around the door. It was very late, she said. They must turn out the light. In the half-dark, their faces illuminated only by the glow from the hall, Lily held on to his hand. Her eyes glistened, brimmed.

'Daddy,' she asked, 'you are really back now, aren't you? You're not going away ever again? Promise me.'

'I promise,' he said, leaning in. 'And now, you promise me to sleep. No getting up.'

'You'll be here in the morning?'

'Of course.'

'Yes,' she said, 'I promise,' and closed her eyes. He kissed her cheek and waited a little, imagining Evelyn at the dressing table brushing her hair, rising and turning as she heard him come in. He hoped she was not tired, or if she was, that he could revive her. He stood as quietly as he could and then crept away, closing the door gently behind him.

But Lily was far too happy to sleep. She heard her father go to her mother's bedroom, their laughter. For long minutes they were quiet and there was only the flap of her curtains, a door closing downstairs, where the landlady lived, and distant voices from outside. Then the bedroom door creaked open and her father walked into the narrow bathroom between the two bedrooms. She heard him pee and flush. He splashed for a long while in the sink, draining and refilling it several times before finally cleaning his teeth. The bedroom door clicked shut again and after that, they talked in low murmurs. From the start, the words were impossible to make out, but quite soon they were not even words, just sounds half familiar, half strange. Lily sat up in bed, and strained to hear more clearly. It was like the sounds of animals or birds, and at the same time, it was almost a kind of music. She was only a little bit scared.

BLUE

'I hope we're in time,' Evelyn's mother said as they hurried along Westover Road. The rain had let up but the wind gusted still, tugging at their scarves and hair. Thank goodness it was a Saturday, Evelyn thought; Harry could cope for a while and then later on he could take Lily and Val to Irene and Bob . . . Her mother grasped her arm.

'I hope he knows you,' she said. 'And I hope you can forgive him and say a good goodbye. But I've got to warn you, Evelyn, that it's very hard to see what your father's come to.'

Minutes later they pushed through the gate and into the dimness of the house, hung their coats on the hooks by the door, continued without pausing up the familiar narrow stairs. The district nurse had gone, and Fran from next door left as soon as they arrived.

'Teddy, dear, it's Evelyn,' her mother said, beckoning her towards the bed.

He was yellow. Sunken eyes, huge. Loose skin. Yellow. Hollow cheeks, cords in his neck. Yellow. He hauled his breath in shallow, desperate gasps. Under the covers, the whole shape of him was wrong. A tube full of dark fluid snaked from beneath the sheets, disappeared under the bed: the source, probably, of the stench in the room. She would stop noticing it soon, Evelyn told herself, swallowing.

'Teddy, dear, Evelyn's come to see you . . . It's Evie, Evie,'

her mother repeated, louder, and her father's famous eyes –
the whites of them now that awful colour – moved slowly
towards her, as if pushing against an opposing force, then
settled on her face. Did he see her? See something, at least?
His face was slack.

'Say hello to your dad, Evelyn.'

Hello? It did not seem the right thing to say, yet what would be?

What would I have liked to say, Evelyn would ask herself
when she thought about it later. *Why the hell? What do you want
to say to me? How dare you do this to my mother? I'm glad this is
almost over. Are you?*

Because it was a very long story. Because sometimes they
didn't see him for days on end. Because sometimes Evelyn,
returning from school or an errand, would detect him in the
crowd outside the Halfway House or the Leather Bottle and
change direction so that he didn't call out to her, and fairly
often, her mother had to go and find or collect him.

When home and awake, he occupied the chair by the fire
in the room next to the kitchen.

'Come to me,' he'd say, and get her to stand so that he could
shakily brush her hair out of her face or wetly kiss her on
the cheek, or rest his hand on her shoulder and solemnly, in
slow, careful words, say how she was his *best girl*, and that he
believed she had his eyes, which she did. Large, liquid-looking
eyes, the irises a deep colour but somehow changeable . . . A
handsome man, everyone said. That was why her mother had
fallen for him. Fallen was the right word. Into a deep hole,
almost bottomless.

I think I've got a present for you, he'd say, yet he could rarely
find it. He'd left it somewhere, or he had sat on and broken
it, and then he'd laugh and say *never mind, next time*. If he gave
her money instead, she knew to give it straight to her mother,
who said he couldn't help how he was, and always believed

his promises because she loved him. Her mother would wash him with a flannel when he was too far gone to do it himself, and kneel on the floor to undo his boots. *Give Daddy a kiss to help him feel better*, she used to say.

And then, one Saturday morning, downstairs in this very house: her mother at work and she, about nine at the time, sat in the sun on the back step eating a slice of bread and butter with sugar sprinkled on top. 'Evie, help me!' she heard, dropped the slice of bread on the step and ran in.

He'd thrown his jacket on a chair and was on his hands and knees, doglike. Huge, barking coughs, in between them a terrible wheeze.

'Can't breathe – '

'What do I do?' she asked and put her hand on his back which arched and then fell as a torrent of brownish liquid gushed out of his mouth. What was it? She jerked her hand away. He turned his face up to her, gasping. Was he going to die?

'How do I get the doctor?' she said.

'No!' he mouthed at her, 'No bloody doctors,' his face slimed with mucus and vomit. His eyes were bloodshot and rimmed red.

'Next door?'

'Help me, Evie.'

How?

He sat back on his knees, chest heaving. 'Outside,' he said. He pressed on her shoulders until he was up. Took small, unsteady steps. Then sat on the step where she had been, right on top of her bread, his hands and arms shaking.

There were rags and a chipped enamel bowl under the sink so she got some water and did her best to clean up his face. But without warning he stood and made his way down the three steps and across the paving to the outside toilet. He slammed the door then moments later opened it and called for her again: he couldn't undo his pants. 'Hurry up!' he said, but it was too late;

his warm pee drenched her hand, and then she had to pull up and fasten the soggy pants in case the neighbours were looking and get him back in to the house to take them off again. She put them and the awful underpants to soak in the bucket by the door, then threw the floor cloth over the worst of the vomit and scrubbed her hands with the bar of yellow kitchen soap.

Wearing only his shirt, her father crawled up the stairs to the bedroom with the faded pattern of bunches of violets, peeling away in one corner.

It hadn't changed.

'Bronchitis' was what her mother had told her then, and 'chest infection'. This was long before they knew he was tubercular as well as a drunk, long before he took to his bed, became a living skeleton, still smoking, still drinking, long before he walked out of the sanatorium that was treating him for nothing. That was twenty years ago, more, but she remembered it still. Her father had been dying all his life.

He had been listless and inactive over the summer, rarely leaving the bedroom, let alone the house. Often, even in broad daylight, he had been upstairs, asleep, or 'resting' when she visited, but she had assumed he was, as usual, simply being lazy and leaving it to her mother to provide.

And then her mother had arrived, soaked, as they were having breakfast in the flat's kitchen. She refused to take her coat off or sit down, but drank a cup of tea standing up.

'It's terrible news about your father. The doctor doesn't think he can go on much longer.'

'But I thought that the last treatment worked. They said his lungs were stable!'

'Yes, dear . . . But it's his *liver*.'

'From drinking?'

'What does it matter what it's from?' Her mother stepped forward, and Evelyn wrapped her arms around her and stroked her back as she sobbed her way through the rest of it: How he finally agreed to see the doctor last week. What an angel the district nurse was. How she'd said no to the hospital even though it was free now because Teddy hated them so.

He hated them because they wouldn't let him drink, Evelyn thought.

The two of them stood, locked together in the kitchen. Evelyn's own eyes smarted, but she kept her tears back. In any case, they were for her mother, and what she felt towards her father, now more than ever – even in the face of his terrible frailty, even though he was now, surely in his last hours – was rage.

'Say something to him, Evie,' her mother repeated, gesturing at the kitchen chair that had been brought up and put next to the bed.

She could hardly bear to look at him, let alone speak, but she stuck at it, and managed to break the silence.

'Dad. It's Evelyn. I didn't know you were so poorly.' It wasn't a word she normally used now. 'I'm very sorry, Dad.' His gaze slipped from her face. He tugged a bony yellow arm out from beneath the sheet and scratched at his chest, groaning as he did so; her mother reached forwards, took the hand and held it still.

'He can hear you. I'm sure he understands,' she said. 'Sometimes, at least, but the doctor told me his poor brain is being poisoned. And he's got fluids building up inside. They try to drain it. He had an injection for the pain . . . Why don't you take hold of his other hand, now.'

She didn't want to, but did it for her mother's sake. The hand was cool and damp, felt more than halfway dead. She knew he was not contagious, and saw how her mother pressed and stroked the hand she was holding, yet her own flesh shrank from the contact.

She knew what her mother wanted her to say: *I love you, Daddy. I won't forget you.* And surely she could say it, true or not, if it made a dying man – the man who had brought her into being – feel better? Surely she could say those words for her mother, if not for the man on the bed? For her mother, and let him have them, too? Why not. There was no good reason, and yet it was impossible. The whole of her – lips, tongue, jaw, throat, heart – locked against it.

'I hope the injections help, Dad,' she said. 'I think the district nurse will be back soon.' He stiffened as she spoke.

'Off! Get the hell off me!' he barked out.

'There, there, Teddy.' Her mother stood; he shouted 'No!' several times, and then fell silent, apart from his desperate breathing, which conveyed more than any word could have done about the nature of his emergency. Tears seeped from beneath his closed lids.

'There, my love, it's all right now,' her mother said, 'It's just me and Evie,' and she dabbed at his face with her handkerchief, then sat down again and kissed his cheek. Straightening, she glanced over at Evelyn, half plea, half smile.

Give your Daddy a kiss to help him feel better.

Evelyn looked back at the man on the bed.

'It's a shame, Dad,' she managed to say. 'I'm very sorry it's come to this.' It was the absolute best she could do.

He did not reply.

They sat there, holding his hands until it grew dark outside, and the doctor came again, and then the district nurse with another injection.

'He'll be peaceful now for at least a few hours,' she said. 'You two should try and sleep.' Her mother would not hear of it, but encouraged Evelyn to go into her old room over the kitchen and lie down.

The bed creaked in a familiar way; the depression in the

middle was both comforting and repellent, but she settled in to it, pulled the bedspread over herself and closed her eyes. She intended just a short nap, but lay for a long time hearing noises, thinking she should get up and keep her mother company, and also wanting to use the WC outside, yet postponing the move out of dread of going back into the room, or even passing the open door and glimpsing him again . . . She did not think she had slept at all, yet she must have, because she woke to her mother shaking her shoulder, telling her time after time, 'He's gone, Evie! He's gone!'

Her father lay on his back with his eyes closed. He was still yellow, but his face had relaxed; the terrible breathing had stopped and the room seemed extraordinarily quiet in its wake.

'There, there. Come downstairs, now,' she told her mother, and soon she had her seated at the table drinking tea laced with a splash of the brandy that Fran next door brought over.

'He had his weaknesses, but he loved us in his way. Poor dear man.' May held her handkerchief ready, but let the tears run down her cheeks. 'I've money put aside for what he needs now.'

It was sad to think that her mother had to deny herself whatever it was – new shoes, a bit of cheese, coal – to such an end . . . And yet at least it was an end. May was only fifty and her life would be in many ways easier without her husband to care for. She could stop wearing herself out, come with the family on seaside holidays, play with her grandchildren; when Evelyn and Harry moved into their house, whenever that would be, there would always be a room for her.

While they waited for May's sister Beth to come, for the doctor to sign the certificate, for the undertaker, Evelyn set to washing the pans, cups and plates that had accumulated in her mother's kitchen. After that, she wiped the cupboards down inside and out, cleaned the window and scrubbed the floor. On her mother's instructions, she went into the front room to close the curtains. It was the proper way to announce the death, and yet it seemed a pity: the silver morning light flooded in and she felt a great surge of energy, a manic heat pushing through her veins – a fierce desire to push back at the forces that had defeated her father, to banish all darkness. She stood in the middle of the room, feeling her own vitality, and thought of her husband, Harry, who had survived the war and come back to her, of his strong limbs and clear speech, his devotion to her, not mere words, not just kisses and caresses, but actions: work, money; his methodical plans, the drawing he had made of the house they would live in one day: its large windows, the garden in full sun, the positions of the trees, the accompanying calculations. How he sat on the floor and played with the girls. She had made the right choice. Just once she had been tempted, but she had resisted . . . Evelyn drew the curtains, walked quickly out, and closed the door behind her.

After the funeral, about thirty crammed into May's: family and neighbours mainly, along with two women May had worked for. There was only one of Teddy's so-called friends, Dickie Weston, a rake of a man with glistening eyes and an unkempt wedge of iron-grey hair who drank most of the bottle of brandy and then stayed on far too long after the rest, even Harry's parents, had gone and she, the girls, and Harry were sitting with her mother and Beth in the front room.

'Dickie, it's very late and we're going to clear away now,' Evelyn told him, and he looked across at her, not moving. The sort that would not be told by a woman what to do. She was not having it, and looked right back at him.

'I'll just finish this,' he said, raising his glass, and she noted a tremor in his hand. As soon as the glass was empty, she walked him to the door, opened it, thanked him for coming, told him goodbye, and stepped smartly back to avoid the kiss she could see him thinking of. She pushed the door shut, and ignored him when he rang the bell.

Valerie, sitting on the floor in front of Harry, had fallen asleep, her head lolling against his leg. Evelyn took Lily to the kitchen to help her make more tea.

'I don't think I like funerals,' Lily said as she counted the four spoonfuls into the pot.

'You're not supposed to, my love.' Evelyn gave her a squeeze before they set off back to the others with the tray. Despite the coal fire burning it felt damp in the front room and she shivered as they entered it. Her mother, flush-faced, was slumped in one of the armchairs by the fire and her Aunt Beth, plump, younger-looking despite being the elder, sat opposite; Evelyn set the tray on a footstool, then returned to her place on the old sofa next to Harry. She was glad when he put his arm round her, pulled her in to his warmth.

'May,' he said, 'we'd like to do something to help. We've been wondering, would you like me to redecorate your bedroom for you? As and when we can find such a thing, I'd be happy to hang some new paper and slap on a bit of paint.' Her mother offered a watery smile. Lily began pouring milk into the cups.

'I think those violets have been there since before I was born,' Evelyn said. The redecoration was her idea. She was haunted by the memory of her father in that room, his yellow sunken face; she was thinking too of the germs that must be there, how scrubbing would never get it clean and a new mattress and a wipe around with disinfectant was not nearly enough. 'It wouldn't be any bother, Mum,' she said.

'That's very kind of you, Harry, dear,' her mother said, 'but I won't put you to the trouble just yet. Teddy put that paper up.'

What? It was extraordinary to think of her father ever doing such a thing and then, for a moment, Evelyn imagined him, sober, in overalls – saw him climb a ladder, the damp paper in careful folds, and then lean in to line it up and press it down, pushing away the bubbles of air. For a moment, this version of him, one she had never known, entranced her and flooded her with tenderness. But of course it was not her own memory. She still wanted a bright new start, a better story.

'Just say when you're ready, or if there is anything else we can do,' Harry said.

The bedroom was gloomy at night, with just the one lamp on an extension cord placed at Evelyn's side of the bed. The girls had taken over an hour to get to sleep, first hungry, then tearful, disturbed by the idea of death, and now Evelyn lay on her back, stared at the ceiling while Harry undressed.

'A difficult day. How are you doing?' he asked.

'That Dickie makes my blood boil!' she said, stiffening.

'You did well with him,' Harry said as he climbed in next to her. 'And it's over with. And as for your poor mother, we tried. Maybe she'll call on me later.'

'She won't,' Evelyn told him. 'She'll stay with Beth in Walthamstow for a week or two and then go back and live in that miserable little house just as it always was!' She switched out the light and in the sudden darkness he reached out for her, but she pulled away, turned her back to him. 'Leave me alone!' she said, her voice beginning to crack. If only, she thought, biting her knuckle to stop herself crying out loud, If only she had been able to do what her mother wanted. Yet for the life of her she could not, and that was the end of it . . . Except that it wasn't, because without meaning to she spun back to face Harry and was saying aloud in a voice not her own: *If only – If only I –* Her fingers dug into his back. She pressed her face into his chest.

'Shh, shh, you did everything you could,' he muttered into her hair, their bodies clenched damply together, 'everything you could.' Gradually, her sobs subsided, and then, when he kissed her gently on the base of her neck she felt the touch of his lips on the skin there with her entire body.

Don't stop, she said.

ANOTHER MAN

Beyond the windows, the new leaves of plane trees toss and gleam in the rain. Somewhere must be a rainbow. But here and now, it's Timber, Labour, and Economies of Scale with Multiple Units, while behind him the radio plays and the girls squeal delightedly in their bedroom across the hall. It is just like the army only without the noise and excitement and he can think of an infinite number of things he would prefer to do, but instead, he must pick up the slide rule, then adjust, read, double-check, record his answer: *Each unit with cavity walls will require 17,800 common bricks and 17,800 facing bricks, 2,500 ties, and 1,800 roof tiles*, and then move on to the next item. A machine could do it and one day will.

Meanwhile, for him, three evening classes a week for three years, and now, on top of that, it's full marks or fail and so now he must shut himself away from Evelyn, Lily and little Val to study this drivel on a Sunday afternoon, the edge of the dining table butting into his stomach, the chair excruciatingly hard beneath his buttocks, yet another practice exam in front of him and Auden's *Nones*, bought in Charing Cross Road three weeks ago, still in his briefcase with not a single poem read. At the beginning of the war, his competence with numbers put him in the artillery and possibly saved his life; now it's offering him a profession – so yes, he should be grateful, but will he ever be able to find his way back to the lovely slipperiness of words, the feeling of them running away with him?

Drops spatter on the glass. Slither down.

So far as *writing* goes, he's ready to admit facts and resign himself. If not by now, never. At the most, keep a notebook. Try again later. When things ease up. On retirement, if he lives that long! But at this rate will there ever be time to even *read*? *Oh*, he tells himself, *shut up and knuckle down . . .*

Evelyn pushes through the door just as he's adding the per-unit total for copper pipe.

'Which shirt do you want me to iron for tomorrow?' she asks, and the figure he was carrying from one column to the next evaporates. He flings down his pencil, twists round to face her.

'Pardon?' he asks, though he heard well enough.

'Which shirt are you wearing tomorrow?'

'I've no idea.' Is it unreasonable to expect an hour's quiet? After all, the bloody exam is for their benefit. 'Frankly, I don't care! I just need to be left in peace.'

'Don't be such a bear!' A phrase which, said another time, could have been an affectionate reprimand. In this case, it's not: he knows immediately from the sudden set of her mouth, the way her jaw skews.

'You're welcome to do your own ironing!' Evelyn slams the door behind her, and he should follow her out and apologise, hear her say how sick she is of the chores and the rain, but he wants *her* to know how *he* is feeling, to commiserate, and so he, at least part knowingly, makes things worse still by returning to the figures. Strict, tedious, functional things. He hates them even more than ever.

Starts over. Can't concentrate. Hears Evelyn hustle the girls into their coats and prepare to go out, Valerie asking in a loud whisper whether Daddy will come? Lily telling her no, hurry up. *But I will come,* he tells himself, *just as soon as I finish this one* . . . And a few minutes after the downstairs front door slams shut, he slips the slide rule into its case, pushes his feet into his shoes and sprints down after them. The rain has just stopped and halfway down the still-glistening street, Evelyn, her spine straight, her shoulders back, strides ahead with the two girls in her wake, Valerie wobbling along on the scooter he made for Lily.

He soon catches up, walks next to his wife. *Dear Evelyn, you are the sweetest wife* . . . he used to write to her in his letters home. *Dear Evelyn. My dearest.*

'Oh – ' She looks straight ahead as she speaks, 'I thought you said you wanted to be left in peace. And *frankly,* so do I.' *Touché.* He has to admire her skill with the rapier; though at the same time, it brings him to the brink of tears. Why? What are they doing? Such a waste! He walks beside her, but says nothing. He's at a low ebb, needs to gather his resources.

He never imagined they would be like this. But once you live together properly, you learn fast. How dismissive he can sometimes be. How very sensitive Evelyn is to that, or to any criticism or lack of respect, whether real or perceived. How, thinking herself slighted, she will put everything she has into self-defence. How she can be vicious as well as sweet. What an art it is, once that begins (normally because of some sudden, stupid, sticklerish inflexibility on his part, or sarcasm, or superiority of some kind) to talk her back down. A direct approach rarely works. Even trying to talk about the arguments, between episodes, is an aggravation: *What are you accusing me of?* Finding the way out requires creativity, energy, perfect timing.

Are these umbrages, these dudgeons of hers within her control? Hard to tell. Perhaps no more than his own sudden snaps or lunges. The important thing is to prevent them from escalating. And he knows, too, that her pride and temper are the extreme end of something that draws him to her, that he could not have Evelyn's fiery, wilful strength without also having her tendency to overreact. Without sometimes finding it directed his way.

At St Ann's Hill he drops back to walk with the girls.

'Where are we going?' he asks.

'The windmill,' Valerie says, craning her neck to look at him and nearly falling over. What a smile she has! What dark, glittering eyes. She looks hot in her coat.

'Watch out!' Lily tells her sister.

Lily is not yet sure which parent's side she will take, though it is very clear to her that since she doesn't know how to ride it and isn't prepared to wheel it, Valerie is at fault for bringing the scooter along.

'Why don't *you* ride it for a bit?' her father asks her as they thin out to pass a well-dressed woman with a Dalmatian on a lead coming from the opposite direction: she's probably from one of the big houses at the other side of the green, Harry thinks.

'I'm nearly eleven!' Lily tells him. 'And the handles are far too low for me now.'

'When we get to the edge of the common, we'll hide it in a bush,' he announces, 'and collect it on the way home.' A mistake: when they get there, Evelyn, watching him conceal the scooter, breathes out, noisily: almost a snort. She is, he knows, castigating him for giving in to the girls, for risking the loss of their property. Yet it was she who brought the damn thing out. No matter.

'Run ahead,' he tells Lily and Valerie. 'See who gets to the windmill first. Wait for us there.'

'I don't want to run,' Lily says, but already Valerie is pulling away. Much as she dislikes it, it is Lily's job to keep her sister safe, so she sets off in pursuit. It will certainly be Daddy's fault if the scooter is stolen, she thinks, and at least part of her hopes that it won't be there when they return.

He matches his pace to Evelyn's.

'I'm so very sorry, darling. I was just in such a bloody mood, having all this work to do on the weekend and the exams tomorrow.' Evelyn, looking ahead, maintains her silence.

He knows better than to reach for her gloved hand, or try to slip his arm through hers. 'It's a strain,' he says. 'Studying and working, paying for here and saving for the house . . . Not much fun *now*, though it will pay off and I'm glad to do it, but sometimes I get frazzled. Of course, that's no excuse. And of course, I know it's not easy for you, having us all in that cramped flat, with me always cluttering up the table, and moody too. Once we've moved, it will all seem worthwhile.'

So he hopes. Part of him longs to push it all aside – the job, the need for security, the bank balance, the constant thinking of the future, the house itself. To live instead an *unsettled life*. Read for hours every day. Hike for weeks on end. Travel, live miles from anywhere in the country, perhaps hand-make the few bits of furniture they need . . . But the girls need schools and a regular life, and then there's Evelyn herself: not averse to travelling, but not one to sleep in a hedge. Remember: she might not have chosen him. She could surely have done better; her school friend Jennifer, despite being plain and dull, married a barrister after the war, moved to a very large house near Tunbridge Wells and has a woman come to clean every day.

'I wish I hadn't snapped,' he says. Avoid at all costs the second-person plural. Shoulder all of the blame. No ifs or buts . . . It's the only way, and already he senses from the set of her jaw and mouth, from the slight softening of her shoulders, from something subtle in the way her feet touch the path, that her hostility is becoming less vehement. In silence, they walk on through the oak woods where the smells of leaf mould and humus thicken the air. Spears of new grass and weeds shoot up at the edges of the path. The red-tinged greens of the new leaves burn against a sky scoured blue.

'You know, it's not really like me to be so bad-tempered,' he continues, 'and I expect this sounds odd, but it feels, well, almost as if that was another man . . . As if the man who sits there doing sums and getting grumpy is someone I become in certain circumstances. For long periods of time, as needed. But he's not who I am, and I don't feel *at all* like him now that we're out here, walking together in the woods. Hard to explain! Maybe he's related to the man I had to be in the war, he's a man all about the means to an end, and doing what has to be done. He gets hired and paid . . . I have to be him, but he's not me. Because there's also another man who wants to walk and read and write and feel and think, to stroke your hair and gaze at you and make love all day and forget all the rest. He's the one I think of as me.'

She looks at him now, and he holds her gaze.

'Well, I can tell you there's only one of me,' she says.

'I know.' She lets him take her hand and kiss it. They walk on.

'We are almost through,' he continues. 'I'll qualify, and we'll be able to afford the house. We'll be living in it in another couple of years. We'll be in the garden, making friends with the neighbours, all that.'

'It seems so long,' she says. Her eyes glisten, but she doesn't let her tears fall. She doesn't cry often, except for at a certain time of the month. She's a warrior, not a weeper.

'It is and it isn't,' he tells her.

'All together, it'll be longer than the bloody war.'

True, yet not so bad as the war, nothing like, and so . . . They walk a little slower.

'What shall we put in the garden?' he asks her. 'Besides your rhododendrons?'

'Daffodils,' she says, not quite smiling.

'A host!'

'Roses.'

'Of course.' He pushes aside thoughts of Blake's invisible worm, his dark, secret love. 'Pansies,' he suggests, as he slips his arm around her. 'Though maybe not: I think it was the juice of them on her eyelids what made Titania – maybe you remember, the queen of the fairies – fall in love with the ass when she woke up? Unless *I'm* the ass, of course.'

He's happy to be one, so long as she smiles back at him.

'Where are they?' Valerie asks Lily. The air is still and the windmill's sails don't turn. When they peek through the fence there's no one in the garden, just a marmalade cat, which won't come however hard they call. They stand with their backs to the mill and stare back down the path.

'Shall we make up a story about the windmill?' Valerie asks, 'Or run back to them? Are you sure they are coming?'

'What else would they do?'

'Don't be snappy.'

'Don't be spoiled.'

'I'm not spoiled!'

'No? Don't you realise how lucky you are to have both of them here, right from when you were born? For there to be *no bombs*? To see Daddy *every day*? And do you realise how much *she* lets you get away with?' Lily loves Valerie – very much at times – but she finds that once she starts like this, she doesn't want to stop, and that she at least half likes it when Valerie begins to cry. The way her face blotches red . . . Because of being so spoiled, she deserves to sometimes feel bad.

'But I can't help any of that,' Val wails.

'Now you're being a baby,' Lily tells her, just as their parents come into view, and Valerie runs, tear-streaked, towards them. Lily follows at walking pace.

'I really didn't mean it,' she says, calmly, with a little shrug of her shoulders. 'I'm very sorry.'

Harry hauls Valerie up onto his shoulders. Why not, he suggests, walk in a loop, have tea in the village, and then take the train or the bus home? But of course, he remembers once they've set off, the bloody scooter! He's very tempted to pretend to forget it, since the others have, but sees trouble looming that way: Valerie suddenly wanting it again, Evelyn pouring scorn and asking him do they have money to burn. And so, where the path divides, he says, taking off his jacket and handing it to Evelyn, that he'll run back to the bushes and get the thing, then meet them at the tea shop.

Running through the leafy lane, his shirt damp with sweat, his body warming to the work and liking it, his eyes growing sharper and taking in the almost-bursting buds and the spiderwebs bejewelled with glistening droplets, Harry forgets the argument completely. And it comes to him that as regards the other man – or men – there's no knowing which one of them he really is, or how much of each would eventually be in whoever he turns out to be, if he ever does – but at times like this, outside, they could all be there, enjoying the same freedom, the vast and intricate world that they inhabit.

After dinner, Evelyn sets up the ironing board and plugs the iron into the bedroom's single electrical socket, awkwardly placed by the door. Humming to herself a tune part made-up, part forgotten, she plucks Harry's pale blue shirt from the basket and drapes it over the board, checks the iron with a quick tap of a wet finger, and then presses the two front

Kathy Page

panels, first slipping the point of the iron between the pearly buttons, then rushing carefree up the side with the holes. It's pleasantly familiar: the faint scent of outdoors, the dull hiss when she presses down on the piece of muslin, first wetted in a bowl then squeezed out, to steam away a stubborn crease. Sides, back, shoulder, yoke. Wrinkled, then flat. Sleeves, cuffs, collar. She slides in its stiffeners, slips the shirt over a wooden hanger and onto the hook on the door. It will wait for him there until morning when he'll feed his arms into the sleeves and button himself into it.

He herds his parents and Evelyn's mother across the road from the bus stop, then leads them slowly up the avenue, passing one by one the decaying Victorian mansions destined to become old people's homes, apartments, and new developments. It's warm, even at ten. After a pause at the postbox to catch their breaths, he steers them down and right, past the Cheshire Home for the Disabled and the rambling turn-of-the-century property across from it. Thereafter the plots and buildings on the road, while still detached and well-built, are somewhat smaller and lower.

He brings the party to a halt and indicates the house with a sweep of his arm: 'There it is!' It's less than half the size of the one behind them, but even so, there are gasps and his mother takes hold of his arm.

'Everything so crisp looking!' she says. 'Like a painting!'

'So many windows! You'll have to pay someone to clean them.' Evelyn's mother chimes in, adding, 'And aren't you afraid the neighbours will spy on you?' The windows, Harry points out, are metal-framed, with hardwood sills: very low-maintenance.

'Well, well,' his father says. He stuffs his hands into his pockets and gazes at the width and height of the place as if it were a spaceship come to land. 'Nice bit of brickwork. Well, well. So that's the house.'

The House. Those words, on their lips twenty times a day for years on end, not to speak of in their minds. It took nine months to build. He had to visit and inspect the site almost every weekend. The plot, a third of an acre, his choice, slopes gently from the back towards the street: good for drainage, and excellent for looking at the back garden from the house.

Like all the others, the house begins thirty feet from the road, runs across most of the width of the plot. It's fifty-two feet wide, and thirty feet deep. It's built with cavity walls, he explains to his dumbstruck audience, in a blend of London stock bricks for the facing and cheaper engineered bricks for the inside skin. Metal ties and weep holes have been used as per the regulations. The major load-bearing wall that runs the length of the house is also brick; other internal walls are studwork. 42,000 bricks were used to build the house, and 2,800 roof tiles; the builder tried to cheat them by charging for twenty percent more than he used, but Harry spotted the discrepancy.

'Swindler. Picked the wrong man. We sent him packing!' he tells them. 'So let's cross now and go in. Evelyn will be waiting . . . I think she's made a cake. Of course, there'll be a lawn to either side of the path here . . . '

The front door is solid oak; internal doors, as they'll soon see, are veneered mahogany – no panelling, no dust traps, the modern look. Central light fittings, he tells them, pausing on the open porch, in every room (two in the living room); electrical outlets on at least three walls in every room, and, of course, new curtains, made by Evelyn, in all the downstairs windows. He doesn't mention the cost of them, or that the upstairs ones are, as a result, just borrowed nets. They'll have to wait until at least the end of the year for something more substantial.

She nearly died when she first saw the price: almost an entire month of Harry's salary. But she was in love with the fabric:

cotton, weighty but supple, with a pattern of hand-drawn triangles and diamonds in a rich range of greens: sap, leaf, olive, viridian, with here and there a brown. 'Forest Depths' it was called, the only thing in the entire shop that she liked. She could see it, in her mind's eye – the curtains closed at night, softly lit. You could look and look at them and not grow bored . . .

Impossible.

'Madam? It's a good price for this quality.'

'Well, it's more than I'm budgeting.'

'I expect you know that we are never knowingly undersold.'

'We have a lot of expenses at once, as you can imagine.'

And so they trailed back to the outdoor tones, to look for something similar but more economical that Evelyn might somehow have overlooked. Useless! She liked just one thing in the entire shop, and that was the end of it. Miss Laney-Smith reached for her scissors to cut a sample. Maybe the little girl would like a piece of the velvet? It was at this point that they realised Valerie had vanished, though at first they did not take it seriously because the tables and racks seemed perfect for a bored child to hide amongst.

Evelyn and Miss Laney-Smith, along with a plump woman in a pale, belted coat who had been waiting her turn, hurried between the rows of rolls and bales, the bins and racks. They peered around corners, under tables, pulled back swathes and drapes. At any moment she would surely reappear.

'Where are you? Valerie?'

Nothing.

'Come here, please, Val. Where are you hiding?'

'Valerie! I'm getting fed up with this, Valerie!'

Several staff cut short their coffee break. Together, they searched Bedding. Took the stairs down and walked quickly through Gentlemen's Clothes, unlikely to have attracted Valerie.

Ladies Outerwear. Ladies Fashions. Underwear. Perfumes. *Have you seen a little girl? Excuse me. Brown hair and eyes.*

The lower floors were crowded. They jostled their way through, made sure to look behind the clots of customers.

'I'm sure she'll be found soon, madam,' the bespectacled man from Furniture repeated as he accompanied her through Hosiery and Handbags where they saw no children at all . . . Had some deranged childless woman or soft-spoken but evil man lured or snatched her? Evelyn burst out into the May sunshine and the din of the street, turned right, where, according to the bespectacled man, a police officer always stood not far from the store. She ran, her bag bumping into her leg . . . And there the officer was, solid and dark blue, walking towards her hand in hand with a little girl barely visible beneath a large straw hat decorated with a flowing scarf and silk flowers.

'Thank goodness!' She crouched down, there in the street. 'What on earth are you doing out here in that hat? Look me in the eyes!' The pink face, staring back at her. Glistening eyes. Sick of curtains! Hated shops. Wanted to try the sunhat in the sun.

'You begged to come with me! I certainly shan't bring you again.'

The policeman's barely concealed smirk.

Damp with sweat, she dragged Valerie back to Millinery, where the hat, left on the table by a customer who had then later returned to buy it, had just been missed. An apology. More tears. And then, because she had hung her jacket and scarf on the back of a chair in the fabric department and Valerie had a horror of escalators, she had to trudge up the three flights of stairs again, dragging her weeping daughter by the hand. She was determined not to spoil the children the way she was spoilt by her own mother, and a sharp slap on the back of the leg was what she felt the situation called for: something to make her think twice before doing it again. But it was awkward to do on the stairs – and besides, there was Miss Laney-Smith, just completing a sale.

'I'm glad to see you safe and sound, young lady. Madam, I have your jacket and the samples.'

The feeling of 'Forest Depths', lovely but ruinous, returned, an ache in the chest.

'Thank you,' Evelyn said, not feeling grateful at all, until Miss Laney-Smith leaned forward and said, her voice very low, 'Madam, I really shouldn't tell you this, but given the difficult morning you have had . . . in confidence . . . It might be wise to come back next month when we have our summer clearance.'

They went for ice cream before setting off home.

It came out at fifty percent off. Though even then, it was dear.

'Eleven pounds? Bloody hell, Evelyn,' Harry said, filing the receipts. 'We budgeted for *seven*.'

'It includes the lining. Very good quality for the price,' she told him. 'A false economy not to get them. Besides, there was nothing else I liked. You'll see.'

Pins everywhere. The great stiff swathes of fabric, the terror, even given careful Laney-Smith instructions, of measuring, marking and then cutting, there on the thrice-cleaned, too-small dining table pushed up to the bay for the very best light . . . *To avoid confusion, work one curtain at a time. Allow four inches plus ten inches extra length to allow for the pattern to be matched. Measure twice, cut once.*

The panels matched, pinned, tacked, then sewed on the borrowed machine. The hem pressed. The cream lining made up four inches narrower and three inches shorter . . .

Mum, no, wait! It's not straight . . .
What do you mean, of course it is!
No! Look!

The two panels joined right to wrong side, then the whole huge thing turned out the other way . . . Roll and press the edges. Mitre the corners. Turn over the top edge and pin the tape in place (knot one end first). Sew through all three fabrics . . . A faint smell of rubber from the machine. *Please don't break!*

Harry, after work, took it to pieces, cleaned it, adjusted the belt, added the tiniest, translucent drop of oil. Then: tighten the strings in the heading tape, adjust the gathers, thread in hooks . . . At this point, a trip, heart in mouth, to the almost-finished house to make sure that everything hung well. The painter doing the windowsills winked at her from the other side of the glass. Mrs Symonds to the right commented *It's very brave of you. I always get mine made up.*

Repeat three times. Just a few strips left over and done in time, just before the move.

'Yes, I do like them, very much. But *eleven pounds* – '

'It's worth having something we like. And they'll last. They won't fade.'

'Point taken. But are you absolutely clear it means we can't spend any more on anything else. Not *at all*. Upstairs will have to wait.' Evelyn said nothing, just stared into the middle distance.

She packed. Harry hired a van, took Friday off, arranged for a friend from work to meet them at the house.

'What's the matter? Your face is like thunder!' she said as they crested the hill at Crystal Palace, the pub and the big old houses to the left, the park to the right.

'Don't look at me, then,' he said. Neither of them had slept well and the girls had wept when they left the flat, and then again when they were dropped off with his mother, and Harry had no desire to explain how driving the van, the rattle of it and feeling of the gears, reminded him of the bloody war.

'If you're going to be like this, I'll get out and walk!' she said, and reached for the door handle, but they were doing almost thirty and just then went over a pothole. Also, they weren't even halfway there.

'Slow down!' she said, but he ignored her. She did not insist on getting out and they plunged on through Penge and into Beckenham, where the streets were leafier and the mood began to lift. Four trips over two days and then back to the office on Monday.

Now, everything is in its place. Harry presses on the electric bell, hears from outside its piercing sound; the door swings in to reveal Evelyn in a navy blue fitted frock, lips reddened, hair freshly waved.

'Mum, Adeline, Albert, welcome!' She takes Adeline's jacket first, slides open the double closet door.

'Is that just to hang your coats in?' His mother grins at him as she says, it, but even so, he's not pleased.

'Yes! Now come on everyone. Don't hang back, Mum,' Evelyn says. There's a brittle sound quality downstairs in the house, due to a scarcity of rugs, pictures and furniture. Voices ring out that bit too loud as, beside the closet, beneath the lamp, the women remove headscarves, exchange quick kisses on the cheek with Evelyn, breathe in each other's scent, powder and hairspray. Their parents, Harry notes, have dressed their best for the visit, May in a floral print on a dark background and fine denier stockings; his mother in a new dark green dress. His father's jacket has been pressed to a shine.

'That was a fair old walk,' Evelyn's mother says. 'You said it's even further to the station?'

'Keeps me fit!'

'You can all rest now . . . This is the hall,' Evelyn adds, and gestures at the space around them, bigger than her mother's back room, papered with the weave-effect paper, carpeted brown, eighty percent wool. She gestures again at the low table and chair under the stairs, upon which, she hopes, a telephone will eventually sit. Lily and Val, crouched on the staircase that runs behind this, peer down through the banisters.

'These are the stairs!' Lily declares, and they both collapse into giggles, quiver in each other's arms.

'You monkeys!'

Valerie, who often came with Harry on his inspections, likes the house. Lily does not. Granted, she now has her own bedroom, and got to choose the wallpaper (a subtle geometric pattern, far easier on the eye than the horses in Val's), but the House takes up so much time. Once, they used to bus to the museums on the weekend, walk the city parks and listen to the bands, or rove the local commons. Now that the House is built they must keep it nice, must plant and tend the garden, and, it seems, talk about it over every meal: House. Garden. House. She misses her old school. She's trying, but it's hard to see the point.

Evelyn gestures at the mahogany doors, their gleaming steel handles. 'Kitchen behind me. Spare room there, downstairs toilet there – '

'Two toilets for one house?' Harry's father mutters, bewildered. He's made clear before that he thinks outside is a better place for such things.

'May I pop in and use that right now, if you don't mind?' her mother asks, and of course they can't stand there, just feet away while she does her business; Harry leads the rest of them past the stairs and the front window into the living room, which runs from front to back of the house, a good thirty feet by fifteen. There's parquet flooring and picture windows at each end. These, Evelyn points out, will come into their own once the garden grows in.

'So much light! You feel gawped at,' May says as she joins them again. 'It's like being in a magazine!'

'This furniture,' Evelyn explains, 'is all wrong, of course, but it's just for now.' In the ensuing pause, everyone examines the dark red sofa and the two tan-coloured fireside armchairs, each with its own footstool and little table, then Adeline asks:

'What's wrong with it?'

'It doesn't match. And in any case, it's far too small for a room this size,' Evelyn explains. 'We need something more modern – and some pictures on the walls, too.'

The older generation looks back at her, not saying what it thinks.

The fireplace, Harry explains, is designed to vent hot air to the dining room on the other side of the wall. They go there next, and examine the special brass vent and the French windows that lead out onto the patio. Low brick walls demarcate the two lower flower beds, which are currently hosting a few geraniums to give a sense of what they might eventually become. A set of broad low steps leads to what will become the lawn.

'This table will go, of course,' Evelyn says. They move on into the square kitchen with its cupboards painted cream to maximise the light and minty green easy-wipe Formica worktops. The miraculous gas stove. The coke-fired boiler.

'Where do you keep your coal?' Harry's father asks, so Harry takes him on a side tour of the bunkers in the concreted yard just outside the back door. It can all be hosed down, and Albert is more impressed by this and the drain in the middle of the yard than by anything else so far.

'One of those metal sinks!' May exclaims. 'But it seems very small.'

'Stainless steel,' Evelyn corrects her. 'This is the size, now, Mum. And here, under here, look: this is my washing machine and wringer.' She flips up the hinged counter, demonstrates the hoses, the handle of the wringer, how easy it all is. 'Lino on the floor,' she points out. 'Extractor fan!'

May peers into the tiled larder with its own little window and space for the refrigerator underneath. By the back door: a cupboard for mops, brooms and cleaning supplies, 'And this one, Mum, just for trays!'

Back into the hall and up the carpeted stairs to the carpeted landing, past the upstairs toilet, into the bathroom, where not all of them can fit at the same time. Blue-grey tiles, shiny chrome fittings. 'This is the sink!' Valerie announces, and there's more giggling as they follow the soft carpet, softer yet because of its rubber underlay, into the main bedroom. The bed with its old-fashioned wooden headboard, also 'to go', seems very small, but Harry draws their attention to the built-in wardrobes.

'How many clothes are you going to buy to fill all this! And so much space,' says May, 'just to sleep in! It's like being outside. I'm not sure I could. I do like a cosy bedroom.'

And downstairs again in the enormous living room, everyone, even the girls, silent, and no one seems to want to sit, until, finally, under pressure, Evelyn's mother settles on the not-new sofa, carefully, as if she might break or spoil it.

'I never would have thought!' she says, looking up at the rest of them, 'I do so wish dear Teddy could have seen this . . . But all that outside, what will you ever do with all that?'

'You have to imagine, May.' Harry gestures as he speaks. 'Rhodos at the back. Shrubs. Roses. Vegetable plot with a path up beside it. Lawn – it's sown already, but we're fighting the drought and the birds – '

'So you won't be lolling around in your deckchairs for a while!' his mother interrupts, smiling. She settles down next to May and now both of them, their hands in their laps, look as if they are still riding together on the bus. They've not arrived here yet. Can't quite believe in it. 'What are the neighbours like? Very la-di-da?'

Valerie giggles again. Lily shushes her.

Well, Evelyn tells them, there is a solicitor and his wife next door, their daughter the same age as Val; a couple with two older boys, in business, probably, to the other side; a doctor, a specialist of some kind with a pale, rather downtrodden wife and large family in the older house diagonally opposite; a dentist and his pregnant wife two doors along.

'You'll not need to worry for your health or your teeth, then!'

'No! Not that we do. Tea, coffee, or some nice cold lemon barley?' Evelyn asks. No one responds. They're still taking it all in: Solicitor! Dentist! The parquet and the pelmets. The lawn-to-be that, if it ever grows, will surely take hours to cut.

'How much do you owe?' Harry's father asks.

'Plenty,' Harry tells him. 'No rest for the wicked. It'll get easier every year, though.' Sometimes he gets night sweats at the thought of it, but forty years – forty years – is a long time. Numbers don't lie and the current rate is two percent. He knows that he will advance himself in ways his father never could, however skilled at the lathe he might be, and however hard he works. Foreman's the limit.

Office work is different. Defined steps. Regular rises. Opportunities. He has grasped the salary ladder with both hands and will climb it as fast as he can, will do everything in his power to provide his children a good life, to give Evelyn what she desires. Standing there with their parents, in the living room of the finished house, he remembers how he walked her home the day they met, how, passing the big detached villas at the side of the common she turned to him, said, 'Imagine living in one of those! Imagine looking out of your big bay windows on all of this.' How it both touched and aroused him. And he still loves the fierce, physical way Evelyn wants whatever she wants. He is her agent. She articulates an aim, he finds the way; together, they work for it, and so yes, he will don every day a shirt with a starched collar, a tie and one of two suits; he'll take the 7.20, carry a briefcase, bring papers home, change clothes and start work on the garden or the house. Sometimes, if he does not fall asleep, he has time to read on the train –

'Mum, look,' Evelyn says. She takes hold of one of the curtains and draws it part way out, so they can see the pattern and the hang of it. 'Remember, I told you how I got this material half price? How I borrowed Cousin Betty's machine to make them up?'

May peers at the pattern, a modern thing that she doesn't much appreciate: and wasn't it *eleven pounds* that Evelyn paid for the stuff, even half price? Just for curtains. She pauses, eyes on her daughter's face, her lips feeling out the words ahead. 'Very nice, dear. But it's not what we're used to, and like I said, it's such a long way and the thing is, I'm going to miss being able to drop by to see you and the little ones.' Her eyes fill with tears; Evelyn lets go of the curtain and takes half a step forwards, but it's Lily who gets there first, who kneels on the parquet, reaches out, and buries her head in her grandmother's flowery lap. Her shoulders heave.

'I'll miss you, Granny!'

'But I'll bring them over every other week,' Evelyn says, 'and you can come and stay here, any time you want. It'll be much nicer once everything grows and we can sit out there to shell the peas and listen to the birds.'

'We'll see,' her mother says, stroking Lily's hair and looking steadily back at her; years later, when Lily is married and she and Tim announce their plan to emigrate to Australia, Evelyn will remember this look, the awful blend of love and reproach; now, she stands, resisting it, and Adeline reaches across, rests her arm across May's shoulders and gives her a squeeze.

'Even the air here is different! It just takes getting used to,' she says, as Lily, wet hair glued to her face, struggles to her feet, 'doesn't it, Al? But what a place! I'm sure you'll all be very happy here.' And only then, finally, with some kind of blessing given and agreed upon, are they ready to drink tea (served, thankfully, in familiar cups), and then to move to the dining room for pork pies, pickles and salad, and then back to the living room for more tea with large slices of home-made sponge cake to fortify them for the journey home.

'At least it's mostly downhill to the bus!' May announces as they set off on the first leg of the journey back: a phrase Valerie will repeat until it no longer makes anyone laugh.

And soon, Harry and Evelyn, stripped down to their under-clothes and holding hands, will lie, side by side on their backs on top of their bed, surrounded by the sheer enormousness of the room, by all the cupboards and drawers that yearn to be filled.

'They'd just far rather we lived in a hovel close by!'

'Though of course, if we *hadn't* done this, you can bet your mother would be complaining I wasn't good enough.'

'True. I suppose she'll come round. And even if not, well – '

'Evelyn, do you remember,' he says, 'that day we first met? Walking past the big houses on the edge of Wandsworth Common?'

'Mmm . . . ' she says. Neither a yes nor a no.

'We'd only known each other about half an hour,' he reminds her, 'but I knew right then that you must have your own house with a garden. Big and clean and light, the opposite of the sooty little terraces we grew up in. I knew I must get it for you.' He studies her face. The soft skin of her eyelids, her full lips, smiling now.

'I do remember. You were wearing a dark blue suit.' She takes in a breath, lets it slowly out. Her hand grazes his leg, settles next to it – he can't but react: the blissful, familiar rush of blood. 'I just wish the garden would grow faster,' she says as he turns towards her.

SO GOOD

The walk to the surgery: down the avenue to the few shops at the green, right up the main road (unless she caught the bus, but they never came on time), and then left through the residential streets on the edge of the town, would take about half an hour at a brisk pace. It was probably a waste of time, since that feeling she sometimes had was very likely nothing. Still, it was pleasant enough to be out on a bright November day, and everything was going well, apart from Valerie and the lipstick, and the damned news, because if the Russians weren't throwing their people into camps or pretending to have turned a new leaf, then they were hurling a dog into space, putting down the Poles or the Hungarians, or exploding nuclear bombs, making everyone else follow suit, so that it would never be possible to relax and feel safe. Already those poor people in the Lake District had radioactive milk. But those ban-the-bombers, geniuses supposedly, were lunatics. You could not give way to threats.

And perhaps Harry was right that she shouldn't listen to the radio since it upset her so much. 'Try not to dwell on it,' he had said, lying behind her in bed and kneading the tight muscles at the back of her neck. 'We survived the war, after all.'

'I couldn't bear another one.'

'I'm afraid it's the way of things that there will always be another one,' he'd said, his hands falling still for a few moments before resuming the massage, 'but I also think we'll be lucky and miss it. Don't let the thought of it spoil things. There's not much we can do about it. Just look at what we have.'

Hardly comforting.

Though it was true that the garden had matured beautifully and the air in the suburbs was very fresh; the shops were bursting with whatever you could imagine, and, despite the Russians, they had, as Macmillan had rather crudely put it, never had it so good. Best to look at it that way. And then, yesterday's school visit: what a pleasure to sit in the study by Mrs Phillips' desk, smiling and nodding as they were told *You should be very pleased with your girls. Both of them are University Material.* An odd phrase, she and Harry had agreed afterwards, proud of course, though Evelyn was uncertain that she liked the idea that the girls would be cut up and made into something, curtains or dresses or whatever. 'That's what happens,' Harry told her.

'How do you feel about your daughters undertaking a university education, Mr and Mrs Miles?' No one in the family had done such a thing. Most of them on both sides had left school at fourteen. Her studies in the matriculation class at the grammar school and Harry's scholarship made them exceptions.

It would be up to the girls, Evelyn said, though of course she and her husband knew that education was generally a very good thing, and that was why they had encouraged them to sit for the school's scholarship exam.

Encouraged? *Insisted.* Who in their right mind would not take the opportunity? Look what it did for your father.

When Mrs Phillips nodded, the gold chain fastened to her glasses twinkled in the light from the desk lamp with its art nouveau stained-glass shade. Lily might study law, she said. She could become a solicitor, or even a barrister. It was unusual, yes, but *possible* –

'Lillian has a strong sense of justice. She easily takes in complicated ideas, and at the same time she often notices details that other others might miss . . . Valerie, on the other hand, seems more practical and scientific, but also artistic – a great gift, though of course not so reliable in terms of a profession. She could eventually consider medicine, though admittedly it may be too early to say.'

Medicine? Valerie, who had lied to her about the lipstick.

Sometimes, Mrs Phillips said, Widmore girls went as far as assisted places at Oxford or Cambridge. Though of course, whatever their potential, most still did want to get married. At the very least if they went to university they were likely to marry a little later, and choose a more educated and affluent man.

Oxford or Cambridge!

Though it would be easier if they were boys. More straightforward.

'We certainly wouldn't stand in their way,' Harry said, and they both shook Mrs Phillips's bony but surprisingly warm hand before going to see the subject teachers and then the performance of *A Winter's Tale* . . . And now, running it all over in her mind as she strode up the hill, keen to escape the noise of the main road, she remembered a day trip before the war: the intense greenness of the river at Cambridge, and Harry with his sleeves rolled up, punting while she reclined . . .

Despite having unbuttoned her coat, she arrived flushed and damp at the surgery, where the receptionist's duties had been taken over by Dr Ransome's unmarried daughter, a woman of about thirty with an unfortunately horsey face. It could not be much fun, Evelyn thought, to still be living at home, and working there too, since the surgery was most of the downstairs of the doctor's large, detached house. To have never got away and to spend all day in a drab room surrounded by people exuding germs . . . In the ladies' room she ran her wrists and hands under the cold tap, splashed her face. She was still feeling perfectly fine.

'Come in!' Dr Ransome called, and she pushed into the consulting room, originally the front lounge of the house. Ransome, a trim little man now sporting silver tufts in a circle around a bald pate, sat at a large desk with his back to a bay window. Ransome had served them well over the past few years, though everyone agreed that he talked too much and liked to show how good his memory was.

'Take a seat, Mrs Miles,' he greeted her, 'a pleasure to see you. How is the family? How old are those girls, now?'

'Seventeen and twelve.'

'Doing well? Both at Widmore House? And your husband working for the London Council still? Is he happy there? Progressing?'

'Yes – '

'Working for government has its disadvantages, as I can testify! But the holidays and pensions are certainly good . . . And so what brings you here, Mrs Miles?'

Evelyn straightened her back. Cleared her throat. Was surprised to hear a tremor in her voice.

'I sometimes have a feeling that my heart is thudding in my chest.'

Only last weekend, long after Valerie had admitted the truth, wept and apologised, and despite almost being able to accept that buying a lipstick was a relatively trivial thing – after all, Harry pointed out, she could have stolen it – Evelyn had lain awake on her back, feeling the awful relentless knocking in her chest. *Hearing* it. It was a shock to realise that both of her hands were clenched into fists, and to distract herself, she had gone downstairs and cleaned the oven. Harry eventually followed her down and found her there on her knees, wearing rubber gloves.

'It's half past two!'

'So what?' she'd replied. 'Am I supposed to just lie there?' She told him, then, about the hammering in her chest, and in the morning, he had made her promise to see Ransome, just in case.

The lie had come about because Valerie had wanted candy floss when they went to the circus on the common, but had no pocket money left and so pretended it had been stolen from her purse. Harry took this at face value and treated them all; later, Evelyn, feeling for some reason suspicious, searched the patent-leather handbag, a cast-off of hers, and found the lipstick, an expensive one in a gold-coloured holder, the colour *rouge intense*, printed on the base.

'You're far too young for lipstick,' she said. 'And no wonder you've run out of pocket money!'

'I was only wearing it at Angela's, just for fun. She didn't want to share hers with me because of germs.'

'How am I supposed to believe that? You told me you were going there to do maths homework together.'

'We *were*, but we tried out the lipstick, too . . . I'm sorry. Very sorry.' The tears were real enough, but what other lies had she told (and what others were to come)? It was intolerable to be lied to, even if, as Harry (why must he always insist on seeing two sides to the thing?) said earlier that night, before she got up to clean the oven, that experimenting with cosmetics and dishonesty might well be a natural part of childhood. He was unable to understand why it upset her so much – was amused, even, by the idea of the two girls, scarlet-lipped, calculating the square of the hypotenuse or whatever it was.

He said he had done similar things – not with lipstick – but lies and even stealing, yes, and so, surely, had she?

'I don't think so,' she had said, refusing to look at him . . .

'And the dentist says I clench my jaw,' she told Ransome.

If people do not stick to the rules, and if you don't have the facts, how can you know what is real and decide what to do? If someone refuses –

'It's probably nothing. I just thought I had better ask.'

'Always worth checking.' Ransome leaned back, whisked off his glasses, reached for a little square of cloth, polished the lenses as he continued: 'Is this thudding at the normal rate, or would you say your heart is beating faster, too?'

'Just thudding.'

'How long has it been going on,' he asked. Because she had ignored it, it was hard to know. 'Weeks, months, or years?'

'I've noticed it more this year,' she said. Ransome stood and reached into his drawer for the blood pressure cuff. In silence, he slipped it on her arm, stood in front of her to pump the sleeve. They both waited for it to sigh and deflate. 'Rather high,' he observed.

'How does your heartbeat feel right now?' he asked as he slipped the stethoscope inside the vee of her dress.

'Perfectly fine.'

'And so it sounds . . . How are your periods?' he asked.

'Regular. Heavier than I'd like,' she told him. She admitted to some moodiness beforehand, and a propensity to both irritability and tears, and yes, the thumping of her heart did occur during those times, but also at others.

'I think we had better do a proper exam. Take this, and pop behind the screens.'

Pop! she thought, what am I, a three-year-old?

The screens were wheeled metal frames with fabric stretched between horizontal bars. She had been behind them before, several times with Lily, who had disliked her new school to begin with and went through a phase of mysterious internal pains as well as an actual chest infection, chicken pox and so on. If something was going round, she would catch it. Valerie, on the other hand, was a sturdy child and rarely sick. A post-war baby, she remembered Ransome opining on a previous occasion, might well be healthier as well as more confident than a wartime one.

Slipping off her shoes, she noted the narrow adjustable examination table, a standard lamp, and a chair, along with various supply cupboards and a place for the doctor to wash his hands. There is nothing wrong with me, she thought: certainly there could be nothing that merited the garment Ransome had handed her, a pale green thing with white tapes. Which way did you wear that? She removed the outer layer of her clothing, struggled with the zipper on the back of her dress, and then peeled down her roll-on girdle and stockings, deciding to retain her knickers and bra.

The examination table was awkwardly high and a portable step had been provided. She adjusted the thin pillow and pulled up the sheet.

Ransome scrubbed his hands vigorously with strong-smelling antiseptic soap, dried them on a blue paper towel. He then pulled the sheet down, lifted the smock.

'Oh,' he said. 'All right. I'll examine your abdomen first, but I can't get to your cervix if you are still dressed. Could you please push those down a bit.'

What, she thought, can my cervix possibly have to do with my heart?

His fingers prodded the flesh of her lower abdomen, travelling systematically from one side to another, and then up a little and back the other way.

'Any discomfort?' No, though he seemed to be being excessively diligent. What was he expecting to find? She didn't ask.

'Marital life satisfactory?' A rather intrusive as well as irrelevant question, but she nodded.

'I imagine you've finished your family now?'

'I think so.'

'Are you taking precautions?'

She would far rather have been asked about all this sitting up and clothed, but since it was easier than explaining in detail, and also because she felt that it was what he wanted to hear, she told him *yes*. It was not too far from the truth: she had used, intermittently for several years after Valerie's birth, a diaphragm. A series of them, in fact, each falsely purporting to be easier to slip in and less of an interference than the last. To her mind, it took the remaining romance out of things so they had abandoned it.

'So what if we have another?' Harry had said. 'I wouldn't mind at all.'

He didn't do the having, though.

'Well, do be careful,' Ransome told her 'You're thirty-seven, if I remember correctly? Pregnancy is still possible, but not advisable. I'll take a look inside now.' He vanished briefly while she removed her underwear, then returned, instructed her as to the positioning of her feet in the stirrups, washed his hands again, and, she was glad to note, ran the horrible-looking steel thing under the hot tap.

'Relax,' he told her, at which her heart began to thud in her chest: *You try it*, she thought as he bent over to push the thing inside her. 'Fine,' he muttered, 'fine . . . Very good.'

Back in the main room he congratulated her: 'Everything in the pink. If the periods get any worse I can refer you to a specialist. As for the blood pressure, it could certainly contribute to what you're describing. Best thing for that is exercise. But I tend to feel that while the problem could be part hormonal, it is mainly psychological.'

'What do you mean?'

'Well, when does it occur?'

'At all sorts of times.'

'But are there particular circumstances, moods, that you associate with it? Does it just happen randomly, or does something provoke it?'

'Well,' she said. 'There is normally some particular thing that upsets me.'

'Well, that's something to observe. What kinds of thing cause the stress that makes your body react this way?'

She stared back at him, unable to reply.

'And here's something else to consider – and this is just a hunch – your two girls are growing up. You're still young and energetic. Soon you will have more time on your hands. It's fair to say that an intelligent, lively woman such as yourself may need something other than housework to occupy her time. I'm not necessarily thinking of paid work, of course, especially if that's not necessary – '

'It's certainly not – '

Briefly, now, she recalled her desk in the reception room at Willis and Smythe: the ring of the telephone, the calm pleasure of answering it, and of greeting the clients as they arrived for their appointments. She remembered going in to take dictation, the pile of typed letters to be checked and signed. Thick, creamy paper with the address embossed . . . Both partners often praised her work, yet they handed her a termination notice the moment she told them she was going to get married. Career or husband. Not both. Not then. How she'd wept. Though surely she would have tired of it. Would it be so very different now, even if you studied law at Oxford? And besides, what was so wonderful about work? Harry was not dreadfully enthusiastic about his.

Perhaps, Dr Ransome suggested, some sort of *voluntary* role?

'Please tell me how that is supposed to help with my heart thudding in my chest?'

'Just a hunch. Something to throw yourself into. The WI is rather passé, I realise. But I know the hospital always needs lady volunteers.'

'I'm not fond of hospitals,' she told him, aware again of her heartbeat strengthening, of the organ seeming to take up too much space in her chest. 'They're very depressing. Apart from the maternity wards, of course. All that disease and death . . . '

'I would say that most people come out far better than they went in,' Ransome said, peering at her in a rather unnerving way.

'My father hated them.'

'Well of course,' Ransome said, displaying his famous memory again, 'Tuberculosis is much better understood and treated nowadays. But back then, it must have been very hard for you and your mother.' He leaned in a little closer.

'Yes. He was in and out of doctors' surgeries and hospitals and clinics for years,' she told him. 'And of course, depending on your luck and who assessed it all you sometimes had to pay, then, and my mother could ill afford it. He drank. And smoked, so that didn't help. They did eventually put a stop to the TB, but then his liver failed . . . ' Ransome nodded.

'Hmm,' he said, 'very difficult.'

'My mother brought me to come and sit with him,' Evelyn found herself telling Ransome. 'He held our hands and cried. It was the most awful thing. I couldn't think what to say.'

Back then, she had been terrified, furious and sorry, all at the same time, but she had not cried. Now, without warning, her face is drenched with tears.

'It was ten years ago, and I'm not normally like this!' she told the doctor, patting her face with the tissue he provided.

'There, there. I'm sure he appreciated you being there . . . Good to get it off your chest,' Ransome said. 'Clearly, volunteering at the hospital would not be a good idea, but I'm sure there are other things. Think it over. Meanwhile, I could perhaps offer you, just for a few months, a mild tranquil-liser.' She dropped the tissue in the waste-paper basket, sat straighter in her chair.

'Isn't that what they give mental patients?' He smiled in what she felt was a rather condescending manner, and glanced covertly at his watch.

'Not exactly, no. It's a low dose, suitable for everyday prob-lems. It can be very helpful to regulate moods and is increas-ingly used in this kind of situation.'

As if I were a cow or a sheep, to be subdued! Managed. *Handled.*

'I think I can manage without that,' she told him, under-standing, as she spoke, what it was that made her heart thud: it was when people broke the rules, when they lied, when they ignored or seemed to mock what she had said, when they pretended a superior understanding they did not possess and when they tried to dismiss her, lord it over her, drag her down, or pull a fast one. It was when they did not and would not understand what she meant, and behaved appallingly, or idiotically, or in order to frustrate her –

She stood and he followed suit, offered his hand over the desk; when she took it, he brought up his other one – damp and hot – to give hers a squeeze. Uncalled for.

'Don't hesitate to book a further appointment,' he said. 'Always a pleasure, Mrs Miles.'

She should, for form's sake, say *thank you*, but could not bear to. Did he take her for a fool? Why did he have to stick that damn thing up her when she was asking about her *heart*? And she most certainly would not be working in a hospital, or any other place, for free. What sense did that make?

By the time she reached the high street her face had dried. She purchased dust bags for the Hoover, a box of Surf, and a bottle of 1001 for the carpet upstairs, and then, feeling she deserved a treat before taking the bus home, stopped at the Silver Spoon.

An elderly waitress, wearing the café's uniform of severe black dress and frilly white pinafore, came to her table bearing a tiny notepad and an equally diminutive silver-coloured pen.

'Madam?'

'I'd like a milky coffee and a buttered currant bun, please.' She watched the waitress retreat with her order: she limped a little and her thick, flesh-coloured stockings did not conceal the dark, almost green-looking, raised veins that writhed up one calf, or the way that her feet swelled over the sides of her shoes, despite how sensible they were.

Service was notoriously slow, so she left her table and went to downstairs to freshen up in the ladies' room, which was papered in an embossed pattern vaguely suggestive of royalty. An area separate from the sinks and stalls featured three padded stools and well-lit mirrors above a shelf with brass hooks where you could hang your handbag, rather than put it on the floor. Surprised by how pale her face was and wanting to brighten things up, she delved in her bag and found, along with her own lipstick, the one she had confiscated from Valerie, *rouge intense*. On impulse, she uncapped it, leaned in to the mirror and carefully followed the contours of her mouth before pressing her lips together to spread the colour. It was brighter than her own, yet also, in its way, just what she needed. Without asking herself why, she recapped the lipstick and tossed it into the waste-paper basket before stepping back to smile at the woman in the mirror, who stood straight and proud now in her belted, teal-coloured coat – the mother of two girls who would go to university – her black leather gloves in her right hand, the left slipped into her pocket, and absolutely nothing wrong with her.

SOUNDS

Valerie had *Black Beauty* open beside her plate and she had already started to eat. Bits kept falling out of her sandwich.

'Well,' Harry announced, 'a good day so far.'

'I'm glad you think so,' Evelyn said, and, from midway between the doorway to the kitchen and the dining-room table, hurled a salad bowl in his direction. It was thick Spanish pottery, a present from the Hallidays, and when it hit the wall behind him, a foot or so to the right of his head, it did not break, but thudded and bounced forwards; it caught the corner of the table with a hard crack and split into several large pieces, which broke further when they landed on the parquet in a brief, brittle tattoo. Lettuce and cucumber that had erupted during the flight reached the floor at roughly the same time. There was a moment of absolute silence and then Evelyn, massive in her smock, burst into tears.

'I should have got that,' Harry said, pushing his chair back.

'I'm sick and tired of this whole damn thing! When is it ever going to be over?' Evelyn said. 'Don't you *dare* tread on that, it'll ruin the finish on the floor!'

'Val – fetch the dustpan and brush, please,' Harry said, and his soon-to-become-middle child, coming up to thirteen, left the table and walked behind her mother to the kitchen to get them. Evelyn pulled out her chair and sat down. 'I never wanted this,' she said, her cheeks glistening, her arms, a moment ago so tense, resting loose in her lap. Val began to sweep up the pieces.

'Thank you, dear,' Harry told Val. 'Don't worry, your mother's just very tired because of the baby being late . . . '

'I know,' Val said.

'Do you want to eat something?' he asked Evelyn.

'No,' she said, as she picked up her sandwich and bit into it. 'Val, remember to wrap those pieces in newspaper before you put them in the bin.'

'I know,' Val said again, and when she returned to the dining room it was only to collect her book and plate prior to vanishing upstairs.

'I should have done something about this baby!' Evelyn glared at the wall ahead of her, still eating, the first half of her sandwich almost gone. 'Well, it's too bloody late now.'

It was best not to touch her.

He stayed in his chair, watched her finish her lunch.

'I know it's very hard . . . ' How could he know? But still. 'Of course it's not fair that you have to do it all, the biological side of things . . . But I'm sure you'll feel better once it's born.'

'You are, are you?' She looked up at him, her eyes, always extraordinary, now dark and fiery and liquid all at the same time.

'Yes,' he told her, looking right back. 'What can I do?'

'Nothing,' she said, and when she reached for his plate, he thought for a moment she was going to throw that, too.

He was pretty sure he knew the occasion. One Friday in July, they had come home in a taxi from a retirement party. The champagne cocktails served and the rumours of an ensuing promotion for Harry put Evelyn in a very good mood and, dressed for the occasion in high heels, a silver-grey, sheath-like dress, and a pearl necklace he'd splashed out on, she leaned against him and let her hand rest on his leg throughout the taxi ride home. It was a clear night with a half-moon, and once the driver had been paid off they walked through the quiet house and out into the back garden, which was at its utter best, lush even in the dark, and full of the smell of roses. The air was the temperature of skin, with just the faintest breeze stirring through the leaves, and they spent some time there, right on the lawn, kissing, until Harry had by chance glanced up and seen Valerie's small face in the corner of her window, where she'd pulled the curtain back. The moment he saw her, the curtain fell and she vanished, but even so, he thought it was best to go inside. He was pretty sure that must have been the night.

They'd become rather lackadaisical about precautions and the pregnancy was, so far as he was concerned, a happy accident, but it had become, as he had recently told Lillian, on their weekly call from her college digs, a rollercoaster. His memory of the previous two, admittedly fading, was that Evelyn had become a softer version of herself when she was pregnant: still energetic, but less so, and at times almost languid. More sensual, too.

This time was different. She was older. The morning sickness had been terrible, her moods unpredictable, intense and dark.

It helped to have a change of scene. They didn't yet have a car, so they slowly walked around the block, past the neighbours' gardens, and left at the end, past the larger houses with stone walls and gates, and back down the other side. At the end of this, she had returned to the more everyday version of herself, and wanted tea.

'I can't say how glad I will be when this is over and done with,' she said, stretched out on her chair with the footstool, the bellyful of baby looming in front of her.

'Won't be long.' He set a cup of tea on the side table. Almost a week late – the doctor was threatening to induce labour, if nothing happened by Monday.

'Lillian told me she's scared people will think it's hers. And all Valerie cares about is not sharing a room. Really, what a thing to do to ourselves, just as we were getting clear. It'll be twenty years, now, before this one's grown up and off our hands. I'll be *sixty*.'

Sixty!

'Impossible!' he said. 'It'll all be fine once it's born. Anything else I can get you?'

'You could rub my feet. It's bound to be another girl. Look at our track record.'

'I like girls,' he told her.

He knelt by the stool and tugged her slippers off. Her feet were slightly damp in their stockings; his fingers slid easily over the nylon. He bent the toes back towards the sole, then ran his thumb along the arches. As he began pressing into the ball of the first foot, he realised from her breathing that she was already asleep. Her face, emptied of tension, looked just as it had when he first knew her. Her mouth, slightly parted, was very appealing, but he mustn't wake her.

'Quiet, now,' he told Valerie, who was clambering up the stairs with her skinny friend Joanna.

He had almost finished pruning the rhododendrons, had just paused to wipe the sweat and leaf-dust from his forehead, when a thrush began its song: a short phrase, repeated three times, and then another longer sequence. He soon saw it, sitting on one of the lower branches of the mountain ash at the end of the bed, a plump, speckled bird, its beak upraised.

What was it about those little sequences of sound, those repetitions and pauses that made him stand still, just to listen?

What made it so touching? He'd heard it sing before, seen the bird, its mate, too, banging snail shells on the path, pecking through fallen leaves, and hauling worms from the compost heap. So what was it?

The bird sang on. A few gritty chirps, and then a trickle of song repeated, three times. Another. More. Like water poured over your head.

Valerie had gone through a phase of birdwatching and so he knew a bit about the thrush: blue speckled eggs, omnivorous, very territorial. Its Latin name, *Turdus philomelos*, was both the stuff of schoolboy giggles and an allusion to a myth that would make no one laugh – and was particularly awkward to explain to your twelve-year-old daughter. A woman raped by her sister's husband had her tongue cut out to silence her, but managed to tell her story by weaving it into a tapestry and sending it to the sister, who took revenge by killing her own son, the rapist's spawn, boiling him, and serving him to the rapist for dinner. Both women were turned by the gods into birds: suffering and cruelty into song. Transcendence. Did singing really make cruelty and suffering any better? For the sufferer? For the audience? But why think like that, or think at all . . . He wanted only to hear the bird sing.

An ascending trill, repeated four times, a single rising note, and then something between chattering and a cry, every note distinct and pure. He could see the bird's throat and abdomen pulse as it pushed out its breath and shaped it, the narrow beak chopping the sound into fluid segments. Its whole body was involved, probably even the feet clinging to the branch; there was no separation between the thrush and its song. No speculation, hesitation or self-doubt. Oneness. Was that what Thomas had been getting at in his poems about the thrush? Perhaps he'd look them up when he got in. But for now, leave me alone, he told the thrush-fancying poets, all of them, but especially Edward Thomas, who, since Whitehorse made him read 'Adlestrop' aloud at school, had a habit of intruding . . . That, though, was a blackbird. *Step aside and let me hear it for myself, will you?* he told them. *Just listen*, he told himself, *listen now*.

The brief little tunes, repeated always four times, swooped and soared. Liquid and yet sharp, these sounds were unlike any made by a human instrument, though perhaps a flute came close. Running water. Between these phrases or tunes the pauses, contrasting voids, expectant spaces, were also part of the song. There were bird arpeggios. Twists and curlicues. Sounds that could almost be jokes, or frogs' croaks. Tsk, tsk. Whee! Imperatives. Grace notes. Were these words? Perhaps. But even if they were merely sounds, at most signals, even if the bird did not know that it sang, what a thing it was to feel at one with a winged creature singing with every cell of itself to mark its place – to yearn to make those sounds with it, and feel that he almost could.

The thrush repeated a three-note upwards-leaping sequence four times, fell silent, and flew away over the hedge, its wing-beats a faint feathered blur.

At that moment, he felt sure something was happening indoors. He left the clippers and barrow, hurried back to the house. Evelyn was up, walking around, pausing at intervals to grip the edge of the table or a windowsill and let out a low groan. 'I'll need to go in,' she told him. He arranged for Valerie to go home with Joanna, then hurried next door but one to borrow the Hallidays' car. Only about half of the people in the road had a car.

At the hospital, Evelyn refused a wheelchair, saying she felt better on her feet. They had to take a lift to the second floor, and, following rather infrequent signs to Maternity, traipse, very slowly, through long swathes of gleaming grey lino corridor starkly lit by square overhead lights. Occasionally they met a nurse or an orderly coming the other way with a clanking bucket and a mop or a squeaking cart full of clean sheets, but otherwise it was eerily quiet apart from their footsteps and Evelyn's heavy breathing.

'Harry, I'm ravenous,' she told him just before they reached the desk – a high counter, really, almost a booth, with a sign saying MATERNITY suspended above it on wires – rather precarious, Harry could not help thinking. Just as they arrived, a sound half groan half scream filled the air. It could only have come from one of the closed doors in the corridor to the left of the desk.

Ignoring it, the pasty-looking nurse there checked over Evelyn's paperwork.

'Someone will arrive shortly, dear,' she said, then took the bag Harry was carrying and instructed him to go away for a few hours. He waited until two more nurses appeared and led Evelyn into the fourth room along, and then drove to the fish and chip shop; it only took half an hour but when he got back with a packet for each of them, things had moved on.

'She's far too busy to be eating,' the pasty nurse said, laughing, 'you'd best go home and get some sleep.'

'She said she was starving,' he said, uncomfortably aware of the smell of the fried food and the way it fought with the carbolic and bleach of the hospital.

'Believe me, it would come right back up,' the nurse told him, but she took Evelyn's package and said she would keep it in the staff room for after, just in case, and yes, she smirked, pass on his love. Maybe she would eat it herself, he thought, but what more could he do? He knew the drill from the other two times: they just didn't want you in the way.

He wolfed down his own cod and chips in the car with the windows open, then drove home, arriving at about half past eight. He parked the Hallidays' car on his driveway; they'd said

171

to keep it. Inside the empty house, the windows glared blackly at him. He closed all the curtains, prowled round, tidied up, and prepared his clothes for the morning. He ran a bath and after that lay on top of the bed, restless, waiting, not even trying to read. Funny: he couldn't think of a single poem about the situation he was in, or about what Evelyn was going through. Where were the poets when you wanted them?

He remembered the other two births: Lillian's on the weekend, a long labour; he had seen the two of them for a couple of hours afterwards, and then had to go on manoeuvres for three days, which had seemed utterly perverse: you did not want to be thinking about how best to kill people when you had just seen a life begin. A week later, they'd returned to the flat Evelyn had found not far from the base, and then less than a year after that, he was in action. When Valerie was due, Evelyn's pains started when they were visiting her mother, who had insisted on coming along with them to the hospital. He'd had to take her to the pub to calm her down. And then those damned stairs to yet another flat, this one at the very top of the house . . . No problems in either case, gas and air at the end and a quick recovery, yet with such a primitive thing as birth, one person pushing another out of themselves, you couldn't but feel the risk. Evelyn's age was something the doctors had made a point of mentioning, but she was very strong, and had done this twice before . . .

He found one of his abandoned notebooks in the drawer beside the bed and tried to write some thoughts down. How they shared this with the beasts. The sheer physicality of it all. The joy in creation. He crossed that out, because it was mawkish and because, at the same time, sex was *serious*. And after it came luck, and risk . . . Excitement, terror. And mystery: he had sometimes been convinced they'd started a child, yet it turned out that he was wrong. So his anxieties now were probably groundless . . . *Absurd*, he wrote. *The separation now is absurd, given this began with the two of us as close as you could possibly be.*

At midnight, more than six hours since he had taken her there, he phoned the ward in the hope of a progress report. No one replied. The mechanical ring-back tone on the line sounded time after time, infuriating, tireless. He hung up, tried again, thought of the phone ringing there, at the desk where he had been. Why was no nurse sitting there under the sign that said *Maternity*? Was there some kind of emergency? The thought got hold of him so he dressed and sped back to the hospital, stopping under a light right by the entrance. He shoved through the double doors and half ran up the staircase and back along the bright but deserted corridors to the ward. There was, now, another man sitting, tousled and hunched, in the waiting area, but no nurse at the desk, just a wilting bunch of flowers that he hadn't noticed earlier on. The phone was ringing – disconcerting, he felt, having not long ago been calling himself. He strode on towards the room he'd seen her taken into, fourth on the left, knocked, pushed open the heavy door.

The light was brighter still. Evelyn was propped up in a complicated metal bed, legs akimbo. Two nurses, twin blurs of white and pale blue, bent over her, one each side, studying the flesh between her legs, the livid, swollen opening with some-thing – it must be the head! – pushing through. Her face was both puffy and tight, her mouth open as she pushed: *Aaaah!* a deep moan, almost a grunt. Appalling. Thrilling. Her gaze was on the mound of her stomach, absurdly draped with a pale green towel. She did not so much as glance Harry's way, but an elderly doctor in glittering bifocals who stood by a sink at the back of the room noticed him and barked, 'Leave this room at once! No fathers! Wait outside!' Harry did not obey.

'Again,' the nurse said and he saw her reach in as the head and shoulders of the baby slid out from between Evelyn's legs, smeared with blood and muck. 'One more, now,' the nurse said and then the entire baby, purplish, streaked with grease, gushed out into her gloved hands, trailing the blue, pulsing cord.

'Wonderful, dear, well done!' The nurse – the younger of the two he now saw – folded the baby into a towel. The older one leaned in. He saw her take the cord in her hands and then her body, mercifully, obscured the view. But something was missing! And then *at last* – it felt that way, though it had taken only one or two minutes – came a sound, thin and strong at the same time, a rhythmic wail, barely human. A sound before speech, but from which it would be made. It came again, again, grew a little louder. Of course, until you heard it, that tiny but enormous sound, you'd forgotten that the source of all your words was this first need. The cries came faster as the first nurse carried the baby – their baby, the cord cut and clamped – to a wheeled stainless-steel table. The doctor slipped his stethoscope into his ears. 'A healthy girl,' he told Evelyn, ignoring Harry completely. The baby's mouth was wide open, a black hole. Her cries strengthened as the nurse dabbed at the vernix on her skin. Harry's legs were shaking. He dragged a chair over to Evelyn's bed, sat down. Her head was immobile on the pillow but her eyes turned towards him.

'How come you're here so soon?' she said.

'I had an odd feeling,' he told her. His face was wet. 'Evelyn, I saw her come out.'

'That's more than I could do!' Evelyn replied, then winced. One of the nurses was messing around with her. He reached for her hand. No wonder poets were scared of this enormous thing, so astounding and so tender at the same time. They could never do it justice. No wonder they preferred to write about birds.

And how strange, he thought many years later, recalling the birth and how lucky he had been to be there, that after such a beginning, Louise turned out to be more trouble than the other two put together.

It cost three and sixpence, but after the endless fuss about the trial on the radio and in the papers, Evelyn couldn't not buy the book when she saw it in Smith's – even though DH Lawrence was to her mind very unprepossessing: small to the point of puny, with far too much facial hair and a sharp, rather foxy-looking face – not to mention being dead, too. Even the manner of his death was a mark against him: tuberculosis, her father's disease. For years she had been frightened that she or the girls would contract it.

Evie, he used to call her.

She had buried her memories of him very deeply and rarely consciously thought of him, but his habitual smell – beer, spirits and stale cigarette smoke with an undertow of sweat, urine, damp wool – and the feelings she'd had when dealing with his sickness, feelings of helplessness, and then of pity going sour and solidifying into contempt, all that was still with her. Even now, years after his death, she would not let anyone shorten her name. And if she passed a down-and-out type, or walked past a pub just as the doors opened, releasing a wave of inside air, she'd be reminded of her father, and feel grateful that Harry was healthy and hard-working, that their children grew up in a modern house surrounded by a garden full of flowers, and the doctor was free if you needed one, though she rarely did, and it paid to be wary. Some of them were over-keen to have you taking pills.

Lawrence having tuberculosis was very off-putting, but on the other hand, the arguments about the book's sexual content and potential to deprave had been in the papers and on the radio for weeks. Obscene, or not? Following the verdict, half-page advertisements and posters in shop windows declared *Now YOU can read it*. Harry said it was a cheap trick, but she was curious. There was a large stack of the books on a table by the cashier, and an unusual number of people, mainly men, milling about.

'You're lucky,' said the overly plump girl at the till. 'All those'll be gone by lunchtime. We had a crowd lined up outside the doors last Saturday morning. Is it really filthy?'

'I've not read it yet,' Evelyn told her, slipping the book in its paper bag into the back of the pushchair. She planned to start it while Louise had her nap after lunch. Valerie returned from school at five, Harry from work at six, and Lillian would not be home until the weekend. Tonight's shepherd's pie just needed heating up. If *Lady Chatterley's Lover* held her attention, she'd have plenty of time to get the measure of it. She'd settle in with a cup of tea in the big armchair with the view of the garden.

Outside in the high street, she crouched down and smiled at Louise, swaddled in her coat and blanket and almost asleep, her blonde hair flying out of its bunches, her lids sinking over her eyes. 'Let's see if you can walk all the way to the bus stop,' she suggested. 'Come on.' She lifted her out and gave her a hug, then set her on her feet.

'Why?' Louise asked.

'You'll be warmer this way. Hold on to the side there, love, and let's see how fast we can go. You can have a big sleep when we get home.'

There was another walk at the other end of the bus journey, uphill, and the cold air was tiring, of course, so it worked like a dream. What would she do when the napping stopped, Evelyn wondered as she slipped out of Louise's darkened room, her stockings rustling softly, her feet sinking into the new wall-to-wall carpet.

She relied on naptime to keep her level. Harry had been delighted, even when it turned out to be another girl and this was touching, yes, but he wasn't the one doing the work of it: the endless barrage of questions and wanting things and messing up the house. There would be the pre-nursery group next September, school itself the year after. Meanwhile, the house was temporarily perfect: clean, warm, absolutely quiet, and all hers. She settled into her armchair, put her feet on the stool, and opened *Lady Chatterley's Lover*.

Connie was a nice enough girl who had the bad luck to be married to Clifford, who came back from the Great War a cripple, so that Connie had to act as a kind of maid to him, which can't have been pleasant. On top of that, he was a writer obsessed with his own fame, and she had to help him with his writing: Evelyn felt sorry for her, of course. They had money and servants, but Connie's life wasn't her own, and their house, Wragby (what a name!), was surrounded by gloomy, pheasant-filled woods. You could imagine the birds squawking and shrieking as they were being shot and it was not surprising that no one was happy. Really, it would have been better if Clifford had died. But even so, Evelyn was shocked when, with no warning or prior thought, Connie slept with a dubious-seeming playwright called Michaelis. The inclusion of details about what they actually did together surprised her, as did the dinner party discussions about free love, and, even more so, Michaelis's eventual boorish complaint about Connie not reaching a climax at the same time as he did, and how that forced him to hang on inside her, gritting his teeth with the effort of it. She thought Connie should have slapped the man.

Yet Clifford, although he changed in other ways, remained very devoted. She could see how Connie might despise him for just that reason, especially since she wanted children and he, unable to perform because of his injury, couldn't provide them . . . As for Mellors! At first Evelyn was appalled, but he improved somewhat once he dropped the idiotic accent. For a while it was almost entertaining, and then, after the initial lovemaking scenes in the pheasant coop and in the forest, the story started to upset her. Was the whole rest of it going to be them either *fucking*, as they insisted on calling it, or talking about it? So it seemed, but a little of that went a long way, she thought. If you thought too much about sex, it put you off. And why insist on that word, which didn't sound like anything you'd want to do?

She set the book aside, and went upstairs to check on Louise, who lay with her arms flung wide, breathing with her mouth half-open. She crossed the landing to her and Harry's bedroom: like the lounge downstairs, it ran from front to back of the house and looked out over both gardens. She crossed to the back window and opened it, glad of the cool, damp air. Connie and Mellors had woven forget-me-nots and other flowers into the hair around their private parts! What a thing to do. Was that what a garden was for?

At this time, although the lawn glowed deep green, most of the shrubs and trees in their garden had lost their autumn colours, and there wasn't currently a flower to be seen. It would be a long time until the snowdrops and hellebores emerged, let alone forget-me-nots, which they did have, growing by the front path and around the foot of the magnolia. They worked very well with tulips and daffodils in springtime flower arrangements, she reminded herself, struggling against a sudden rush of tears.

It was a silly book, but the trouble was that it had some-how put her in mind of what happened in Torquay during the war – had set her remembering how she and her mother, sweltering in the dust and heat of London, had escaped there for a week away. The town had been bombed earlier in the year but they told themselves that was no worse than home, and at least the public were still allowed on one of the town's beaches. She'd not been to Devon before. They got a very good price for the trains and buses and a budget room on Brandon's Cliffe: no sea view, but a decent size and pleasant enough. It was relaxing to be away.

And she remembered how after supper – no better than you'd expect, but not the point – and Lillian's bedtime story, her mother took to playing cards with the owner, Mrs Briggs, in the lounge and the pair of them listened out for Lillian – she must have been about four – and Evelyn could slip out for some time on her own. It was a delicious time of day, still warm, the sea turning to violet and pink, the air smelling first of garden flowers and then of the sea.

Of course, the place was full of servicemen and someone was bound to try his luck. Her strategy was always to keep walking, but when on that first day she did eventually pause to take in the sunset on the water, the man who appeared out of nowhere and approached her had something about him that made her pause long enough for conversation to begin. He was not especially tall or muscular, quite slender, in fact, but from the beginning she felt an intensity, a strange kind of assurance and authority about him. And at the same time, he was very polite. He stood at a distance, called her madam, introduced himself with a slight bow:

'Aleksander Grutowski. Polish Air Force. My squadron was evacuated when the Germans invaded and we are in this country now to train in exile. I can say no more than that . . . But I hope I may I have your permission to walk with you, unless you prefer to be alone?'

His being in the Polish Air Force was part of why she agreed to the walk, but it was also something to do with the way he held himself, his quaint manners, and the quick, definite way he looked at her.

They walked at a more leisurely pace than the one she had kept before. It was very lucky, she ventured, that his squadron managed to get out when the Germans came.

'Yes,' he said, and drew in a long breath, 'yes, but I had no chance to say goodbye, and now I am afraid to say that my father, mother and sister are missing. Look – '

He stopped by a stone wall covered in nasturtiums and took from his pocket first his passport, and then a photograph of the family, glossy-haired and posed formally in a drawing room bristling with gilded furniture and picture frames.

'All gone!' he said.

Looking at the picture, at his sister in her jewellery and elegant calf-length dress, and the parents in their dark formal wear, at the youthful, fuller-cheeked version of the airman himself, it had seemed impossible.

'Perhaps they're hiding somewhere safe,' she said. He agreed to hope so.

His father was a count.

'One day,' she told him, close to tears, 'we will punish Hitler for what he has done to your people and their country.' She put her hand on his arm as she said this, then quickly removed it.

'Even now, we punish the Germans quite often,' he said. He pulled a quick smile, continued. 'Of course, it is never enough, and at the same time, it is not what anyone wants to have to do. Shall we turn around at the bay?' The sea was extraordinary, shimmering orange and gold.

He would be very happy to walk with her again, he said. He could see she was a married woman, and would be very interested to hear about her husband and family. And then, when they parted at the end of her street, that little half bow again . . . He was very easy to talk to, and it turned out that they walked together every day of that week except the Saturday, which she had to miss because it was her twenty-fifth birthday and her mother had something arranged.

'You seem no older than nineteen!' he said when she explained this, and she blushed. 'With me,' he said, 'I am a similar age, but I rather think it is the opposite way around.'

Her heart thudded when she so much as thought of him. Nothing untoward had happened, but she was incapable of turning away an opportunity to meet him, and this was in a way appalling to her, degrading, somehow – yet she admired Aleksander Grutowski very much and that made it less shameful. She wept into her pillow at the prospect of not seeing him again when the holiday was over.

'The day after you leave, I will return to base to resume my duties,' he told her. 'I will be both sad and glad. We are different men, in the air. I climb into the cockpit, and I already feel lighter,' he told her. 'My shoulders release – ' He stopped in his tracks, frowning.

'Relax?' she suggested, and a smile flashed across his face.

'Thank you . . . The roar of the engines, the moment when the plane takes off . . . This is beyond description. And when I look down and see the little world spread out below, I forget my troubles then, for a while at least. I love to fly. Though unfortunately it is now a very deathly business.'

Most of them only lasted a few weeks. She willed back tears, and the noise in her throat when she swallowed was so loud that he must have heard it.

'None of us asked for this,' he said, taking her hand, 'but it cannot be avoided. The important thing is to live, to really live for as long as we have.' They had come to a halt at a bend in the path and he pulled her into a kiss.

She allowed it. Much more than that: she felt the kiss spread through her, she tipped her head back, and opened herself up to it. She had relished his hands on her waist and buttocks, the heat and pressure of his body against hers. She wanted it all, wrapped her arms around him. No one else was around. How far would it have gone if he had not pulled back at the end of the second kiss and said, smiling, 'So this is what you want?'

And then she remembered who she was supposed to be. She too pulled back. Breathing hard, she looked right into his eyes.

'No,' she'd told him. 'No. I'm married.'

'I'm sorry,' he said. 'Extraordinary times do perhaps call for extraordinary behaving, but I certainly mean no disrespect for you, or to your husband.'

He released her completely and then, with a foot at least between them at all times, they walked briskly back to the guest house, resuming polite conversation about halfway there: the spell of good weather, how long it would take her to get home to London, her favourite parts of the city. The sun sank below the horizon; colours were softer and somehow richer. He accompanied her right to the door of the guest house.

'I do very much hope all goes well for you and your family,' he said, bowing to her before he walked off into the dusk.

It was around that time that Harry had written to her, from Tripoli, about a man in his troop getting a divorce when he learned his wife was having an American serviceman's baby. *I like to think that after the first shock of it I'd be more tolerant,* he wrote, *but please, don't test me.*

In the letter she wrote to him when she got home from Torquay, Evelyn mentioned the Polish airman and his birthday compliment, though she didn't say that she had walked with him every evening, or that she had kissed him and more than liked it.

Of course, she had no idea then, of the horrors to come. The Warsaw Uprising – the misery and starvation, the hundreds of thousands of civilians killed. How, at the end of the war, Poland would be betrayed, handed over to the Soviets who had engineered their defeat. *That Polish airman*, she'd tell Harry then, *the one I told you about. How would I face him?* Though of course, the odds were that he was dead. She felt it was better not to try and find out, and as time went on she rarely thought of him.

Just once again, years after the war ended, prompted by a documentary about Poland on the radio, she had spoken to Harry of the airman she'd met on holiday.

'I was quite sweet on him in a way,' she said 'But nothing happened.' They were taking a walk around the garden, looking at what was coming up.

'Understood,' Harry said. He glanced at her, slipped his arm around her waist for a while. By then they had two children and a mortgage; they'd long ago left the streets they grew up in and were almost middle-aged.

But if he had not asked me if that was what I wanted – if I had let that kiss continue, Evelyn thought as she looked out on the green lawn, the rich mud of the vegetable plot, the shrubs, mature now, but dormant, the cypress tree and the hedge at the back, at the neighbours' gardens to the side and back, all large and well-kept – would I have been *carried away by the last blind flush of extremity*? Would I have found *the very heart of the jungle of myself*? Would I have become *a passive, consenting thing, like a physical slave*? She felt stirred up.

Harry was a conscientious lover. He took his time and wanted her to enjoy sex, and mostly she did, but there was no jungle, no being a *consenting thing*.

What a way to think! she told herself on the way downstairs.

She decided not to finish the book, and put it away in the back of her stocking drawer, where no one would look. Modern novels in general, she felt, were perhaps better avoided. You never knew what was going to jump out of them.

Something was going on: Evelyn's eyes seemed brighter than usual, Harry thought, and her jaw tight. Louise was asleep upstairs and Valerie had already left the table to do her homework, so he asked, 'What's bothering you?'

'I don't know what you mean,' Evelyn said.

'You seem a bit on edge.'

'You're imagining it,' she told him, and he should have known to give up then, but he said, 'Maybe you're tired,' at which she stood and said, 'I'm getting tired of this,' and began to gather the plates. Oh, not again, Harry thought.

'I'm sorry,' he said, 'I just – '

'Don't *just* me,' she said as she made for the kitchen. He followed her.

'You're being completely unreasonable,' he said, though he knew, by now, that reasonable was beside the point, and challenging her a stupid thing to do. But he wanted to know: 'What *is* the matter?' he asked. She had her back to him and her hands in the sink.

'I've told you,' she said, 'and will you get it into your thick head that there is nothing the matter with me.'

'I'd rather you didn't speak to me like that,' he said, another mistake: he shouldn't have given her the opportunity. *Rather*. She turned to face him, her eyes wild.

'Oh, you would, would you?'

'Don't shout.'

'I'll do what I damn well like!' He hesitated – *almost* said something along the lines of 'When have you ever done anything else? I'll leave you to it, then,' and *almost* walked out of the steamy kitchen, as he'd done before – out into the cold, soggy garden or the garage where he'd find some kind of distraction, and could at least smoke. But instead he took a step towards her, stood close enough to hear her breathing. Her chest rose and fell. She stood proud, her hands fisted at her sides, her back and neck long, her chin a little tilted, her enormous eyes larger than ever, glistening, and fixed on him. It was not a simple thing. He saw that she was furious, but heartbroken at the same time.

'What's that, then?' he said quietly, with half a smile, 'What would you damn well like?' She didn't answer, just looked at him.

'I know what I'd like,' he told her, then closed the gap between them, put his hands on her shoulders. He cupped the back of her neck, kissed her, then walked her back to the pantry door, the only part of the kitchen you could lean against.

'Valerie – ' she reminded him. Valerie would be all right, he told her. He half pushed her up the stairs, and in the bedroom said he didn't care about the damned girdle marks and why did she wear the thing anyway? Off with it, please. They stood together in the dusky room, running their hands over each other's skin – that was the bit she would remember – and then got down on the floor beside the bed and *fucked*, as Lawrence would have put it.

A decade later, around the time things started to go off the rails but long before the visit to the police station, Louise, snooping one afternoon when Harry and Evelyn were at the Starks' for dinner, found the book still there, in the middle drawer of Evelyn's bedside chest. It was buried beneath a tangle of stockings of various thicknesses and similar hues, which looked like the cast-off skins of a nest of large beige and tan snakes.

INCHES

The building was the colour of dried blood, and the door slammed heavily behind them. Inside, it stank of cigarettes. Several benches were bolted to the black-and-white tiled floor. The office was to the left; a pink-faced young police officer with very short hair slid open a much-smeared window.

'Yes, madam?' he said. Earlier, Louise had thought of jumping out of the car, and now she thought of pulling free of her mother's grip and running, but where? She was wearing flip-flops and had no money on her; also, part of her wanted to know if this could possibly be real, and if so what would happen next. Her mother's fingers dug into her arm.

'Constable Ryan? Mrs Miles. I called earlier. I've brought my daughter in because she's beyond my control,' she said. The officer switched his gaze to Louise, standing there in her jeans and T-shirt, and she stared back at him, noting a fold of neck fat that bulged above his collar. 'I'd like to make a formal complaint,' her mother said, and the officer picked up his phone. Her mother's grip loosened and Louise tugged her arm free.

'Constable Ryan. A mother with a teenage girl beyond parental control,' the officer said. 'Yes. Mrs Miles. Please sit down and wait,' he told them, gesturing at the benches behind them, and obediently, they both did.

'Look what you've brought me to,' Louise's mother said, clutching her bag on her lap.

187

'I didn't ask you to read my mail.'

'Mail that you were having sent to your friend's house!'

'I wonder why.'

'Don't you take that high tone with me – '

The door next to the sliding window opened abruptly, and the short-haired officer motioned them to come in.

They followed him to a small but very high cell-like room where a much larger, older and completely bald officer sat behind a metal desk. The door closed behind them with a loud metallic clang.

'Sergeant Whitney,' he told them. 'What is the problem, madam?'

'I believe my daughter has been having underage relations.'

Call it instinct. She was vacuuming. It was a Friday afternoon and she was doing the stairs and landings and main bedroom. Monday and Tuesday were for the washing and then the kitchen and bathrooms and Wednesday and Thursday were for the living and dining rooms. The house was finally under control and things were much better since she'd spoken with Harry about the accumulation of books and the fussy, old-fashioned effect it gave a room, especially since his book jackets did not match. He had eventually agreed to limit himself to three shelves on the unit to his side of the living-room fireplace. After all, she had pointed out when he chafed at this, he was not actively reading most of them, and was there not plenty of storage in the attic, as well as a huge, free public library in town?

On the matching shelves to her side, she kept her Du Maurier collection and a few other good-looking hardbacks, along with framed photographs and ornaments, so the look was not really symmetrical, but the chaos had been contained, and the two landscapes that hung above each of the sets of shelves, Cornwall and Box Hill, were the same size and framing and so had a soothing, balancing effect. And as for Louise's dreadful room, the rule was that she had to pick everything up and vacuum on Sunday mornings, or else forfeit her pocket money, and that worked fairly well, too. Valerie had been untidy as a child, but grew out of it, so there was hope! Lily, of course, had always loved to have things nicely put away.

She had finished vacuuming the upstairs landings and for some reason opened the door to Louise's room. There was that ghastly smell of incense. She noted the curtains still half closed, the plant on the windowsill dropping its leaves. The new carpet covered in papers, a stapler, staples, Sellotape, used cotton balls, T-shirts. The mirror and a clutch of cheap cosmetics beneath it, coated in dust. The bed made, but only just, books scattered and piled beside it, the bedside table stacked with cups and water glasses, pencils, erasers. The waste-paper basket empty, but maddeningly surrounded with balled-up paper . . . Her eyes settled on the desk, the surface of which was invisible beneath the accumulation of notebooks and yet more books. The titles, *Being and Nothingness, The Doors of Perception, Self and Others,* were enough to make your eyes roll out of your head. Was that what they studied at school now? Or was it something Harry was encouraging? And then she saw it, in a half-open drawer, a blue envelope.

'You seem to be getting a lot of letters from someone,' she had said when those envelopes had started appearing.

'Yes.'

'Who is it?'

'A penfriend,' Louise said, flicking her hair out of her eyes and frowning as if a mother did not have a right to know who her children were in contact with. Boy or girl? Boy. David. Living in Lancashire. What were they writing to each other about? Art, books and music, ideas, things of that sort. It sounded plausible.

How did they get each other's addresses? Louise had looked up at her then and said, 'At school, Mum, it's a scheme,' and despite knowing Louise to be the worst – and also the best – liar of all three girls, she had believed her. Weeks passed before she realised that the letters had stopped coming to the house. She meant to ask Louise why, but forgot. And now this: the letter was addressed, in that small, very regular hand to *Louise Miles, c/o Miss Andrea Marsden.* The thing had gone underground. She took the letter downstairs and sat at the dining room table to read it.

Dear Louise,

Thanks for your letter. I'm sorry to hear that you have been feeling depressed. It sounds like breaking up with Andy last year was unavoidable, and probably even a good thing, because of the difference in your ages and him wanting to go travelling before university and all that. It would be far worse if he went off and then came back six months later only to tell you he had met someone in Peru or wherever, or lied about it and then dumped you when he went off again in September. Or even if he didn't, but expected you to just wait around for him to come back at Christmas and then who knows.

He sounds like an OK bloke. And at least you have had a relationship of some kind! I'd be happy to say the same, but even though I do go out and socialise more these days as you suggested, I still find it v. hard to approach girls.

I was very interested in what you said about the physical side of things between the two of you. I've never thought how it might be for a girl the first time she sees an erect penis! We are very used to seeing them ourselves but I can see that it might be a shock, even if you have felt it through cloth before. So how big would you say his was? From what I've read in magazines and agony columns and so on I know there's a lot of variation, but most are about six inches long when erect but they can be much less and a fair bit more. The width can vary too. Do you think girls might even prefer them not to be too big? Mine is fairly standard . . .

Sergeant Whitney leaned towards them over his grey metal desk, the pen dwarfed in his huge hand. He frowned and looked from her mother to Louise and then back again, giving each of them several seconds of his attention.

'I see. Just to be clear, ma'am, it's the boyfriend your daughter used to have that you are complaining about, not the one who wrote the letter?'

'Yes. That boy – young man – Andrew Smiley – betrayed our trust. He sat in our living room having tea while this was going on. He is nineteen now. At the time, he was eighteen, and she would have been underage, so yes, I certainly want to report it.'

'I don't!' Louise said, the clarity of her voice, its almost-steadiness, startling all three of them. Sergeant Whitney returned his attention to her. 'No one did anything wrong,' she continued, 'and anyway it was months ago, and it's *all over*.'

'You could be pregnant!'

'No, Mum – '

'Of course you could. Would you stop interrupting me!'

Whitney ran his hand over his bald pate, then placed both hands heavily on his desk.

'Let's all calm down now. Do you have that letter with you, ma'am.'

'Yes!' she said. But when she looked in her bag, it wasn't there.

'I think I left it on the kitchen counter,' she said. That was where she must have put it, on her way to the low chair by the phone, where she sat to call the police and then to wait for Louise to get home from school.

'Please get into the car,' she'd said to her as soon as she came in through the front door, careful not to say why, in case she refused.

'Why?'

'You'll know soon enough,' she'd said, waiting until they were on the main road to announce, 'I've read that letter from David Armstrong.'

'What letter?'

'The one in your desk.'

'Oh,' Louise had said, staring out of the car window and smiling, as if it was nothing, *nothing*. Goading her: 'What was it about?'

Whitney drummed his fingers on the metal desktop, studied the pair of them some more.

'Well, we'd certainly need to see the letter,' he said. 'Meantime, I'd like to have a word with the young lady.' He picked up the phone and called for someone to escort Evelyn back to the waiting area.

Louise sat very still. Whitney was a big man and part of her wished her mother was still there, though another part was glad she had gone.

'Your mother's very concerned about your behaviour,' Whitney began. *Stop staring at me*, she wanted to say. 'She's worried that she can't keep you under control so that you stay safe. If I was your parents, I'd feel exactly the same. And if you go on like this, you'll end up on the streets . . . Believe me, we see girls from nice homes in that line of work and it's not a pretty sight.' The whites of his grey eyes gleamed in the fluorescent light.

'I haven't done anything wrong!' Louise told him, in the same, almost steady voice. 'And I have no intention of ending up on the streets.' Her hands had balled into fists. She willed them to relax.

'Let me tell you, life is not about what you think you intend,' Whitney said. He pushed his chair back, half stood, and, propped by his arms on the desk, leaned towards her, breathing heavily. 'No. Life is about *consequences* – ' he jabbed his index finger at her ' – how one thing leads to another.'

Despite her efforts, Louise's eyes welled up. She wiped the tears away with her sleeve, stared back at the lowering face, the grey irises floating in their bluish whites. She knew it was very important not to look away or down. 'Now, tell me, did you have – ' he lowered his voice, 'did you have *sexual intercourse* with – ' he studied his notes – 'Andrew Smiley?'

'No!'

'What *did* you do, then?'

'I don't want to talk about it.' Her hands were shaking now, so she sat on them.

'Well my advice to you, young lady, is that it's best not to do things you don't want to talk about.' Whitney let out a gust of stale breath and sat back heavily in his chair. 'Now,' he said, 'listen carefully to what I'm going to say . . . ' He paused. She stared back at him. 'What we need in any investigation is proof. In this case that would have to include a physical examination of you by a police doctor, in order to establish whether intercourse has taken place – '

'What?' She didn't decide to stand, or to knock the chair over as she did so.

'Pick that chair up and sit back down, please!'

She picked up the chair, didn't sit, but took a step back and stood behind the chair, holding the back of it. He glared at her, she stared back, ready – whether to fight or to flee she had no idea. She was pretty sure the door was not locked, but what about the one at the end of the corridor? She noticed, behind him, a yellowing poster of a car crash.

'Your mother,' he continued 'says you were *fifteen* at the time of the sexual activity, but you are *sixteen*, now?'

She gave a small nod. Beneath her shirt, sweat ran down her spine.

'So in that case, we'd need your authorisation for the physical examination. We can only proceed if you are in agreement.'

She was crying properly now, face in hands. Whitney walked around to her side of the desk and sat on it, his navy blue pants stretched tight over his thighs. He seemed far too close. She could hear his breath.

'Well I'm not,' she said.

'Then it's very unlikely that we can proceed, and I'll tell your mother that when I talk to her . . . You should bear in mind what I've said to you.'

It was dusk when they emerged from the police station. Her mother's eyes seemed larger than before, very shiny. She gripped the steering wheel as if to throttle it.

So what *did* you do?

Silence.

Did this happen under our roof?

No.

Where?

Silence.

In his house?

Silence. She would not be saying, in his room above the kitchen, with the books and paintings and the single bed. His long, bony body. The rough stubble. How they took off her blue top, but, by agreement, not her jeans. How his face flushed as he struggled with his zip, pushed his jeans and underpants down. And then, the way his penis sprang out from the confines of the clothes, livid, taut, huge-seeming – though probably, in retrospect, about sixish inches – and how he had asked her to touch it, and then, the instant the skin of her fingers met the skin of his penis, which he called cock, and maybe she would too, the sperm-stuff blurted out. *Sorry*, he said then, grinning. They'd both laughed.

'Believe me, the police may be spineless, but I'm not leaving it there. There are going to be consequences for you, and I'm going to take this up with Andrew's parents.'

'It's nothing to do with them! Or any of you.'

Louise, crying again, was thinking about how Andrew had ended it, walking in the woods near his home on a damp day, beads of water on the spiderwebs, and both of them had cried, and then hugged at the bus stop before she climbed on; how she had been pleased with herself for not pestering him when she felt low in the aftermath, never once calling or sending him a note. None of which her mother would ever know. All of which would be ruined if –

There was a near miss when the vehicle in front stopped to let out a passenger. Another at the roundabout.

'Mum!'

Evelyn struggled with the gearstick.

'You're making me ill. I can feel my heart banging in my chest.'

Evelyn, her bladder at bursting point, left the car on the drive to avoid parking it in the too-narrow garage, and rushed inside to use the bathroom; Louise found the letter on the kitchen counter and, to the sound of her mother peeing in the next room, stuffed it into the boiler, saw it catch fire before slamming the door closed, then ran up to her room and locked the door.

Harry arrived, with the steak and kidney not even started. They had to settle for poached eggs on toast . . . It was hard for Harry to make sense of what had happened. An incriminating letter about penises that had disappeared. Andrew, who had come to the house a couple of times and talked about physics and modern art, and then another boy, this David, in Lancashire, to whom Louise was secretly writing about things that should never have happened, but in any case should be private. But then, the police! Utterly ineffective and spineless, she told him, to think we pay their wages! Surely not the best place to start, he thought . . . What was she thinking? And now, this idea that they should call Andrew Smiley's parents, people they had only occasionally glimpsed in a car and twice chatted to on the doorstep, and make some kind of accusation.

'I'm not at all sure that's a good thing to do,' he said, pushing aside his plate with its smears of egg.

'Are you telling me I'm wrong? That we should let our daughter do whatever she pleases?'

'No – '

'Are you afraid to deal with them? Because I'm not.'

'But what would be the point of it? I think we should try not to blunder about and I'd rather think it all over.' The phone rang and Evelyn took the call: Valerie. Louise had called her from upstairs.

'The thing is, Mum, times have changed. These are the kind of things teenagers do. It's all fairly normal. And from what she says, they were pretty responsible. Though I do think the letter-writing thing is rather strange.'

'Did we ask for your opinion? And does being a trainee vet qualify you to pronounce on this?'

'No, I'm just offering it, Mum, for you to consider. Of course you're right to be concerned in case something's amiss or she's pregnant, but I don't think that's the case. She's quite upset and – '

'Do you think *I'm* not upset?' Evelyn hung up and, even though it was after midnight over there, called her oldest, Lillian, in Perth, who after all had studied Law.

'What do you think?' she asked.

There was a long pause.

'I'm out of touch on the British legislation on the age of consent, but I do expect the police officer knew what he was talking about,' Lily eventually said. 'I can see both sides, of course. It must be worrying for you, but on balance, I think it's best not to aggravate things. And no, I really wouldn't call the boy's parents.'

'I expect you'll feel differently when your two are teenagers,' Evelyn told her, and again, hung up.

Neither she nor Harry slept very much.

He got up as soon as it was light.

'Are you going to speak to her or not?' she asked him when he came in from the garage where he had been sanding an occasional table that she wanted refinished.

'In due course.'

'When would that be?'

'Please stop hectoring me,' he said, and knew as the words left his lips that it was a mistake.

'So somehow I have become the one in the wrong here?'

'No. Please, Evelyn, let's not talk like this.'

'Like what? All I am asking is for you to do your part . . . And remember, please, not to leave that book on the table. It goes on the shelf.' *For heaven's sake*, Harry did not say, *this is ridiculous*!

'I do sometimes think you're doing it to spite me,' Evelyn said.

'Doing what? Reading?'

'You know full well what I mean. Leaving your things all over the house.'

'I left that book and my notebook on the dining-room table, so far as I remember. I was reading it with my coffee before I went out to revarnish that side table for you, and I intended to return to it. Why shouldn't I leave a book on the table? Where else do you want me to put it?'

'Away. On the shelf, or is that too much to ask?'

'I intended to return to it.'

'How many times do I have to say – '

'Evelyn, you're being unreasonable.'

'Don't patronise me!'

Unreasonable, he felt, put things mildly – truth was, there was a line between strong-minded and outrageous that Evelyn now crossed with increasing frequency. Though sometimes it was his fault, for goading her. Or, according to his daughters, for letting her get away with murder. Or even, as he admitted to himself, because there were still times when he found Evelyn's anger arousing, and enjoyed making up afterwards . . .

'I am reading it,' he told her, sitting down and reaching for the book. 'Or will, when I have a chance.'

Hadn't he already read at least one biography of Edward Thomas? she had asked him when he brought the book back from the library last weekend. Didn't she send one to him, during the war? Why read another?

Fair enough, he thought, searching now for the page where he had left off in the early hours, but the war was a very long time ago and this was not a biography but a pair of memoirs, written by the poet's wife. And he couldn't really say why he was so drawn to it, though one thing was that you began to see where the man's poems came from, how much of his life went into them, and how much reading, too. He was being given an intimate glimpse of a man by turns depressed, desperate, brilliant, and also a picture of an unequal marriage: how the two of them struggled, how impossible the whole thing was, even though Helen put a good face on it. He sometimes wished he could speak to the pair of them – make Edward see what luck he had to be so thoroughly loved, or else commiserate with him for his inability to accept her gifts; he wished he could warn Helen that she would never get back the measure of what she gave, and yet at the same time, encourage her to continue . . . For what else could she do, being who she was? Some people could not help but love, and most people were the prisoners of their own natures. He identified with both players in the Thomas marriage, but especially with Helen because she was forever fitting herself around someone driven and intransigent. And it was oddly gripping, he had tried to explain to Evelyn, though also strange, to learn about the intimacies of another couple's married life.

'When are you going to fix that side table?' she had asked. And now, the question was: When would he talk to Louise? *Talk to.* He stared down at the page, but the words would not open themselves to him, stayed sealed, like some sort of hieroglyphics.

She appeared at about noon, white-faced, dressed in jeans and a grey granddad vest that Evelyn particularly hated. In silence, she filled and plugged in the new electric kettle, reached for the jar of Nescafé, spooned, poured, stirred.

'Your father wants to talk to you,' Evelyn announced. Louise did not reply, or offer to make a cup for anyone else. Now, it seemed, he had both of them against him.

'Let's go outside, just the two of us,' he suggested. Evelyn would not like it, but it was the only way; she would hover otherwise, and interrupt. It was hard enough without that.

They sat at the slatted garden table, out of earshot of the house, she with her back to it, shivering in the breeze.

'Do you want the rug?' She shook her head, but he went to the shed and fetched it. 'You have upset your mother,' he began, and paused, waiting for her to point out that she, too, was upset. She did not, so he cleared his throat, began: 'The main thing is that we're concerned for your well-being. Even if there is the pill and a different approach to sex now, that doesn't mean it's wise to rush into things . . . You still need to think carefully about what you do with your boyfriends.'

'Actually, I do,' she told him, staring into her black coffee, hair like a curtain, shutting him out.

'How did you feel about Andrew?' he asked.

'I liked him a lot.' She glanced quickly up at him then, gulped a mouthful of coffee.

'Were you – in love with him?' Excruciating, he felt, to pry like this – yet oddly, she did not seem to mind.

'I'm not really sure what it was,' she replied.

'Then why go so far?' he asked. She shrugged, leaned back, cup in hand. The sun was on her hair and face now and she looked more like herself again.

'I liked him, and I was curious,' she said. 'And Dad, it's just a part of the human body.' Well yes, he thought, but also, no. No just about it.

'Don't reduce sex to the physical,' he said. 'Your mother and I were very much in love, when we . . . '

Her gaze landed squarely on his face.

'How has that worked out, then?' she asked, the pure cheek of it catching him off guard and rendering him speechless. 'You really should stand up to her more,' she continued. 'Hold your ground. Don't give in so much.'

In their different ways, all three of his daughters seemed keen to tell him that he was too accommodating with Evelyn.

And he could see why. Of course he should be able to leave a book on the table! It was not as if he lacked backbone. He had withstood playground bullies, the Germans, and countless liars and fools at work. Evelyn, though, was a different matter. Part of the problem was that he didn't see it just as *giving in.* It was doing what he could to make things work. He could bend, she could not.

'The thing is, that makes for a pretty miserable atmosphere,' he told Louise. Again, the shrug, the stretching of her neck to the side, up, to the other side, down again. Her blonde hair all over the place, the fringe obscuring her eyes. She, the last child, was the one who most resembled him. Same eyes, everyone said. She flicked the hair away, stared right back at him, 'Have you ever thought about giving up on it? I mean, sometimes I do wonder what's keeping you two together. It can't be me.'

Harry took a deep breath.

'I love your mother,' he told Louise, his throat suddenly raw.

'Dad,' she said, just sixteen and sitting in the sun with her feet propped on the garden chair he had made when she was two, 'Dad, these days, lots of people get divorced, you know. You two might be happier apart.'

Was he unhappy? At this moment, yes, but in general? Marriages were not equal or fair: Look at his own parents, look at Evelyn's mother's senseless devotion to a man who did nothing for her. It was stupid to pretend otherwise.

'I can't imagine being without Evelyn,' he told Louise, bliss-fully unaware that she would, within a year, abscond to France with yet another boyfriend, causing further months of worry and argument. 'People aren't perfect. But neither are you, and you love them even so, and even though you know it won't ever change – '

'It'll probably get worse, in fact,' Louise said.

A step too far.

'I didn't ask for an opinion and we're supposed to be talking about you,' he told her, speaking more loudly than before, as if to a larger audience. 'Whatever you think, we are your parents, and we need to know who you are seeing and what is going on. This is our house and you are only sixteen and we don't want – that kind of thing – happening in it, in our house I mean, is that clear? And I think this correspondence with the boy in Lancashire has to stop. And it would be very helpful if you apologised to your mother for all the worry you have caused.'

There was a long silence.

'I'll do that if you stop her from calling Andy's parents,' she said.

'I'm not sure I can do that,' he said. 'I will try.' Louise shrugged, stood, stretched.

'I'm going to stay at Sandra's,' she said, and walked back to the house, leaving her mug on the path.

Evelyn was glaring at them out of the kitchen window and he did not feel like going in. He just wanted the whole thing to be over. To enjoy the damn weekend! But best to get it over with.

'Well?' she asked as he braced himself on the door frame and eased off his garden shoes.

'I think she is sorry to have upset you . . . ' Evelyn said nothing. She was wearing her apron and her hands were wet from the sink. 'And I expect she'll apologise. I did stress that she can't just do whatever she wants in this respect.' The kitchen tap, he noted, needed a new washer. It was drip-dripping into the stainless sink, making a dull, enervating, plopping sound. He tried not to hear it, put his arm around Evelyn's shoulders. She stood unyielding, her eyes on his face. 'It's been difficult and I think we should just see how things go from now on . . . As for calling the Smileys, let's not. Not now. I really don't think it will help.'

'You are all the same,' she said, pulling suddenly away.

'What on earth do you mean?'

'All three of you, ganging up against me. No, don't try and touch me!' He stood in the kitchen, stunned, heard her rush upstairs and slam the bathroom door.

'Don't be so bloody stupid!' he shouted, then flung the back door open and strode outside.

Most of the vegetable bed was ready or planted but he still had some double digging to do at the far end. He yanked the spade out of the earth, shoved his sleeves up, and set to work on the next row. It was about fifteen feet across the width of the plot. He kicked the blade in hard with his heel, levered up the heavy spadeful, tipped the earth down next to the trench. A house full of bloody women! What the hell was he supposed to do now?

He dug on. It was dense soil, with patches of two kinds of sticky clay, one grey, another yellowish: remediable, and already far better than it used to be, but still hard work. Fat pink earthworms slithered through the clods of earth. Occasionally you found an old bit of pottery or a clay pipe. He pushed on, worked up a sweat. As the end of the row he switched to the fork and roughed up the compacted ground at the bottom of the trench. He threw in some compost, then began again, turned the new spadeful into the waiting trench. He worked steadily now and began to feel more like himself.

She could not help it. That was the thing. It was best to keep right and wrong out of the equation.

He finished the digging, hunted down a pair of secateurs and set off around the rest of the garden. He found late daffodils, narcissi, tulips, cherry blossoms, and, in the circular bed at the back, roses about to open. He added some asparagus fern and two kinds of early peonies, which not only smelled wonderful, but were one of the consolations proposed in Keats' *Ode on Melancholy.*

The flowers in one arm, he again pried off his boots at the kitchen door. Both it and the front door were locked, and the key under the brick was gone.

He'd worked on mines in the war, so it only took him half an hour with some strong wire and pliers. Even so.

The house, filled with a thick, unnatural silence, seemed to resist him as he arranged the flowers in a vase found under the sink, then set it on a table mat on the dining-room table. The house responded: So what? Upstairs, he tapped on the bedroom door, and hearing nothing, cracked it open. The curtains were closed. Evelyn was either asleep, or pretending to sleep; he wanted to lie beside her but he was filthy and it was in any case a bad idea.

In the ensuing week, he slept in Lily and Valerie's old room with the geometric print wallpaper, slipped into the bedroom for fresh shirts and underwear while Evelyn was not occupying it, made his own toast for breakfast, and ate dinner before he caught the train home.

Downstairs, they were never in the same space unless passing through. He spoke to Evelyn whenever she appeared: he was very sorry for his part in the misunderstanding; could they sit down together and talk it over? Was there something he could do? She did not reply; acted, indeed, as if she neither saw nor heard him. It was, he felt, both magnificent and pathetic at the same time. Infuriating, too. Evelyn left him notes: *Kindly wash your teacup. The gas bill has come. I am not doing your washing.*

On the train to and from work he wrestled with a letter to her, struggling to move it beyond the stock phrases that first came to mind: *I hate it when we are estranged. We should not let small differences come between us. No one could mean more to me than you do. I love you still as I always have . . .*

On Friday, he left work early, stopping on the way to the station to buy a card to write it in. At home, he sat in his shirt-sleeves in the dining room (the flowers had been moved from the table to the sideboard, and were all but dead), trying to read Winston Graham's *The Black Moon*, when he heard Evelyn emerge from the living room to answer the phone.

'Evelyn Miles speaking. Yes, I did, thank you for calling. Thank you. Yes I am still – ' He found it strange to hear her interrupted, but when she spoke again, her voice rang out proudly: 'The grammar school. Including French. Shorthand and typing. Two years at a city legal firm, Willis and Smythe, and then over twenty years' experience of running a household . . . ' Again, she fell silent, and Harry sat at the table, motionless, listening with his entire body. 'There have been some changes here, so I think it is time for me to move. Yes, a live-in position is exactly what I am looking for . . . ' Again, she fell silent. 'It's a fairly small household,' she continued, her voice a little less confident. 'Four . . . No experience of supervising staff, not as such, but it's certainly something I could do – '

He understood immediately how, on Monday, she must have waited until the two of them had left the house before getting up. Still sick with rage, she had put on her sunglasses, walked to the newsagents and bought the copy of *The Lady* that he'd noticed on the phone table that night, and, next door at the baker's, a croissant, something she never could resist. At home, she'd have searched the classifieds at the back. There were advertisements for housekeepers under 'Help Wanted'. She'd have chosen which vacancies to apply for on the basis of how soon they wanted someone and how much she liked the name of the house: Hartcourt Place, Withinden Manor, Somerset Court, then typed the letters of application on the portable she kept zipped up in its vinyl case in the spare room, signed them with her full name, Evelyn Anne Miles, and carried them to the postbox at the end of the road before making early dinner for herself.

'I understand,' he heard Evelyn say now. 'Thank you.' She could not bear to be slighted and he knew how her pulse must be thudding through her, that she could hear it when she closed her eyes. He heard the faint *ping* and the dull clunk of the handset as she hung up. There was a new kind of silence, and then an awful moaning sound. He made his way to the hall where she sat on the low chair by the phone, her hands fisted, weeping. It was the most terrible thing. He knelt on the parquet and took her in his arms.

'What idiot was that?' he said, 'And why would you go away when I want you so much?'

And there, hanging on the wall behind her was the still life they had bought years ago in the local art sale. And on the phone table, the *Sunflowers* notepad she used, open, blank, the pen ready next to it.

He knew she would not answer, and that they would never speak of this humiliation or of what had led to it. But he felt her relax just a little and let him take her weight.

BLUE

Not the best way to start. He was lying in his swimming trunks on the bed in the cabin when she, halfway between tears and rage, burst out of the bathroom wrapped in a white towelling robe. Her swimsuit looked terrible, she said. She hadn't thought to try it on at home. It was too tight and worn thin in places. She must have put on a lot of weight.

'Why didn't you tell me?'

'Because I didn't notice and just thought you looked very nice,' he said, sitting up. 'We're both bigger than we used to be. It's that time of life. Show me.'

It was a brown suit, with white dots and a bow at the bust. There was nothing wrong with it that he could see, but she was glaring, as if hypnotised, into the huge mirrored panel behind the bed – doubtless there to catch the light and make the cabin look more spacious. 'Venus de Milo,' he told her, 'but with arms.' He remembered a similar moment of his own, a view from the side. You saw and admitted your youth had long gone. Though time had been kind to Evelyn. Her face and voice were lively, her back straight, her movements vigorous.

'I can't sit by the pool in this,' she said, tugged the robe back on, and stood at the window – not an actual porthole but a rectangle with rounded corners – with her back to him. He had been going to say, all right then, let's just get dressed and walk around a bit, when he remembered the shop on Deck

Two. They might have something she liked, he suggested. Even if they did, it would be hideously overpriced, she pointed out. Still, he countered, it would be even more costly to waste the holiday, not cheap despite the food and excursions being included. They'd shelled out a fair bit so it was worth using the amenities. But she couldn't face the shop. Did she want him to investigate? How on earth would he know what she liked? He told her he would just see if they had anything. What size, he had to ask.

The shop was dark, cave-like, packed with stands bearing cosmetics, jewellery, chocolates, watches, hats, scarves, and sunglasses, their preposterous prices attached on tiny hand-written stickers. At the back was a whole section of clothing, including a row of swimsuits, all of them skimpy and low-cut; the assistant, a slender Italian woman, assured him this was the fashion now, even for the mature woman, but directed him to the end of the rack where there were some which she called 'elegant'.

Whatever had possessed him? He was bound to get it wrong, but badly wanted to succeed. In the end, he chose something in a bold black-and-white design, with a kind of skirt, almost like a very short sundress. It was the most expensive of all the outrageously priced items on the rail. He paid for it on the understanding that it could be exchanged or refunded, unworn, that same day, and carried it back to the cabin. Again she vanished into the bathroom.

It was eleven by the time he had changed it for the next size and they'd found their way to the pool: it was a small pool, but there was something pleasantly surreal in it being there at all, about a boat floating on the water, containing water. They were ushered to two reclining chairs with associated towels, blue umbrella, and table, and offered a drink. By then, he felt in need of one.

'Why not have a glass of the fizz?' he suggested.

She ordered tea; he a whisky and soda. The tea came with biscuits, the whisky with a bowl of peanuts. The food was all in: it was not a place to worry about your weight and he hoped she wouldn't.

They had barely finished the mutual anointing with sun cream and settled down when the man reclining next to him sat up and wished them good morning. His wife, rather sleepy-looking under her floppy hat, did the same. 'Julian and Mary Russell-Smythe. Very pleased to meet you . . . ' Beneath thick, rather long iron-grey hair, Julian's face and neck were deeply tanned. He was on the lean side, and sat unnaturally straight, as if suspended. He seemed very keen to keep the conversation going; it was almost as if he had been waiting for someone to sit next to him.

'How are you finding it so far?' he asked as soon as the pleasantries were over.

'We enjoyed Rome,' Evelyn told him.

'As for being at sea, it remains to be seen,' Harry added. Office life had conditioned him to the point that he found it a little odd socialising without a shirt on.

'It's our first cruise,' Evelyn said, at which Mary leaned in. She had a head of blonde curls, rather unnatural looking, and a blank expression, which dissipated when she spoke, which she did with surprising enthusiasm:

'Well,' she said, 'they attract a good sort of passenger and if anything isn't right, you only have to say the word. Though of course, you can't move cabins if the ship is full. I do hope you're on the port side?' They were, as it happened. 'I hope you don't mind my saying,' she added, speaking directly to Evelyn, 'that's a lovely suit.' A moment after she had finished speaking, her face drained of life again. It was as if a switch had been turned off.

'Time for a pre-lunch dip?' Julian suggested.

'I hope they're not too persistent,' Evelyn told Harry in the cabin as they changed out of their swimming things.

'He's a bit pushy, but likeable enough,' Harry said. 'What do you make of her?' Evelyn shrugged. 'Not much,' she said. 'Actually, I think there's something wrong with her.' She had recovered from her earlier feelings, and peeled her suit off in front of him. Her breasts and haunches glowed white in the shade of the room, the skin there pale and unmarked, just as it had always been. Alabaster, he thought. Or marble. But warm. He remembered Pygmalion, from the *Metamorphoses*: an unusual story in that the man got what he wanted, with no penalties.

The Russell-Smythes had commandeered a large, well-positioned table in the restaurant. Mary had applied lipstick and thrown a lacy sundress over her swimsuit; Julian now sported a short-sleeved shirt and beige slacks. He ordered a bottle of sparkling wine as an aperitif.

'On us, of course,' he said.

'I warn you,' Evelyn told them all, 'I'm not used to drinking. Just a sip goes to my head.'

'Evelyn only drinks bubbly,' Harry explained.

'You're clearly a woman of excellent taste,' Julian told her. 'Now,' he continued, turning back to Harry, 'I don't think we met during the hostilities, but I'm pretty sure you served. Am I right?'

Hostilities? What a way to put it. And why not keep your guesses to yourself, Harry thought. Was there nothing else to talk about? He hoped the man was not a retired major, or worse, still expecting respect.

'Ten out of ten,' he replied, evenly. '58th Field.' Any minute now, Harry thought, he'll be asking which school I attended.

'I can always tell. It's something about the way a man speaks and carries himself,' Julian said. Oh, really. One of those *best years of my life* types, Harry thought, as Julian told them how he had been in tanks in Egypt and Italy, and how he had ended up, like Harry, as a captain.

'So your paths might have crossed,' Evelyn suggested, smiling at them both.

'There were a lot of us there, we were fairly preoccupied, and it's more than thirty years ago,' Harry pointed out. Evelyn was always interested in the war, in the part of it she had not experienced; only natural, perhaps, but still, it was the last thing he wanted to think about now. His one qualification, when Evelyn had come up with the idea of a cruise, was that they avoided anywhere he had been as a soldier. Though of course the whole of Europe had been ravaged. Those years of destruction and death were something he carried without being much aware of them, and he wanted to keep it that way.

'I prefer not to think of it,' he said, and raised his glass. 'We and our children seem to be living in better times.'

'To better times!' Julian chimed in. The waiter materialised, and they ordered plates of seafood all round. Julian requested another bottle of the spumante.

'So as for children, where have yours ended up?' Evelyn asked Mary, whose vague gaze had drifted towards the blue glow of the windows during the talk of the war.

'Actually I don't have any children,' she said, bringing her attention back. 'I'm Julian's third wife. He has two very handsome sons from his first, lovely young men, but I can't really claim any credit because I didn't get to raise them when they were young.'

'Oh!' Evelyn said, just as the food arrived, various pinks and whites arranged on a bed of vivid green, ringed with sliced

211

cucumber and studded with lemon wedges, absolutely nothing like the food at home.

'What about your family?' Mary asked.

'We have two married daughters, both of them university graduates,' Evelyn told her. 'The other one, my youngest, is a worry. Moody and wild. Twenty-two, but always changing her mind about what she's doing. She seems very impractical, and hostile to suggestions. Actually, I'm trying to put her out of my mind.'

'That must be difficult,' Mary said. She had peeled a large prawn, and now popped it into her mouth.

'No, not really,' Evelyn told her, smiling. She felt she had said too much. She didn't want sympathy. It dragged you down. 'Isn't the food wonderful!'

Three wives, she remarked to Harry that afternoon.

A virtual harem, he joked. They were on deck, watching Sorrento come into focus: the yellows and ochres and terracottas, the greens, pinks and purples of it all. The mountains, the water and the sky.

'She went through the whole thing exhaustively while you two were smoking after lunch. The first divorced him when the boys were still at school. The second had cancer and died. She's ten years younger than him, though she doesn't at all look it, does she? They've only been married for fifteen years. He's some kind of accountant and she was working in the office.'

Only? True, fifteen was nothing compared to almost forty. A mere dalliance, an experiment! Harry was beginning to enjoy himself. The run-up to departure had been unpleasant: the need for new clothes and a pair of sandals, the withdrawal of his best underwear from circulation, the packing and repacking, the checking of documents, the top-to-bottom house-cleaning, the tension when Valerie and Hugh couldn't caretake the house, meaning they had to ask Louise: very fraught and probably a mistake. The writing of notes and instructions, the reminders about the houseplants and closing windows, the inevitable argument when Evelyn asked whether Louise intended to bring anyone into the house, because if so she hoped they would be suitable, and Louise had said, very bluntly, 'Do you want me to do this or not?'

But now, domestic tensions and habits had dropped away. It was like returning to the days of their courtship. Old-fashioned word! Still. He was, as Evelyn said, a stick-in-the-mud, happiest in the garden and rambling on the downs or in the Lake District. He liked revisiting places. If it had been left to him they might not have ranged further than Cornwall, or Scotland. Paris, at a stretch. Australia, of course, though only because Lillian and Ed were living there. But Evelyn hungered to see the world. She was very drawn by the names of places, so they had embarked on Cruising the Three Seas: Tyrrhenian, Ionian and Aegean.

From Sorrento, the Russell-Smythes travelled that afternoon inland to Pompeii, an excursion that Harry and Evelyn had booked for the following morning. Meanwhile, they rode the ferry to Capri, which, according to the guidebook, was the island from which the sirens once sang, causing Odysseus to have his crew fill their ears with wax and strap him to the mast. Not far in the other direction, on the mainland, the sibyl finally wasted away to nothing but a voice in a jar because she had failed to ask Apollo for everlasting youth to go along with immortality.

Silly of her, Evelyn said.

The air, deliciously warm, was seasoned with birdsong and the scents of flowers. They walked hand in hand through the old town to gardens featuring palm trees, roses and bougain-villea; wandered under a pergola smothered in wisteria, past fountains and walls of shrubbery, gazed up at mountains, down at a vertiginous switchback path that led to a bay below, and out to the astounding sea, from which poked three much-photographed limestone formations. Evelyn, wearing a blue short-sleeved dress and film-star sunglasses, posed for a photo-graph against a wall, the view behind her as a backdrop; after that he slung the camera on his back and drew her close for a kiss.

Just as they were finishing, an Italian in his thirties came up to wish them both a good afternoon, first in Italian and then in English, and introduced himself as Antonio. The man was intrusive, to say the least, and the lavish good wishes, Harry felt, were mainly aimed at Evelyn. Did they, Antonio asked, require the services of a guide? Did they know the true story about the path, which was not at all the same as the one in the tourist leaflet? Evelyn, always curious, might have fallen for it, but Harry, suspecting that money would be involved if the conversation continued, thanked Antonio and said they had to make their way on, *because of the tides*. Having said this, they decided they would after all catch the bus to the Blue Grotto, which they had been in two minds about, fearing it would be a tourist trap.

'And how was it? Did you have to wait ages for the little boat to take you in?' Mary asked over dinner that night.

'No,' Evelyn said. 'Hardly at all.' That, Harry knew, was because she had made sure they sat at the front of the bus, and then had eased her way through the crowd waiting on the little platform for the boats. She had stepped forwards, shielding her eyes with her hand, smiled at the fleet of boatmen, and drawn one to her almost immediately. Before long they were at the tiny entrance to the cave; their boatman asked them to lie down as they slid through momentary darkness into an unimaginable, lucent world. The water glowed like a kind of liquid sky; it exuded light, and cast a blue pallor onto the cave walls and the faces of the visitors in their boats; they were floating not on but *in* colour, and yet when Evelyn trailed her hand in the water it seemed as if it had been turned to silver. You could not but want to tear your clothes off, plunge in and swim, to become all over silver, precious, transformed, young again – though it was, of course, forbidden. From the back of the cave came the sound of a man and a woman singing a duet. The boat rocked gently on the incoming tide. It was over far too soon, and impossible to photograph. Better that way, of course.

And it was, yes, astounding, Harry had thought as they sat on the bus bound for the port, Evelyn's hand resting on his thigh, that they had been to the Blue Grotto in Capri. That they, born between two wars in dense London streets, by a river channelled in concrete and topped with industrial froth, the air thick with the clatter and smoke of the railway, with the smells of the brewery and the factories where most people of their class were expected to work – that they could now be at leisure on an island in the *Tyrrhenian Sea*.

Much as he'd quarrelled with the place, his secondary school was largely responsible for this. And his father, of course, who had listened to the teacher who'd said his son might win a scholarship. Because of his education, and all the damn drilling they'd done after school, he began the war a second lieutenant, surviving it and rising to the rarefied rank of captain. He'd become a certified member of the middle class. He still remembered the weight of his father's hand on his shoulder at the school gate that first day as he told him not to waste his chance.

They found good seats on the ferry. Harry took out the new notebook and pencil he had brought with him, and tried to

215

describe the experience of the cave. It seemed both essential and impossible to avoid the word *azure*, which came, he knew, from the stone, lapis lazuli, and was there in the Italian name of the place, *la Grotta Azzurra*. He ended up with a list: azure, cerulean, royal, limpid, ultramarine, turquoise, ethereal, sky blue, sapphire, electric, empyrean . . . There did not seem to be enough words, and at the same time it seemed as if they were all trying too hard. And then swooning for some reason came to mind. A swooning blue. *Swoo.* There was a point when words dissolved into rhythm and sound, and just before it, he felt, they meant the most.

That evening the Russell-Smythes left dinner early, but reappeared at the last minute in the lounge for Professor Archibald Masson's talk, 'Treasures of Pompeii'. Masson, who had taught classics and ancient history at an impressive string of universities, was not at all the frail, startled-looking academic Harry had expected, but substantial and solid in a way that might have been more suitable for a chairman of the board or a bon viveur of some kind. He had dressed formally for the occasion, in a starched white shirt and a bow tie, and wore expensive-looking frameless glasses as well as a gold signet ring. A lectern and screen had been erected at the far end of the room.

After a romp through the geography and botany of the area, the basics of Roman civilisation, house design, cuisine, decoration and construction, Masson showed slides of the major highlights of Pompeii, and diverted into the story of Leda and the Swan, which featured in several of the frescoes: 'Was this conjunction between woman and bird, as these sensuously rendered images seem to suggest, a seduction?' he asked, pausing and looking around the room. 'Or was it, as WB Yeats depicted it in his poem, an *overwhelming*, even an assault? *A sudden blow: the great wings beating still / Above the staggering girl, her thighs caressed / By the dark webs, her nape caught in his bill*? It depends, perhaps, on the kind of story you prefer. In either case, it was an encounter that resulted in the birth, from an *egg* laid by Leda, of Helen of Troy, and thence the Trojan War, and the *Iliad*, one of the masterpieces of ancient literature! Would we be without that, even if it meant saving Leda?'

'Many artists,' he continued, 'for example Correggio, here, in 1530 . . . have represented the encounter with a degree of explicitness and sensuality that would not be tasteful if a human lover, or a less aesthetically pleasing animal, were involved.' He felt that this said as much about themselves as the Romans' art said about them, and it brought him to his final point: 'Pompeii is a place where you will learn as much about yourselves as about those who lived and died there,' he said. 'You will find that the Romans were surprisingly like us, and yet in some respects very different. Less inhibited, certainly,' he said, 'and perhaps less hypocritical. Material from the excavations is, to this day, locked away in the Secret Museum in Naples, deemed too shocking for the public to view. Only serious scholars are allowed to see what were once serving dishes and garden ornaments . . . ' The lights faded back on and Masson, smiling and polished with perspiration, looked around the lounge as he wound up: 'I urge all who have not already visited the ruins to do so tomorrow. Many books have been written about Pompeii, including one of mine, *Life and Love in Pompeii*, on sale throughout the voyage in the gift shop; I am more than happy to sign copies. Thank you, ladies and gentlemen, for your kind attention.' He bowed, to protracted applause.

'I feel I've already been there,' Evelyn said, yawning deeply. She thought she might write a letter in the other lounge and then make her way to the cabin. Headed notepaper was supplied, and there was an old-fashioned roll-top desk to sit at. *Louise*, she would begin, *Thank you so much for looking after the house. We are living in the lap of luxury and seeing wonderful sights every day. We spent the day in a garden and a grotto, on the island where Gracie Fields has her villa. I have not seen your father so relaxed for a long time . . .* She would begin in that way, and describe the food and poke a little fun at the Russell-Smythes, and then at the end she would find herself saying: *I must say I fail to see how what I said could have caused such umbrage on your part. After all it is our house and the whole point of your staying is for it to be looked after. Some of your friends don't inspire confidence, and you don't look well, so of course I worry about the kind of life you are living. I think it was kind of you to spend time with your friend Tony and his mother during her last days, but I do feel you should be out and about enjoying your own life while you are young, not sitting in sickrooms! I remember my father lying in a darkened room, hanging on by a thread. It was horrible, and very hard on my mother. I wished he had died sooner, and spared her. She was much better off without him. But now she is getting to the point where she is not herself and we will have to decide what to do. Make the most of your youth! I hope you are eating well and getting plenty of sleep . . .*

Once she started writing, it was hard to stop. Harry said that she should let things lie, leave Louise to her own devices more, but he always took the path of least resistance. Where did that get you? And how could she let things lie? The words seemed to push out of her, like so many frogs in a fairy tale. She had a right to speak her mind . . . Why not just write it down, but not post it, Harry had once said. What was the point of that? And did he say the same to Louise? He did, he said. She sealed the envelope, added the stamp she had purchased the day before and slipped it into the little box by the purser's office; after this, she felt instantly relieved.

And as for Pompeii, she was at first disappointed. It was miraculous that it had survived, a whole city, yes, and the forum and bath houses and plumbing and so forth, which Harry raved about, were very advanced, but it was still a *ruin*, the rooms open to the sky, the walls crumbled, the mosaics, apart from the dog, mainly incomplete, the frescos faded. It was a ruin, *and* it was neglected. She preferred grand houses she could picture herself living in, and places that did not make you think morbidly about how life could at any point come to a sudden end.

Here, in Pompeii, you had to imagine ceilings, an upstairs, a roof, that the colours you saw only traces of were everywhere, glowing; you had to imagine the people in the rooms, the smells of food and perfume and probably other less pleasant things, too. You had to know the stories to understand the pictures: Hero and Leander, both drowned. Theseus abandoning Ariadne, the giant Polyphemus spying upon Galatea and her shepherd. Leda and the swan, everywhere. Whoever first thought of *that*? According to Harry, the poem Masson had quoted was about the meeting of the human and the divine, but she was not convinced.

Even so, after an hour, she reached the point where she *could* almost imagine herself living in one of the larger houses, wearing some long, loose robe and clipping lavender in the courtyard garden: pleasant enough. And then, right in the entrance way of the next villa, she was confronted by a painting of a man with an enormous penis sticking out from under his shirt, as long as his thigh, apparently *weighing* it. Beneath it, a large bowl of fruit.

'Oh!' she said. 'Look!'

'I'm sorry if I've been short-changing you,' Harry said.

'Men!' she replied. What on earth was it doing there, in the hall? A fertility symbol. And then again, a well-endowed statue, a former fountain apparently, in an alcove off the kitchen: unhygienic, somehow. Also, nearby, a faded picture of a pasty-looking naked woman with large buttocks squatting over a reclining man.

'Masson did warn us last night,' Harry said.

After the lecture, Julian, on his own because Mary had slipped away for an early night, had persuaded Harry to have a drink with Masson while Evelyn wrote her letter; the man was, he'd insisted, a wonderful source of information and he was keen to know more since he and Mary had missed most of Pompeii. Mary had found the body casts unsettling, so they'd decamped to a restaurant until the bus came.

'I find I have to steer a very careful path so as to avoid offence,' Masson, nursing a large brandy, had told a group of eager men gathered at the bar. 'For example, I'd love to be able to show you my slides of Pan copulating with a goat, executed in marble – an extraordinary thing! Of course you'll find some illustrations, and detailed descriptions, in my book. And then there are my slides of the frescoes from the main brothel near the forum, which is still out of bounds to the general public ... They run the gamut of sexual possibility, I can assure you. But I'd not be invited on board next year if I gave you a glimpse of those. I find the Roman frankness about bodily functions and sex refreshing, but the ladies do tend to be shocked by how very, well, phallic, the Romans were, whereas I think most of us men would love to time-travel for a day or two. When in Rome, eh? If only, eh? You'll find plenty of interest, if you look.'

Though you hardly needed to look. Sex was everywhere, impossible to avoid. They seemed to have liked the woman on her elbows and knees.

'They're not at all slender, are they?' Harry pointed out to Evelyn as they studied a faded fresco in flesh and earth tones.

'Pear-shaped. Rather voluptuous,' he said. Despite the crude execution of the painting, he found the knees and elbows position fairly arousing – a reminder of times when things between them were more spontaneous and varied. He had to keep himself from putting his hand on Evelyn's hip.

'That winding path down to the shore,' Julian said that evening, the second night in Sorrento, all four of them leaning on the rail to look at the lights twinkling on the water, 'the switchback down to the little harbour? Did you hear the story?' He told them how, before the first war, the wealthy German arms manufacturer, Krupp, had arrived on his yacht, fallen in love with the island, and paid for the construction of the path to the bay, at the bottom of which a small locked gate led to a cave that housed a not-so-secret club. 'Outrageous homosexual orgies,' Julian said, his eyes widening. 'Krupp's wife heard of it and complained to the Kaiser, and the Kaiser, being a friend of her husband's, locked her up in an asylum. But eventually photographs leaked out and Krupp had to leave Italy. Went back to Germany and shot himself.'

'Good riddance,' Evelyn said. 'And a shame the firm didn't collapse; it might have saved a lot of lives. What happened to the wife?'

'I don't know,' Julian said, 'but I will make it my business to find out.' He did, too, delivering the answer two days later: she was released.

'Did you two go to the grotto?' Harry asked.

'I trust there aren't any stories about that,' Evelyn said. Though surely, Harry thought, there would be: silvered swimmers lost, found, or turned into dolphins; the ghosts of emperors ravaging teenaged girls.

'We waited almost half an hour,' Mary said, 'but in the end we had to give up. There were so many people. We

221

would have missed our transfer back. We should have gone with you.'

'I hope you're not expecting *me* on all fours, like an animal,' Evelyn told Harry, and actually, he had been thinking about it, but there was no law against that.

'I'm not expecting anything,' he said, kneading the muscles between her shoulder blades. She lay face down on top of the bed, the sheet pulled over her legs and buttocks. 'But,' he added, 'do you remember the fun we had in that first flat? I think we did, back then – '

'Down a bit,' she said.

'I do,' he said, running his fingers slowly down the bumpy sides of her spine until he reached her lower back, another area that she liked him to give detailed attention to. Over the last decade, it had got so that foreplay could take days, a week even, beginning with the first verbal overtures, and often a gift of some kind, such as the swimsuit, and progressing by subtle degrees from there.

'You are still just as lovely,' he told her. If he was lucky and she relaxed enough, she would turn over and let him in. The whole ship, he thought, might well be engaged in similar activities, after their day in the city of the dead, who, before the ash fell, had been so very much alive.

They were at sea the next day, and Harry found that once Evelyn fell asleep, he grew tired of sitting by the pool. The tedium put him unpleasantly in mind of the troopship, going to Egypt. To dispel the association, he walked around the *Calypso* several times, exchanging pleasantries with other passengers, and stopping periodically to study the waves, the sky, and the mysterious place where one became the other. He thought he might manage to get over his inability to write about the grotto by writing instead about the very impossibility of describing its blueness. He leaned his notebook on the cap of the rail and wrote: *Blues must not try to be the blues of sky.* Or sea, for that matter, he thought, looking out at the expanse of it, the darker parts, the shining places, speckled with light, the mysterious stillness. The depths, and the surface, sometimes a mirror, sometimes a skin. The skin of the sea . . . Didn't Homer, perhaps feeling the same impossibility, avoid particularising the colour, and call the sea *wine-dark*? Each blue was its own entity. He'd be better off without the words that existed, must somehow create something new. That was the thing: the experience of being in the grotto with Evelyn required a *reinvention of blue*. He wrote that down, too. There could be a sonnet, he thought, beginning with the attempt to avoid azure, and ending with the search for utterly new words, the need to reinvent, syncopate. And there was a deeper journey, as well as the actual one. What was it about being in that blue that melted him so? What was he really trying to name, keep and pass on? The journey from outside to in was part of it. The little boat – the transition from land to water, the disconnection from the earth, that was the beginning of the whole thing. Wave-jostled, they glided towards an invisible entrance, slipped away from the sun and the sky into that low passage, a narrow neck of rock, blue glowing at the end of it, a strange flame, and all the while the water lapped and the boat rocked, and Evelyn had leaned back on him. All experience was ravishment. It had been like being born, or perhaps the opposite of it, an inverse birth, returning to a womb of light and music, the two of them joined in the experience . . . *Blue womb*. It was contained but at the same time vast, and in it, in the bluelightedness, the blessedness, the impossible blueness, a man and woman together after many years, a heavenly thing –

A shadow darkened the page and he knew immediately that it was Julian.

'Nice morning! And nearly time for a glass of wine,' he said, as Harry snapped his notebook shut. 'What are you up to?'

Harry shrugged, looked out at the ocean's indescribable blues: utterly different to those in the cave, related, yet unique. Perhaps everything that mattered was like that, he thought, beyond expression. Yet how he wanted to be able to set it down. Why? To keep it? No – you couldn't. Out of gratitude? To whom, or what?

'Just jotting down a few notes,' he said, slipping the pencil down the spiral binding and tucking the book in his pocket.

'Good for you. I do so admire people who write.'

'I don't, really,' Harry told him, 'I just have a notebook.'

There was a long pause.

'I must say, your wife is terrific fun,' Julian said. Harry turned to look at him but his face was relaxed and ordinary as he too studied the sea. 'So spirited and full of life. Though I can imagine she might sometimes be a bit of a handful.'

'Excuse me?' Harry said.

'Oh, I didn't meet to give offence. But I can see how, well, *determined* she is. To be honest, I wish Mary had more of that spirit. She was very vivacious when I first met her, but she lost a baby and, frankly, hasn't been the same since. She's on some new kind of tablets now but they're not working. And so far this holiday doesn't seem to be having the desired effect. Sometimes I wonder how long I can put up with it. I don't seem to have much luck with wives.'

'I'm sorry to hear that,' Harry said. The two of them stood there staring at the glittering water of the Ionian Sea.

'Do you suppose,' Julian continued, 'that Evelyn would take Mary under her wing a bit? A new friend might help her shake it off.' Their eyes met briefly; the man was clearly desperate: why else would he make such a proposition. But what on earth to say?

'I can only ask.'

'Much appreciated,' Julian said, treating Harry to a toothy smile. 'What a day, eh? Now, going back to your writing,' he said, 'is it poetry, now, or prose?'

'Nothing, really,' Harry said, 'but verse.'

'I'm only asking because my brother edits a little magazine and they're always looking for things. I could put you in touch.'

'No, really,' Harry told him. 'I'm not at the sending-out stage.'

They reached Corfu at dusk, a time when the colour of the sea was particularly deep and unfathomable. Masson's talk that night featured Calypso, Nausicaa and Odysseus, with illustrations from a variety of painters through the ages, some of them very amusing, and quotations from the *Odyssey*. Calypso, Masson reminded them, had seduced Odysseus and kept him on Ogygia for *seven years*, desperately in love with him even though, despite her attractions, he hankered for his wife, Penelope. Eventually, under pressure from Athena, Calypso released him and he set forth on a raft, only to capsize in a storm, and struggle, naked, ashore here in Corfu, where he stumbled upon princess Nausicaa and her maidens, at which point he admitted his identity and began to tell them the complicated tale of his adventures thus far.

'And thus,' Masson said, 'when we step ashore in the morning, we will be standing on the island where the most famous story of all time was first told – that is, if Homer is to be believed.'

'Nausicaa fell in love with Odysseus,' Harry told Julian, who was sitting to his left, 'but he wouldn't marry her. He sailed home to Penelope. And later on, Nausicaa married his son. More suitable, really . . . '

'Befriend her?' Evelyn had said before dinner, when Harry mentioned Julian's request, 'Why would I do that?' She was sitting at the little dressing table doing her hair. She wore the necklace he had bought her for their silver wedding anniversary.

'He thought it might help. Jolly her along, I suppose.'

'Harry,' she'd said, turning to him, 'I don't like her. We've nothing in common! She's a wet blanket and you know I'm not a do-gooder. We're on holiday! We didn't pay all this money to spend our time being social workers.'

'I thought it an odd request,' he said, 'but I said I'd mention it. I suppose if you were down like that, you might like some encouragement.'

'But I wouldn't be,' she said. 'You can't let yourself fall to pieces like that. I didn't. It's terrible to lose a baby, of course, but it must have been a very long time ago. She has to get over it.'

'It's probably not the whole story.'

'It's quite enough,' she said. 'As for tomorrow, let's do the old town and the monastery, just the two of us.'

It was excruciatingly awkward, but Harry felt saying nothing would be worse still, so he accompanied Julian to the bar after the Corfu lecture.

'Look, I did have a word with Evelyn, but I don't think it'll work out. She feels you probably can't engineer these things.'

'Just a thought!' Julian said, smiling determinedly. 'Women, eh? Very complicated. How's that poem of yours coming along?' Doubtless it was just conventional chit-chat, or the need to change the subject, but Harry felt a sudden and powerful urge to punch the other man in the face: was there nothing of his the man would leave alone? Not even his innermost thoughts, the words he played with in his head, his dreams of what he might have been? But he swallowed his fury, shrugged, and wished Julian goodnight.

Evelyn lay on her side, covered only by the sheet, breathing evenly. He undressed and lay beside her, but sleep eluded him.

He told himself that a day at sea without any real exercise was likely to blame and eventually slipped out of bed, opened the window as far as it would go, and settled into the not-very-generous armchair. He considered finding his shorts and digging his notebook out of the back pocket, but did not do so. The Blue Grotto sonnet was over and done with, spoiled, dead. He would never complete a poem to his satisfaction, much less send one to a little magazine, however much he had once imagined he might do such a thing. It did not matter that he had an ear for verse and had grown up in the same streets as Edward Thomas. He was no longer that boy who had sat on the back step, his heart thudding as he read the sonnet his teacher had assigned him: *Love alters not with his brief hours and weeks / But bears it out even to the edge of doom* . . . And he was no longer the young man coming home to his wife after years of war, vowing not to be ground down by routine, to stay open to the possibility of an ecstatic life. He was none of that now, so who had he become?

A 'keen gardener'?

A career in municipal construction, counting bricks and catching contractors when they tried to cheat, the management of others doing the same, the writing of policy: all that, thank goodness, would soon be over. Four years to go. He was a father and very glad of it; he'd have been happy to have more children, and had taken Evelyn's two miscarriages harder than she had. Despite all the violent emotion, or even because of it, he liked being among women. More than anything, he was a husband. He liked having a wife who, even now, other men noticed and envied him for, a woman who only had to sit on a deckchair or a park bench and a would-be charmer would materialise . . . As for Evelyn, had she changed? She had become more intensely herself. She was sometimes generous and sometimes passionately loyal; she understood duty and believed in

227

it, yet in practice found it intolerable . . . When she wanted something, it drove her. She experienced her own feelings with great intensity, but often failed to accept those of others, especially if they differed from hers. She disliked bullies and tyrants; she also disliked introspection, compromise, weakness, vagueness: these things frightened her, he understood, and also, she saw them as a waste of time, of life. She believed in food, laughter, walking, fresh air. Evelyn would never do a thing she didn't want to do; she was incapable of it. She had always been like this, but seemed more so, now, as she moved beyond the middle years. Perhaps the girls were right that he should have withstood her, defended himself, and them? But he would have lost her, and that was unthinkable.

Her hunger for life seemed starker and more desperate without the distracting glow of youth, also less charming, more primitive. It was growing more powerful; as she felt the pressure of mortality, the life force in her, the ego, or whatever you called it, the thing about her that everyone noticed, pushed back harder. This was Evelyn: strong, hungry, wilful, beautiful, sometimes kind, sometimes harsh: completely extraordinary. The woman he had met on the library steps thirty-five years ago had changed only in degree. He had chosen her and continued to do so. What love was had changed to the point that he no longer understood it, though he knew its scale and depths, and knew that it was most of who he was.

She slept on while he thought these things.

In the morning they would stroll around Corfu, and the next day the ship would dock at Olympia, and from there to Crete, where somewhere, in the nearby hills, waiting to be discovered, lay the Minotaur's cave. They would visit the ruins of the palace at Knossos, where Pasiphaë had mated with Zeus's bull and her daughter Ariadne showed Theseus how to navigate the labyrinth, and then was abandoned on the beach.

But all that was to come. There were gods and there were mortals, Harry thought. Evelyn was some kind of goddess, and he was just a man. She lay on her side, one arm tucked under the pillow; the sheet she was draped in skirted the tops of her breasts and then tucked under the other arm which rested loosely on her side. Her youthful face had restored itself. Her eyes at rest behind smooth-seeming lids, she slept on and gradually it grew lighter, the sea glittering first silver, then gold.

*

Only a month after the holiday, Julian wrote to tell them that Mary had taken an overdose of sleeping pills: he'd returned from work to find her on the sofa, dead. They agreed to invite him for a walk on the downs and a pub lunch, if he felt up to it. Evelyn found that she liked Julian much more without Mary there.

'Your wife's suicide was a terrible thing,' she told him, putting her hand on his arm, 'but you must accept that it was probably for the best, if she felt as she did about life.' It was up to him, now, she said, to make the most of his time.

He was a little taken aback at first, but took this well, and later gave them, without charge, some very useful tax advice.

HOTEL PARIS

CLOUD

During the summertime visit, there was still a kind of comedy to Evelyn and Harry's mealtime negotiations, and Louise did not at first realise how bad things were.

'What do you want? Chicken sandwich or macaroni cheese?'

'Whatever you're having will be fine, dear, thank you.'

'You know it drives me mad when you say that. What do you *want*?'

'Please remind me of the choices.'

'Chicken sandwich, macaroni cheese.'

'I really don't mind . . . '

Evelyn whipped around to face Louise. 'He won't choose in case someone else wants the same thing,' she said. 'Martyrdom. Drives me mad.' But perhaps Dad really doesn't care, thought Louise. Or perhaps he wants neither.

'Macaroni, please,' he said, his eyes fixed on his wife's face.

'I'll have to warm the oven all over again.'

'In that case, chicken.'

Time after time . . . It was even worse at night.

'Have you used the facilities?'

'Will you kindly leave me alone?'

'Why are you so bloody-minded?'

And so at Christmas, when she took the children to visit, she warned them in the taxi to the airport that their grandparents might have *changed* since their last visit. She cringed at the euphemism even as she uttered it.

'Changed into what?' asked her oldest, Zoe. Liam, the youngest, sucked his fingers. Issy, who hadn't wanted to come, stared miserably out of the window at the wasteland of industrial buildings and hotels.

'Growing old is hard. Stress makes them irritable. They were very grumpy when I visited in the summer.' Though back then, it had still been possible to see the bickering as a phase, to imagine that things would improve as Harry recovered from his hip replacement. Now, as the airport came into view, it struck her that things might actually be worse.

'You might hear them say things we wouldn't say,' she told her children, 'or yelling . . . I'm sure they'll try not to, but I thought I'd warn you.'

'I'm *so* looking forward to this trip,' Issy said, turning to look at Louise with big eyes. 'Dad must be devastated that he has the flu.'

Evelyn stood in the doorway that led to the kitchen, her arms held slightly wide from her body. Harry, seated in the velour armchair that gave him only a distant and awkward view of the television, gazed at her, hesitated. She rolled her eyes.

'Ham sandwich, or a slice of quiche? Tell me! Which? Sandwich, quiche.'

He stared back at her, silent.

'What could be simpler? Everyone else has chosen.' The imputation, Louise was well aware – he too, doubtless – was that her father was feeble-minded. It was not true: although sometimes forgetful, he still solved most of the *Telegraph* crossword and had asked yesterday how the two meanings of the word fluke – the whale's tail and the surprising stroke of luck – might connect. But she had resolved not to seem to take sides and managed to stop herself from leaping to his defence.

'I don't mind.' Harry peered at Evelyn over the top of his glasses, which badly needed cleaning. Evelyn, inches shorter than she used to be, but no less forceful, stepped into the room, her fists clenched.

'Tell–me–what–you–want!' She pronounced each sound very clearly, and left long pauses between the words, implying, again, idiocy. She did not seem to mind other people hearing her do this. She felt absolutely justified in it, so far as Louise could tell; later, she realised that it could be that her mother was so desperate that she didn't care what other people thought.

'Whichever is easiest for you,' Harry replied, adding, 'that is the important thing.' His tone sharpened: this blend of sarcasm and accusation was as far as he would ever go in terms of challenge or resistance. Was he playing to the audience?

'You'll have nothing, then!' Evelyn slammed the kitchen door behind her. Zoe's eyes, meeting her mother's, widened. At fourteen, she understood most things. Liam, almost four, and Issy, twelve, both on the floor with their sandwich remains in front of them on the coffee table, sat bolt upright and stared up at their mother like two meerkats, ready to bolt into a burrow, if only one could be found.

'It's okay,' Louise said, though clearly it was not.

Evelyn's heart pumped so hard she could hear its wheeze and thud. She felt the urge to lash out, to break or hurl something: a perfectly good day, one out of the seven of the grandchildren's visit, ruined. He was impossible! Cantankerous. Obstinate. Uncooperative. He was most certainly not the capable, decisive man she had married. A different man. The opposite, almost. Impossible. Idiotic. A pan from lunchtime soaked in the sink and she took the scrubber to it, pushing at the burned crust with all the strength in her arm, scrubbed and scrubbed until Louise came in, asked if she was all right, and could she help with that?

'I can clean my own pans! And I am perfectly fine, except that your father drives me mad!' she said, dropping the scouring pad and turning around to face her daughter. 'He hardly goes out, even though they told him after his hip was done to use it or lose it. A twinge of pain or a breath of wind is enough to put him off, and he won't make his damned mind up about anything. Snaps at me when I tell him he's got to make a habit of going to the lavatory every time he drinks something. He's had several accidents – '

'Oh dear. It sounds – '

'And this deafness of his – '

'I can hear you perfectly well!' Harry shouted from the living room.

'Bully for you. *So what!* Shut the damned door, would you?' But Louise just stood there like a nincompoop, so Evelyn reached past her to yank the door to.

And then Louise said how she really felt it was time to consider getting some 'help'. That again! Did Louise not know that Valerie had been banging on about 'help' for months? Did she not know that some things just could not be *helped*? That you reached a point when you had to accept that something was *over* or no longer worked?

'By help, you mean some useless cleaner I'd have to supervise and make sure wasn't stealing?'

'No, actually, Mum, I meant – '

'I do not want strangers in my house. How many times do I have to explain that if your father was not so infuriating, I would be fine. Though of course, the general direction at our age is downhill. Things are not going to get better.'

'I'm trying to think of ways to make life easier. And actually, by help, I meant – '

'Well, keep thinking!'

Evelyn turned her back on Louise, thrust her hand in the clotted dishwater, yanked out the plug. The answer, surely, was obvious. But it was better if they saw it for themselves.

'Elocution,' Harry told Isabel, and she wrote the letters carefully into the boxes. Her spelling was good.

'Five across. Nine letters. Part of speech, ends with *e*,' she read out.

'Aha. But what do you think? Suppose it began with an *a* . . . What I think you call a describing word . . . Good girl.'

'Five down. Poetic collective noun for daffodils, second letter *o*.'

'Host.' Host was also a thin biscuit served at communion. He was ravenous. Suppose he strode in and seized something from the fridge . . . Strode? Who was he fooling? And Evelyn hated him in the kitchen. He got in the way and messed things up. And the waterworks problem. Unfortunate. But surely –

'Voila!' Louise handed him a plate: ham sandwich.

'Thank you, dear,' he told her. 'You can see how things are,' he added, and despised himself for saying it, especially in front of Isabel. Because what did he expect Louise or any of them to do? Wave a wand? Reverse the flow of time? Make Evelyn forgive him for getting old? Make her realise she was old, too? He most certainly didn't want that, even though she stood in the threshold of the room, glaring at him.

'*All* you had to do was answer a simple question!'

'Nothing's simple with you,' he replied.

'Will you two please stop this!' Louise said, at which Evelyn stormed upstairs, opened and closed drawers in their bedroom and slammed the bathroom door.

The sandwich, thick, salty and moist, was perfect, in its way.

'Sorry,' Louise said, 'but you should hear yourselves! How often is it like this?'

He swallowed, pretended not to hear, asked Isabel, sitting forgotten on the sofa, to please hand him the crossword so he could see how far they had progressed. There was her writing, neat and confident: *ADJECTIVE, ELOCUTION, HOST.*

Lonely as a cloud, he thought into the ensuing conversational vacuum, desperate now to fill that emptiness of things not said, *That floats on high o'er vales and hills . . .* There were clouds in 'Adlestrop', too, which were compared to haycocks. And loneliness. *No whit less still and lonely fair | Than the high cloudlets in the sky.*

'It's to save Grandpa from waking Granny when he gets up to pee in the night,' Louise told Liam, though the truth was that she too found Harry's new sleeping arrangements upsetting: the narrow single bed in the smallest of the spare bedrooms, the saggy mattress with the plastic undersheet, the tiny bedside table. As for being mean, she explained that being mean and loving someone could happen at the same time. Liam, not convinced, sat abruptly up in bed.

'But you and Daddy won't – ' he began.

'Of course not.' Yet how did she know? There was an intransigence in her, an impatience that sometimes reminded her very much of her mother. In another forty years, who knew?

The phone was in the kitchen, beneath Harry and Evelyn's bedroom.

'It's pretty grim here, Val,' she said, keeping her voice low. 'War zone.'

'Now you know what we've been dealing with,' Val replied; she was still angry with Louise and Rick for moving so far away.

'I'm sorry. I didn't know it would be like this and maybe I should have imagined it better. But it can't go on.'

'Agreed,' Val said, softening. 'Hang in. It's very civilised here, and you'll be joining us soon. My two arrived yesterday and are out with their old school friends, and we're listening to Bach and playing Scrabble. Max has stocked up on champagne, which hopefully will have a positive effect. The three of us can go out for a walk and talk everything over after lunch.'

Later still, Louise called Rick, who was just getting up. He sighed, sympathised, said it sounded horrible. He felt much better, but there were no flights available until the 28th and they cost the earth; they agreed he might as well stay home and paint the living room.

Fourteen for lunch. Apart from Rick, only Lillian and Ed's daughter Susanne and her lot were missing, due to Susanne being in the later stages of her third pregnancy. It had gone well, Val thought. Very well.

'A toast to the cook, and all her assistants!' her father had proposed as they began it, thanking her for her hospitality, and noting the range of ages at the table and the panoply of talents and abilities; her mother, resting her hand on her husband's, had smiled in a queenly way as he spoke, and a complete and almost uncanny truce prevailed: a triumph, Max said afterwards, slipping his arms around Val as she loaded plates into the dishwasher. Seriously, he said. Magic.

And then, the 'brass tacks' walk, uphill in a freezing wind: well, that had gone as well could be expected.

'Look,' Val had told the other two as soon as the garden gate closed behind them, 'the thing is, it won't improve. I can handle them, up to a point,' she'd explained. 'If I say: "Listen, I will leave now and drive straight home if you continue like this," or, "I will not be having you two stay in my house, if all you do is bicker," then they'll compete trying to placate me and we might go a whole day without an argument. But as for what happens once they're alone . . .

'Mum does do her best,' she'd told them. 'She's just not a natural carer. The incontinence is actually only two occasions that I know of. But it pushes all those buttons to do with her father . . .

'And Dad's incredibly slow on his feet, and that drives her mad, so he avoids walking, so it gets worse. And he's mainly very indecisive, but can suddenly turn stubborn. She's over-worked, frustrated . . . It's only going to get worse.' Soon they were climbing the hill, warmer from the walk even though their eyes still watered in the biting wind. But such a relief to lay it all out. She kept on: 'They won't move in with us. There's nothing to do here and she'd be dependent on me for trans-portation. *He* won't come on his own . . . *No* to assisted living, *No* to a home help, *No* to someone to help Dad with using the loo, etcetera. Adamant. It doesn't matter what we think. None of it will happen.' They stopped and looked down, breathing hard, at the patchwork of fields and houses, the lights of a few cars creeping along the lanes.

'But surely, if we present a united front?' Lily had asked. How could she not see that would likely have the *opposite* of its desired effect? Why did her older, taller sister still expect that reason and common sense would prevail? Life must be very disappointing to her. But Val had managed to stay calm.

'By all means, try,' she said. 'Another thing is that Mum needs a holiday. Any volunteers for that? Suppose one of you took her somewhere, and the other looked after him?'

'I suppose I just never thought they'd be like this,' Lily said as they set off down the hill in the almost-dark. 'But of course, the thing is to keep it in perspective . . . It's just the last few years that have been difficult. The last one, especially. We must remember that most of it was pretty good. Not perfect, but good.'

'Care to put a figure on that?' Val asked – it was a running joke of theirs. She extracted a torch from her pocket and shone it on the path ahead of them.

'Let's say seventy-five percent good,' Lily replied.

'Hmm . . . I recall about seventy-five percent arguments, ninety percent about nothing,' Louise said, peering out from under her fur-trimmed hood.

'Don't forget,' Val had reminded her younger sister, and immediately regretted it because she could be oversensitive, 'that many of them were about you.'

'Ouch!' Louise said, but she seemed to be taking it well enough.

'Maybe, Louise,' Lily said, 'you just tend to remember the arguments more easily, and forget all the plain sailing between.'

'Remember, Lily,' Val had told her then, 'that at the earliest opportunity, you moved to another country. Pretty much as far away as you could get. And you, too, Lou, you've installed a large buffer zone.' It was a relief to say all that out loud.

'We've visited at least every two years, and I phone every week,' Lily told them as the house came back into view.

'Do you two really think everything was all my fault?' Louise asked, seemingly stricken at the notion, which surely, Val thought, must have occurred to her before.

'Not to begin with, of course,' Lily said. 'You couldn't blame a small child.'

'What does that mean?'

'Enough!' Val had told them, pushing open the gate. All the lights in the house seemed to be on, except for the one in the room her parents were using. 'I'm going to come in at fifty percent, fifty percent of the time. The thing is, Louise,

241

you turned up so much later. You missed some of the best bits. You'll have to imagine them.'

And thankfully all of them had laughed. And now, yet more food provided, her girls out once more, the husbands vegetating by the fire, Val slipped back into her stone-flagged kitchen and turned on the light. Max had swept the floor and put most of the dishes away. It was warm from the Aga and the wood and tile glowed in the soft light from the lamp that hung over the huge pine table. It was time for another drink: after that talk, and after fourteen for lunch, she deserved a few glasses of the best red they had. All of them did. She crossed to the dresser for the crystal glasses her mother had recently passed to her in one of her clearings out, and took three of them down.

'Wine in the kitchen! Girls only!' she called through to the living room.

Girls! Lily thought as she and Louise abandoned Ed and Max, half asleep in front of the TV, and made their way to the kitchen. Hardly. She settled next to Louise on the chair with the striped cushion and watched Val pour the wine. All of them had the same short haircut, she thought, but that was pretty much their only common ground in terms of appearance. Val had green eyes, hers were grey; Louise had inherited their father's brilliant blue, along with fair skin and the little bump at the top of her nose. Not one of them had been blessed with their mother's magnetic looks, though she, the tallest, had sometimes been described, in her youth, as *elegant*. Now the sad truth was that she looked just like any woman her age.

The wine was very good. Rich, almost thick. They clustered together under the light, clinked glasses, drank, and then Val reached for a battered brown envelope stuffed between two jars on the dresser shelf.

'So,' she said, 'these are loose pictures from the back of the desk drawer. Mum's starting to sort through old things and wants to throw them away. But I thought I'd better check.' She extracted a handful of black-and-white photographs. 'Look at this beauty,' she said, and slid one across the table to Lily. It showed their parents sitting together on a beach mat. Both were smiling, smooth-skinned, young. Their mother wore a dark bathing suit and sunglasses, the outfit completed with a necklace of white beads. She sat upright on the mat, knees and calves pressed together and arranged to one side, mermaid-style. One hand connected her to the ground, the other curled into her lap. Their father, in bathing shorts, sat cross-legged, his stomach flat and all of him strikingly muscular.

Behind them, a sandy cliff with scrubby plants clinging to it.

'Where would that be?' Val asked.

'Broadstairs,' Lily told the other two, 'forty-seven or forty-eight.'

She'd not thought of it in the intervening decades, but now it came to her, all in a rush, and perfectly: how her father had crouched beside her and instructed her to stand perfectly still and look down into the window at the top of the camera.

'I took it,' she said. 'With that Rolleiflex Dad brought back from the war.' She remembered how the breeze blustered in her ears and blew her hair about.

'What can you see?' he had asked.

'Mum,' she had told him, the waves slapping the sand behind her, the sun warm on her reddened shoulders that later would peel from too much sun.

'Dad had taken one of Mum, and one of me and Mum, and he wanted one of the two of them. He was very fussy about it all. How I mustn't cut off his shoulder or Mum's feet. How they needed space above their heads . . . '

'If you don't hurry up, I'll have to do my hair again,' her mother had called out.

'Perish the thought. Just do your best,' her father told her and she had looked down into the little square window, and watched him appear, seconds later, in his place. The sea lapped suddenly at Lily's feet, but she didn't move.

'So I pressed the button at what seemed like the perfect moment when both of them had smiles,' she said, 'and I made sure nothing was cut off, but when it was developed Dad had his eyes half closed like this and Mum said he looked gormless, which must be why it ended up in the drawer . . . And I remember we stayed in a B&B run by Mrs Greening. A huge, detached house with a back garden, a bit back from the seafront. The guests shared one bathroom on each landing. Breakfast was downstairs in the basement.

'Val,' she added, passing the picture back across the table, 'I think you are in here too, but not quite visible. Or maybe you can see – ' One by one they peered. And yes, perhaps a very slight thickening around Evelyn's middle.

'There could be worse beginnings.' Valerie refilled their glasses. 'Louise, I'm afraid you're not even thought of at this point.'

'I'll have to live with it,' she replied, chin in hands, smiling. Lily ran her fingers along the ridged grain of the tabletop.

'It's all coming back,' Lily told them. Was it the picture, or the wine? In any case, she couldn't stop.

'I had a room of my own, a box room, Mrs Greening called it. On the same landing as Mum and Dad's . . . ' Was it as small as a box, the child version of her had wondered, or full of boxes, and if so, how would she fit in to it? 'Very tiny,' she told her sisters. 'Just a little wider than the bed and its side table, with a window at the feet end.' . . . The extra charge for it was a bit more than the extra charge for having a small bed brought into the main bedroom, which was very nice, with a bay window and its own little basin for cleaning your teeth. There was space there for the spare bed, but of course it would spoil the look of things . . . When we went to inspect the box room Mum said the white candlewick bedspread was impractical for a child, it was smaller than she had thought. She started to haggle over the price.'

'Oh God,' Louise said. 'I can imagine.'

Her father, of course, had not wanted her in the marital bedroom.

'I think I had a point,' her mother told him as they unpacked, he slipping socks and underwear into the chest of drawers, she hanging her dresses and his short-sleeved shirts in the wardrobe while Lily, listening, had arranged the washcloths and shaving things on the shelf and hooks by the sink.

'Yes, but we may as well have the space to ourselves.'

'It seems rather grasping,' Evelyn said. 'And I'm not keen on this wallpaper. Do you think that's damp in the corner over there?'

'Well, she's a widow after all. Can't be easy. We'll not be here much in any case.'

'I don't like to be taken advantage of,' she had said.

Now, grown up Lily, *old* Lily, could tell her sisters this and they could all laugh at the sheer absurdity of anyone thinking they could do such a thing to their mother, but at the time the phrase had, for her, been full of mystery and scandal.

Her father had cleaned up in the little basin, and she and her mother went to the bathroom at the end of the landing. It was large, with tiled walls. A new-looking Ascot water heater flared into life when you turned on the tap, and she sensed – hoped – that the facilities would gain her mother's approval. As instructed, she took everything off, climbed into the bath and washed with the shower spray while her mother stripped down to her bra and used a washcloth at the sink, humming softly as she did so.

'Do you remember,' her mother said, 'the time we went to the seaside, a different one, not here, with Granny, when Daddy was away?' Lily tried and failed to recall it, decided not to pretend.

'No. Was it nice?' she asked. 'As nice as this? Nicer?' Her mother, studying her own face in the mirror, began to laugh, and then stopped abruptly, turned and said, 'That was in the war, sweetheart.'

They had to carry their damp towels back to the big bedroom and spread them over the backs of chairs.

'What are we supposed to do,' her mother had asked, 'when we have beach towels and wet swimsuits as well?'

'There must be a line in the garden. Don't worry. Everything is going according to plan – '

'Everything is going according to plan, and it'll get better every year. That's what he said,' Lily told the other two, suddenly tearful. She reached for the wine bottle and knocked her glass over; fortunately there was only a little left in it to spill.

Had it got better and better? Well, materially, without a doubt. The car, the longer, better holidays, and even, eventually, trips abroad. And it seemed to Lily now, a lifetime later, as a woman with a degree and half a career, her own marriage and family, a woman with *grandchildren*, a woman who had, because of her husband's work, ended up living in Australia, of all places, that perhaps at that moment in Mrs Greening's B&B her father had been talking, knowingly or not, about something more than the material things, that in some way he understood why these minor deficiencies bothered her mother so much – that they stood in for deeper fears that she would never admit to, such as disease, invasion, poverty, starvation. None of which, as luck had it, came to pass.

Louise tore off a piece of kitchen roll and put it in front of her. She wiped her face, blew her nose.

'And there's something else I remember. The eggs!' Lily said. 'How could I have forgotten! You know what those places are like. The first morning, we went down the brown-carpeted stairs to the basement for breakfast. It's very gloomy and very fussy at the same time. Lace curtains on windows that look out at a wall. Paisley tablecloths. A big room, crammed full of tables, and smelling of fried food. People are talking in hushed tones and clinking their spoons in their bowls and cups. And Mrs Greening's poor plump niece, not much older than me, in an apron serving things . . . She showed us to a table right in the middle, brought a pot of tea, and took our orders. And I asked for cornflakes, which was very exciting because of course we never got those at home.

'The food arrives and I'm shovelling them down when Mum calls out "Excuse me!"'

'Oh no,' Val said, grinning. Her green eyes settled on her sister, waiting for more, but they all waited while Louise went to get another bottle from the rack, held it between her thighs, and pulled the cork out with a satisfying *thwop*.

'*Excuse me!*' she said.

'Yes! So the dumpy girl in the apron reappears, terrified. Stares at Mum, her mouth half-open. 'Excuse me, dear,' Mum says, in that tone of voice, you know, so polite that it's rude, 'but this egg is like a *bullet*. I would like a soft-boiled one, please. The white, set, and the yolk, liquid."

'Of course the whole room had stopped talking the moment she said *Excuse me*, so it's as if we're suddenly on stage. I put my spoon down without making a sound. The big clock on the chimney breast ticked and tocked. The poor girl made a clucking sound in her throat and bolted back to the kitchen . . . '

'Oh, too much,' Val said, her eyes bright. And it was. Had been. Lily remembered the embarrassment, but there was something else, too.

'Well, an egg should be easy to get right, and we are paying for it,' her mother had said, and then very gradually the people at the tables all around started to murmur to each other again.

'I couldn't finish my cornflakes, they'd gone soggy. Mum buttered some toast. And then, the room hushes as the girl emerges from the kitchen bearing the new egg in its china cup on a china plate that she's carrying with both hands, her eyes glued to it.'

And the thing was, Lily thought, pausing for effect, that her mother first signalled what would give her pleasure, and then that it did: that was the other side of her complaints as to what fell short. You just wanted so very badly to please her.

'Bitten nails. Hands shaking,' she told the other two. 'The china egg cup and the new spoon rattling on the china plate as she walked back over. I kept thinking, the poor thing's going to trip, but she made it up to the table and put the plate down in front of Mum. 'Is it all right?' she asked, in this strangled kind of whisper, her gaze now glued on Mum's face, and the whole room staring, and the poor thing stood there, waiting, while Mum chops the top off and peers in to see – '

And why on earth was she remembering this? But she was.

DO NOT RESUSCITATE

'I have to tell you, dear,' Evelyn said, the cordless phone pressed hard to her ear, 'I have to tell you that your father is worse than ever since you left. He has told me what he thinks of me. I have told him what I think of him. And there we are. He is fussy about his food, asleep most of the day, and vicious when awake. And as you know, I am not one to be a doormat. And – ' there was something caught in her throat ' – I'm upset with you, too, Louise. The casual way you dismissed my questions about that pillowcase! You brushed me aside as if it wasn't important – but it is one of a matching set, with a pattern of leaves. You told me it *would turn up*! And it *hasn't* turned up, and if you are going to lose my bed linen, please do not strip the beds next time. Leave it to me. Have I made myself clear?' She had been sitting on her own bed, but got up to cross the landing and examine the room in question: clean, but empty, the mattresses still bare.

'Yes, Mum. Sorry. But I really do think it will reappear,' Louise said. 'It's bound to be somewhere in the house.'

'You said you swapped your pillow with Liam.'

'Yes, he wanted to have a squishy one. But it still should be *there*, just in a different room.'

'Did you check your luggage?'

'Yes.' Had her mother looked *inside* the duvet cover? At the back of the washing machine?

249

'Of course! The kids' luggage?'

'Yes.'

'Those are matching pillowcases for the twin beds, to go with the duvets. The green ones, with a pattern of leaves.'

'I know. I'm very sorry, but we don't have it.'

Evelyn sat heavily on the bed nearest her.

'Well, dear,' her voice unravelled completely, 'it's not a good start to the year!' she choked out. 'Why does he pick on *me* to have a go at? And why should I put up with it? I could be off doing things. The longer we live the more money we've got, but with him like this, I can't go anywhere at all. I *know* I've been very lucky until now. I've been well loved and cared for, first by my mother, and then by your father. But now, with him as he is now, there's absolutely nothing to look forward to.'

And afterwards, she did feel a bit better for getting it off her chest.

And now it was breakfast all over again.

'Louise said that she would stay with you if I went away for a week or so to Cornwall or even France with Lillian. She can bring work and it won't be any trouble. What do you think?' Harry, seated at the table in the dining room, either did not hear, or wasn't listening. But she let it go. She was only asking to be polite. She was fed up to the back teeth and no matter what he said she was going to have a decent holiday, a real break.

She pressed the lever on the toaster, thought of how she couldn't even boil an egg when he married her. Spoiled rotten by her mother, that was the thing. So that first year, they ate a great deal of toast, and sandwiches, or out of tins, with occasional fresh fruit for vitamins, and they went to her mother's for something substantial when they were starved. She had taught herself, bit by bit. It was not so bad, since due to rationing everyone else was having to learn how to cook all over again, and all the food was terrible anyway.

After a while she had the hang of it, and eventually the ingredients improved . . . Breakfast and dinner every day, plus lunch, coffee and tea on weekends and holidays. And now, nearly seventy years later she was still doing it! Buying food, cooking, clearing up the plates! At least, until very recently, he had an excellent appetite: breakfast would be porridge with brown sugar and cream, toast, butter, jam, three cups of tea. But now, the pills: every single morning this week he had looked at them as if they were poison, and asked what they were for.

She took her slice of toast and sat at the table opposite him. He'd only had a bite or two of his.

'Aren't you going to finish that?' she asked, loudly.

'Well – '

'Yes or no?'

'Thank you, dear.' He coughed, abandoned the half slice on his plate, patted his lips with the napkin. She watched him struggle up out of his chair, pushing down hard on its arms. The way he hissed the breath out between his teeth, like a steam train – what was that about? The doctors had said his hip had healed well and there was absolutely nothing wrong with his lungs so far as she'd been told. When he unhooked his sticks from the edge of the table and fumbled with them like that it made her whole body tense just watching it. And as he had said, why did it bother her so much, since it was him that had to use the damn things? But it did. It made her feel like breaking something and, at the same time, sick of feeling that way.

'Are you going to the bathroom now?' she asked, not bothering to swallow her mouthful first.

'I expect so.' That look, as if to say, *Why on earth would you ask me such a thing*? Either he knew exactly what she meant, or he was a complete moron! *Expect*? What was wrong with *Yes*?

Trying to preserve his dignity, Lillian had suggested. Well, it was too late for that.

'Please yourself, you awkward bugger!' she told him. Again, it was a relief to speak her mind. Though did he hear? It really didn't matter. She returned to the kitchen to rinse the plates and pick up yesterday's peelings to add to the compost. She pushed out through the back door and walked around the side of the house. A bright day out, thank goodness, plenty of birds at the feeder. The little bay tree would need repotting in the spring . . . Valerie had given her that. And the hellebore was from Louise, the cherry by the gate from Lillian . . . She tipped her peelings into the compost behind the laurel and looked back at the garden. Even in winter it was pretty – nothing like the garden in their old house, but lovely still, with the evergreen clematis around the window coming into bud. She noticed a dock weed growing by the side of the path and crouched down to pull it out; as she did so, she felt a faint, mysterious tug towards the house, something calling for her attention, which she ignored. She struggled a while with the sinewy root, then gave in and decided to go back for a trowel; it was only as she got close to the front door that the sounds she'd been half hearing made sense, added up to Harry calling *Help!*

He was face up on the floor of the downstairs bathroom, panting like a dog and jammed into the tiny space, red face, burning blue eyes, blood on the side of his head where it had hit something as he went down. His head was by the toilet. His pants were round his knees, soaked, the air in the small room reeking, acrid.

He made a terrible moaning sound.

'Did you twist around? They told you – '

'Help me!' he yelled and she got hold of his free arm and pulled – useless – the size of him! He yelled again so she dropped the arm and hurried to the phone, where she had to yell, too:

the directions and how he'd had his hip done six months ago and probably gone and dislocated it.

'They said they won't be long,' she told him. He just panted and stared at the ceiling as if a message was written there. The skin under his eyes was wet – tears! She'd never seen *that* before, not in all this time . . . She hurried out to open the front door and the gate just as the ambulance men with all their equipment drew up. How on earth were they all going to squeeze into her tiny bathroom? It was the big, bald one who did most of it on his own, straddling Harry then shifting his shoulders towards the door while someone else moved his legs and feet. The scream he let out – she never could have imagined that.

The waiting room was packed with people sneezing and coughing, several wailing babies, and a man with a bloody towel wrapped around his foot, but, thank goodness, Harry was carried straight through. She had to wait with the rest. Valerie didn't answer the phone so she left a message then sat down in the one remaining plastic seat.

'I've got this terrible pain in my side, like a spike stuck in me, and I've been here two hours already,' the woman beside her said.

'Oh dear. I'm perfectly well. It's my husband,' Evelyn replied. 'He had a serious fall. I'm waiting for my daughter.' Saying this, she felt tears rise. People their age often failed to recover from falls. She called Valerie again – still no reply: could be out somewhere, or on her way, impossible to know. 'I'm afraid it's the beginning of the end. Come as soon as you can,' she said at the end of her message. Back at the waiting area, a grimy-looking man with a beard had taken her seat; he did eventually offer to stand, but even so she was very glad when they called her and a nurse led her to a small, dim ward. Harry lay propped half up, very still, eyes closed, with an oxygen mask over his face.

She gasped when she saw him.

'The main problem here is pneumonia,' said the doctor, a tall black man with a tight helmet of hair. The whites of his eyes were startlingly bright but his English was good. 'Did you notice him coughing or wheezing?'

'Well yes, but what about his hip?'

'Dislocated. Luckily the pelvis is fine. What comes out can go back in,' the doctor said. 'It'll be sore and he'll need physio. His mobility will certainly be affected in the short-term, but what I'm trying to say is that the pneumonia is in both lungs and it is advanced. We're hoping it's bacterial. Intravenous antibiotic treatment is normally very effective for that, but not always. I just wanted you to be aware of the situation, Mrs Miles.'

It *is* the beginning of the end, she thought, and her heart started up.

'We both have Do Not Resuscitate on our notes,' Evelyn told the doctor whose name she felt she could not pronounce. You knew, of course, that this kind of thing could suddenly happen, but nothing prepared you. It was vital that they understood what you wanted, that you did not want to be a cabbage, or have to have someone mopping up after you for years on end while you slowly declined, thank you very much, *or* to do that mopping up. You wanted to either live, or not.

'No, no!' the doctor told her. 'That's different. I don't mean to worry you unnecessarily. There's still a good chance this treatment will be successful.'

But looking at Harry, she doubted it: his skin papery, his cheeks hollow, his chest barely rising. The transparent plastic over his nose and mouth, the horrible whiffling of the oxygen machine. Tubes going into his arm. A bag of brownish-yellow liquid. Could he hear her? She asked him several times.

No response, nothing at all.

'Often they can hear, even when they can't speak,' said the Irish nurse who came to tell her that Valerie had called the desk and was just setting out: she'd be two hours, then. 'It's best to talk to him, dear, just in case.'

Screens divided them from other, equally unresponsive patients, none of whom had anyone with them. All you could hear was their breathing and the hum of the machines. It reminded her of the terrible time – half a century ago – when she and her mother had sat in her parents' bedroom with her father while he died; her mother had wanted her to say a nice goodbye to him, yet she couldn't – she was still furious with him and the words just wouldn't come, and the smell was awful, and then, years later, with her mother, she didn't get the chance because it happened so suddenly.

You never knew.

She had always hated hospitals but actually it was better here, with everything clean and people to help.

'Can you hear me, Harry?' she asked again, speaking slowly and clearly. 'This is Evelyn here . . . Your wife. Valerie is on her way. You fell down . . . I've told them about the DNR. It's been a shock . . . ' She swallowed, studied what she could see of the face lying on the pillow. He was like someone from outer space. His skin flaking away. The bristles growing through. He hated to miss a shave. She drew in a breath, leaned closer. 'Look, dear. I do want you to know . . . to know that I know that you – that I've been a very lucky woman.' She took a deep breath. Something in her loosened. The words had been heavy, something she had to make herself push out of her mouth, but now, suddenly, they were coming easier, as if of their own will. 'I remember how you propped yourself over me in the bomb shelter to protect me . . . How strong you were then. How you got the house built . . . Worked in the garden. The lovely holidays we went on. How good you always were, playing with the girls. And it's just a crying shame how things end up but, dear, we don't get to choose.'

He didn't so much as move. She leaned closer. Her lips were only inches from his ear.

'You treasured me,' she said. 'You were a good husband. Devoted. And I never regretted saying no to Aleksander Grutowski. Thank you, dear . . . Did you hear me, Harry?'

He probably didn't.

It was probably all a waste of time.

Or perhaps a good thing.

But she asked twice more, 'Did you hear me, Harry?' and then she had to go and wash her face in the Ladies'. There were no paper towels. On the way out she went left instead of right, got lost, and ended up in Cardiology, and one of the cleaners there had to lead her back. The Irish nurse brought her a cup of tea and a shortcake biscuit, and then Valerie arrived to take her home.

And then, four days later, there he was, sitting right up, alert, if noticeably thinner. He had a bit of a wheeze but no coughing at all.

The arguments, the fall, the ambulance, the excruciating pain when they pushed the hip back without anaesthetic because his lungs were so bad, all the things she had said to him when he lay there apparently on the brink of death? He seemed to remember none of it.

'I'm sorry to have been so much trouble!' he said, smiling at her as if he had never stood in the living room and accused her of being tyrannical, never pretended not to hear what she said in return. 'I wonder,' he asked, 'whether next time you come I could have my glasses and the book I was reading, and perhaps a pen and some paper, or a notebook?'

'Which book?' she asked, but he couldn't remember the title, and when she looked on the bedside table at home, there wasn't one. Maybe she had tidied it away.

What no one seemed to understand was that he was not the man she had married. Not the man who had written those letters in the war, or come back from it and built the house . . . Lillian had those letters now. The fact was that things *ended*. She felt suddenly very weak, sat down on the bed, put her head in her hands and sobbed until there was not a sound left in her.

'Valerie,' she said a few days later, standing receiver in hand by the phone in the kitchen and looking out at the ivy on the back wall, 'yes, Valerie, the antibiotics are definitely working. He's surprisingly bright, especially compared to the rest of them, all lying there with their mouths open. And he seems very glad to see me – even after all that's gone on . . . ' Her voice faltered, then gathered itself together. 'So I took him his glasses and the *Treasury of Verse* and some chocolate. Dr Abiyoe seems very pleased . . . But Valerie, I can't have your father back. I can't. I have cleaned that carpet three times and it still smells. I have told them that no, they can't send him home. I told Dr Abiyoe they'll have two patients on their hands if they do. The nice Irish nurse knows what I mean. 'You're nearly ninety, dear,' she told me. As if I didn't know! I told them I don't want to spend my last months or years on my hands and knees cleaning up impotence. Omnipotence. Incompetence! You know what I mean. So I need your help to find the right place.'

And Valerie let out a long breath, and then said that yes, she would come over in the morning. They would come up with a plan. She was a good girl. The best of them.

And then, 'What kind of place are you thinking of?' Lillian wanted to know. Had they researched it properly? Yes, Evelyn told her: some places were better decorated or more convenient than others, but the fact was that they all charged the same astronomical amount and the government wouldn't help until it had bled you dry. 'We'd have done better to spend everything on a luxury cruise and then jump off the side just before the end,' Evelyn said, 'but in your father's case it's too late for that. I've told Valerie to shove me down the stairs if I can't eat properly or go gaga.'

And then there was Louise, who asked: 'Did you two ever discuss what might happen if you couldn't look after him any more?'

'No.'

'So it might be an awful shock to Dad to suddenly hear that he's not coming home from the hospital. It might be best to tell him gently. To tell him you – '

'I shouldn't think so, dear,' Evelyn told her. 'He's very happy there, reading poetry and chatting to the nurses. He's doing better than expected on his tests. The doctor thinks he was probably depressed at home, and may well be happier in a new environment . . . Valerie and I will take him to see the best of the places we've seen, and the hospital will keep him until somewhere comes up . . . Please leave me to deal with this in my way. It has been very difficult, but this is all for the best. He will be looked after and I can make the most of what's left to me, which I hope you can understand. And now, I've been meaning to tell you that I found that leaf-patterned pillowslip that was lost at Christmas. It was tucked inside a corner of the duvet, after all. I found it when I started the ironing. So, dear: All's well that ends well.'

And after that, on her way up to bed, she took a fresh towel from the airing cupboard and let her eyes linger on the ironed and folded linens lying there on the upper shelves, and decided that even though it was late, she might as well put the leaf-patterned set on the spare beds in the middle room and have everything looking its best.

'So this is your home now, Mr Miles,' the manageress, Sandra Hepworth, told Harry. They were sitting in armchairs in a little parlour adjoining the office. Teacups and biscuits perched on little side tables beside them. Various tasteful artworks jostled on the wall. 'I know this move has happened suddenly. I did have doubts because in terms of your assessment – frankly, you could wait longer before considering care. But people do come here for all sorts of reasons and I think that all in all this will be for the best. It will take the stress out of your domestic situation and allow both you and Mrs Miles to relax.'

I can't have you back, Evelyn had told him. She was always very blunt, a good quality in many ways. And of course, it must have been very hard for her to say. *Sorry,* or *I hate doing this* would have sweetened the pill, but there it was, give her credit: *I can't have you back*. She got that far, and then Valerie took over: how the extra work of looking after him was just too much, especially, Evelyn made a point of adding, the extra laundry caused by his accidents; how she didn't want a stranger in the house, or to move in with Val and Max in the middle of nowhere; how Louise could possibly visit more often, but not move back over, because of their jobs and the kids having their lives in Canada, and how Lillian in Australia was even further away, had her own health problems and couldn't promise to do more than she did. How, because of the strain of the need to look after him more, the extra work – especially the laundry – he and Evelyn had been at loggerheads, and then to cap it all, he'd fallen off the toilet and dislocated his new hip . . . He could remember nothing about that now, but it must have been a terrible shock for Evelyn. She'd had no idea that he was seriously ill with pneumonia, and that was rather dangerous. She just couldn't have him back and it boiled down to there being only one option, and so there they were, his wife and his middle daughter, in the hospital's apple-green day room, waiting for his reaction.

Take it well, or badly – that was his choice. Harry drew breath, caught Evelyn's gaze. Her eyes, always large, now magnified by the large-rimmed glasses she had taken to, would not settle and she was clenching her jaw, as she always did when anxious and fixed on a goal of some kind. He did not like her feeling that way about him.

'I have no desire to be a burden,' he told her, and meant it. Though of course, he had other desires too, which were not expressed. For her to say that she would visit every day. For her to fling her arms around him, as she had when they parted at the bus station in Reading before he embarked. He could remember that surprisingly well. Love made it both harder and easier to bear a separation.

Her face relaxed.

'Thank you, dear,' she said. 'I didn't think you would,' and she leaned back in her chair a little. But it was Val who put her hand on top his.

'It's not easy,' she said, 'but we have to be realistic.'

Over the next few days they toured five places. The Beeches was definitely the best: an elegant building, if ruined by the conversion, with a sunny, interesting garden, not far for Evelyn to travel, and near a bus stop. The staff smiled and looked you in the eye; they seemed busy, but not rushed. Some of the residents were fairly active.

When a room came up, it meant someone had died or degenerated to the point they had to move on. And so here he was.

'You decide,' Sandra continued, 'Meals in the dining area, or in your own room. Many of our residents prefer breakfast in bed, but we highly recommend lunch and dinner downstairs, so that you get some time to socialise and don't brood too much. I've put you at a good table where you'll get some sense talked. Two other men and four ladies, the crème de la crème. You have a television in your room, and a lovely view, too, one of the best. But of course you may want to spend time in the library or the lounge or the sun lounge or the garden, or to go out for a walk with your wife when she visits, or take a bus or a taxi in to town, and all that's completely up to you, just please let us know if you are going out. Do you have any questions?'

Why do we live so long?

'Not at this point.'

'Krista, your lead carer, will talk to you about all this later today, but we offer an activity every day of the week and excursions on Tuesdays and Thursdays, again, all completely up to you at a small extra cost. If you have any questions or problems, please ask Krista or any member of staff, including me.' She paused for a moment, studying him. 'Welcome, Mr Miles. Or would you prefer Harry?'

'Harry.'

'I very much hope that you'll be happy here,' she said. He had felt that both the wish and the smile that followed it were genuine, and the feeling of someone wanting him to be happy was a novelty that made him momentarily tearful.

Since then, he had grown to like Sandra, who did a walkabout most lunchtimes and sometimes knocked on his door to see how he was getting on. A tall, big-boned woman of about fifty with bottle-blonde hair, she wore a different dress or blouse every day, and never seemed flustered, however many people were trying to talk to her at once. The parrot, Godfrey, who lived in a cage by the entrance to the lounge, issued a piercing whistle every time she passed. *Oh, that bird*, she'd say. Godfrey ignored the passing of other women, even the young ones: a good thing, really, given how many of them there were here. Staff and residents alike (inmates, Evelyn would keep calling them) were mainly female. On Harry's corridor there lived just one other man, in the room by the lift: wheelchair-bound, deaf, blank-faced, rarely glimpsed. The carers called him Major Tom, and, for reasons mysterious to Harry, found it amusing to do so.

He could not go back to the house, Evelyn had insisted, even to choose his things. She did not say why, but it was easy to see that she was frightened that if she allowed him in, he might remember what he was losing, and refuse to leave. Make a scene. Or break down and weep in front of her, which he too preferred to avoid, though he did quite often feel like it. Evelyn, Evelyn, he knew not to ask – How could you do this?

Evelyn, Evelyn! He had loved her all his adult life, long after the gloss of their youth and its illusions had been worn away and left them with the essentials of who they were, along with a collection of sometimes contradictory memories . . . He had never denied her anything, material or emotional, that he could provide, and what she desired now was his absence from her daily life. Evelyn! She was frightened by weakness. It did help considerably to understand her from the inside. To align himself in that way with her.

On the morning of the day when he had the afternoon chat with Sandra, he was collected by Valerie and Evelyn from the hospital, driven to the home, and shown his newly painted room. The home's van and driver had already collected his armchair, a bookcase with his poetry books and the dictionary, and a selection of shoes and clothes. He'd asked for the painting of geraniums the girls had given them a few years ago, but Evelyn said it would leave a dark square on the wallpaper above the fireplace, so she had allocated him a Turner print from the spare room. On request, she'd included a framed photograph of herself in a deckchair, from the fifties, along with one of them together taken not long ago. Now there was an ever-expanding gallery of smaller photos, including the children and various grandchildren with their names written on the backs of the pictures. The room struggled to contain all this along with the bookcase, bed, TV set and two chairs, but it boasted two tall windows that gazed out on to the bowling green, the houses and the sky beyond.

'Well,' Evelyn said, 'It's much better than the hospital.' A small table had been arranged downstairs so that they could have lunch together. After Evelyn and Valerie left, he went back to the room, sat on the bed, and sobbed.

A young woman who was bringing toilet rolls for his bathroom sat next to him and put her arm around his back.

'Harry, it is nice place here,' she said. She was from Latvia, she told him, and missed it very much. They would both have to adapt.

And it certainly was an improvement, not being got at all the time, he told Valerie, a week or so later, though it seemed a drastic way to achieve that result.

'There you are, Harry,' said a short, brightly dressed woman wearing thick glasses whom he was fairly sure was called Elspeth. She had introduced herself on the first day, and always encouraged him to sit next to her. Now, she pushed the chair out for him, and summoned someone to take his sticks and put them in the umbrella stand in the corner. 'Sit down and feed,' she continued, 'and welcome to our table.'

'Where's that from?' he asked, detecting a quotation. She'd told him how she used to be involved in the theatre, not acting, but making costumes and sets.

'Ah,' she said, beaming at him as he let himself down into the chair. 'From *As You Like It*.'

'All the world's a stage, and the men and women merely players,' he volunteered, hoping he had the correct play, and then stopped at the beginning of the speech, not wanting, in company as old as this, to mention exits and entrances, or the seven ages of man. Though probably no one could hear, or was listening even if they could. 'I'm not so well up on the comedies,' he said.

'Such fun to do,' she told him. 'I certainly prefer them now. Tragedy seems too close to home.'

'Who would like oxtail soup?' asked a plump girl wearing a white apron and a ring in her nose. Everyone raised their hand, as if they were at school. Soon the soup arrived, glutinous and peppery, along with a basket of soft bread rolls.

'Good day, Harris,' said the man who looked like Humpty Dumpty. The other male, Gregory, seated next to him, was physically the opposite: thin, with a tremor in his hands. He and his wife shared a large room overlooking the garden at the back, but today, he told them, more than once, Eleanor was sick, and not coming down. The rumour was that she drank.

A woman with white curls (Shirley, he thought, or else Joyce) asked Harry whether his wife was visiting today. Everyone seemed interested in the answer to this.

'I don't know,' he told them. 'But normally she comes in the morning.'

'When did she last visit?' asked another woman, with sparse hair dyed an unnatural carroty colour.

Harry thought this was rather rude, so pretended not to hear.

'They tend to start off frequent, and then drop off,' the woman said.

'She seemed perfectly charming when I met her just last week,' Elspeth said. 'A woman of immense character and style.'

'Yes,' said Harry. 'Thank you.'

The girl with the nose ring took the soup plates away.

'I like mulligatawny better,' Elspeth told Harry. 'It reminds me of my childhood . . . I'm so glad you're here. It means a great deal to be able to have a decent conversation.'

'Cod with parsley sauce, buttered new potatoes, carrots and peas,' announced the girl with the nose ring. The piece of fish was rather small, but otherwise, everything was edible. Harry, aware of eating faster than the others, forced himself to chew more slowly.

'Good digestion wait on appetite, and health on both,' he said, setting down his cutlery. He had no idea which play it was from.

'*Macbeth*! Harry, when was the last time you went to the theatre?' Elspeth asked.

'My daughter took us to *HMS Pinafore* last year, if that counts. It was very good.'

'Of course it counts. Gilbert and Sullivan,' she told him, 'are absolute geniuses. Do you have a DVD player?' She had scarcely touched her food, and now it was being whisked away.

'No,' he said, 'I'm rather old-fashioned.'

'Well, that's a good quality, overall,' she said. 'But I have the discs for over a hundred plays and operettas, and I could have lent you something . . . '

'Chocolate mousse for non-diabetics,' announced the girl.

'And here's where I disagree with the Bard,' Elspeth said, 'There is no such thing as a surfeit of the sweetest things.'

After the dessert came appalling, weak coffee in delicate china cups, and a bowl of fruit. What would he prefer, Elspeth asked, peering through her thick lenses into the bowl: apple, mandarin orange, or pear?

'A pear, please,' he told her, and she chose one and passed it to him.

'I used to grow these,' he told her. 'In our first garden. It feels ripe. But I'll make a mess of my shirt if I eat it.' Elspeth made to summon the girl with the apron and nose ring, who, she said, would take the pear into the kitchen and have it sliced for him, but Harry declined. He couldn't tell her, but he wanted to eat the thing whole, and feel the juice run down his chin. The problem was how to get it to his room, given he needed two sticks. The pocket in his cardigan was too small.

'Let me bring it up for you,' Elspeth said, and so they walked past the parrot to the lift, then turned left on the second floor, and he invited her to sit a while in his spare chair.

'In a place like this, you need to have good friends, and good memories. That's a lovely photograph of your wife,' she said. 'It's hard to believe, but I have been a widow for almost twenty years.'

'I'm sorry to hear that.'

'I still sometimes talk to Ralph. Isn't that mad? And if I get maudlin, I remind myself that we had thirty years. There were some difficult times, but in the end, I don't think it really matters, do you?' Harry, beginning to feel tired, but also aware of the need to empty his bladder, agreed. 'Young people,' Elspeth continued, 'don't understand long marriages. My son is on his third wife: a lovely woman, but then so were the other two . . . They live in Hong Kong.

'I'm thinking,' she said next, 'of watching *The Mikado* this afternoon. I could get them to bring in a good chair, if you'd like to join me.' He hesitated. It seemed a pleasant and reasonable thing to do. She was an intelligent woman, kind. But also, the feeling of pressure in his bladder was growing to the point where he could no longer ignore it. 'Your wife wouldn't mind, would she?' Elspeth said. 'Of course, she'd be very welcome, too.'

Yesterday, Shirley of the white curls had been the one to make an invitation: a drive with her daughter, who was taking her out to the country for tea, and had room for two more in the car. For a moment Harry had considered it: the half-familiar landscape rushing by. Trees, fields, hills, rivers, some early blossoms, flowering currant, daffodils. A café somewhere – but he had said no. And now the same to *The Mikado*.

'Thank you for thinking of me,' he told Elspeth. 'Perhaps another time, but I'll stay put today. And I'm sorry to rush you, but I need to use my facilities.'

Elspeth bustled out just in time to avoid witnessing his bladder get the better of him only a step away from the tiny bathroom that divided the bed area from the door. He stood a moment, drenched, considering his next move: whether to be helpful, or at least show willing, by unfastening the pants and trying to remove them?

'Dad, what you really have to watch out for in here,' Valerie had told him last time she visited, 'is becoming institutionalised. Letting people do everything for you. As Dr Hamilton said, use it or lose it. You have to keep on your feet, and do things for yourself.'

Perfectly reasonable. But instead of jettisoning his sticks in order to wrestle with the button and clip at his waistband, all the while tensed against the possibility of a fall, he turned back, and, still wearing the sodden pants, lowered himself on to the cushion, which he knew from experience would go straight into the laundry. He pressed the buzzer.

'I'm sorry,' he told Krista when she eventually turned up. 'I had a visitor,' he added, as an explanation.

'Never mind, Harry.' Krista plucked some gloves from the stash in the bathroom cabinet, and the whole business took almost half an hour; he was very tired at the end of it, when she settled him back in the chair. A rather sweet girl, with very dark hair and pale skin. She mentioned the pads again, but she wasn't angry, and he had to admit it was a relief to be looked after. He liked the feeling of people not minding, or expecting anything particular of you – because they were paid, of course, and because they weren't related and didn't know what kind of person you used to be – and also simply because they were *kind*. Why, at this point, resist? Wasn't the whole point of a place like this that you could let yourself go?

He turned to the photos of Evelyn propped on top of the bookshelf. The photograph he and all his visitors gravitated to was the framed black-and-white enlargement, just her head and shoulders against the fabric of the deckchair. Eyes looking straight into the lens, at him, as he took it, in the back garden of the house on Manor Close. The most recent one showed the two of them together in the gardens at Hidcote Manor, with Val and Max. A passer-by had taken it at Val's request, using her camera. At that point he only had one stick and Evelyn was as elegant as ever in a light-coloured jacket, sunglasses, and a bright silk scarf. It had been, as he remembered it, a good day out.

Did Evelyn remember how they used to be with affection? He could only hope so. Would she mind if he sat and watched *The Mikado* with Elspeth? He couldn't be sure. What had she done all day, and how was she right now, at the end of the afternoon? He was afraid that she must be lonely, even though she had wanted to be rid of him, and he knew that she would be surprised at herself, too, for feeling that way. She would not want to admit it. She would, of course, chat with the neighbours over the fence, find ways to be busy and go out as much as she could, but in the afternoon she would return home, where he no longer was. He didn't like to think of her in the empty house, especially as night drew in. The curtains tightly closed, the television loud.

TO MAKE MUCH OF TIME

The one Harry thought was called Samantha towelled him down, got him as far as half dressed, and settled him in the vinyl chair they kept in the bathroom. She took the new shaver from its stand. 'Cordless. Very fancy . . . From Mrs Miles?'

That was what the gift card said: *Love, Evelyn*, though the shaver was a German brand, which they had always avoided, and everything about it said *Louise*. Still, Harry thought, why not suspend disbelief?

'Yes, indeed,' he told Samantha, who leaned in close, bringing with her a whiff of perfume and a faint buzzing – half sound, half touch. A strange, subtle feeling of exposure spread in the razor's wake: a dry shave. He was getting used to it, though inevitably it set him yearning after the weight of those old safety razors, made him remember how you unwrapped a new blade from its waxed paper and slipped it in – the sandalwood smell of the warm, wet lather and the tender scrape of metal on flesh. And then the feel of your skin afterwards: air-kissed, ready for more intimate touch.

Good, bad: any shave at all was better than none. Serving in the desert, he'd use the undrinkable tea they brewed in oilcans for shaving water, along with carbolic soap and the Gillette Super Speed. How good it was, even so. Near Enfidaville, a parcel had arrived from Evelyn containing books, cigarettes and a tube of shaving cream, which had burst and leaked, but he used it just the same. There were three more years to go, but he didn't know that then, and he sat outside his tent and shaved, hearing not the thunder of the big guns, but the faint scrape of the blade on his skin and an invisible bird that, like him, had somehow survived. He had never felt more alive. *Best shave ever*, he wrote to her afterwards. *If only I were home and you could run your hand . . .*

Pale, clear skin Samantha had, and great green eyes, hooded now, all her attention on his jaw. Perpetually shiny lips, held in the beginnings of a smile.

'Tilt for me, please,' she said, and began on his neck. Apart from instructions, she did not talk while she shaved him and he wasn't supposed to either; the only thing to do was think – for example: how many shaves in a life? Some were missed due to sickness or enemy action, but to balance those were plenty of two-shave days – days when he was calling on Evelyn, or, once they were married, when he thought he might be in luck – that she might touch his face, rub her cheek with his, sigh, say *Oh, Harry* . . . A kiss, then, during which he would settle his arm in the small of her back, and pull her close. No need to rush. And that was another thing you did many times in a life and never tired of, though now it was best not to think of it too much.

Break the sum down: three thousand six hundred shaves in a decade, at a *very* conservative estimate. At least seven decades: he was well up in the twenty thousands by now.

'Did you know,' he asked Samantha, deadpan, when she was done, 'that you have just given me my twenty-five thousand, two hundred and twenty-third shave?' It did not bear thinking on, but it was funny, too – and as he had hoped, Samantha looked into his eyes and laughed.

'Mr Miles. You are something else!'

So you could say he'd got what he wanted (or part of it, or almost) when at some point in the recent past he'd wheeled into the office and asked the manageress to please dial out for him.

The receiver was tiny, modern, with buttons all over which you could easily squeeze by accident. *Careful*, he'd told himself, bringing it slowly to his good ear. The tone was barely audible, but when it ceased, Evelyn's voice sailed down the line, crisp and perfect. Hearing her recite their number – businesslike, firm – he felt his pulse quicken, a feeling of readiness and assent. *Still*, he'd thought, *after all this time*. They had been married longer than most people lived.

'Harry here,' he told her, loudly. TV news played at her end of the line. He could picture the room: the fireplace, its mantel cluttered with photographs; her sofa, one of the old chairs from upstairs brought in to replace the tan leather armchair where he used to sit, from which he had a view of the TV, the window, and Evelyn herself, to his left, with her feet up. He closed his eyes. 'How are you, dear?'

'Is something the matter?' she asked, and he felt an odd, slack feeling in his guts: it was agreed he wouldn't have a phone in his room, since he'd always be knocking it over, and anyway, she didn't want him constantly bothering her with things. He accepted that. And he didn't call often. But why no *Dear*? Why must they cut to the quick like this?

'I need a new razor,' he told her, 'it's broken.' *Bazoukered*, the girl had said, after she'd apologised for the nick on his cheek.

'That electric one?' Evelyn asked. 'You've not had it long!'

'Wasn't it one of Craig's, an old Christmas present he didn't want?'

'No, it was not! I'll look at it next time I come.'

'And when might that be? Look – ' he told her, 'I'm cut to bits and I've got blood all over my shirt!' It was a rank exaggeration, and he certainly didn't believe it himself, and yet for some reason as he said it his eyes watered, his voice rose and then broke. 'Goodbye, dear,' he told her, in a completely different tone, and then his thumb slipped and cut her off.

'Thank you very much,' he told the manageress as he handed back the phone, making sure to smile. Andrea? Angela? Or was it something beginning with an S? He could not quite remember, but he liked her.

And then at some point after that phone call he had woken in his chair and Evelyn was right there, standing in front of him: it took a moment to bring her into focus, dressed today in shades of beige with a yellow and green silk scarf around her neck; he remembered, with affection, another dress from decades ago, abstract print, fitted bodice, zip at the back . . .

'I came earlier,' she was saying, 'but you were asleep in your chair!'

'Very nice to see you, dear!' He struggled upright and she settled in the chair opposite him and explained how she'd taken the electric razor back to the shop but they wouldn't mend it under guarantee because he hadn't cleaned it properly, and the part that needed replacing would cost far too much and wouldn't last unless it was properly maintained . . .

'But I can't clean it. These damn hands. Can't undo the wotsit – '

'The *girl* should do it!' They weren't supposed to call them girls. Or not that way. What was the word – ?

'I don't think I asked her to – '

Carer, he remembered. Which was no good either because it suggested others did not.

'And what did you mean – ' Evelyn leaned forwards, '*Cut to bits*. Where? There's not a mark on you! You'll have to use disposables. Lots of men don't like electrics, anyway. Max swears by the old-fashioned kind. You used to say the same thing.'

'But I don't shave myself now. It's for the, the . . . ' Whatever you called her, the person who shaved him certainly knew a shave was important, and aimed to please: he could tell by the way her jaw softened and her forehead puckered, just a little, as she leaned in close.

'Samantha!' he said. A lovely girl, as most of them were. Washed your balls for you on bath night, too. Though still, he would rather be at home –

'She'll have to learn.' Evelyn settled herself back into the armchair. 'I put a bag of ten disposables on your bathroom shelf. They were on sale.'

You could ask where did it come from, the money saved by not replacing his shaver? An index-linked pension, the result of forty years' worth of long days in the office, the salary that flowed into their joint account, and was then divided into pension, housekeeping, savings and running costs . . . But Harry did not point this out. He didn't want to and he wished it had not occurred to him at all. He closed his eyes and sat, waiting for the thought to fade away. And then again, he was tired.

'I haven't come all this way just to look at you,' Evelyn said, sharply. And that was it. Always, always, it went this way: a last straw, then –

'Thank you for your trouble, dear.' He paused, just so, continued, his voice tightening a degree or two: 'I wonder, though, how would you feel if your electric kettle blew its fuse and someone decided it was easier if you just used a pan on top of the stove?'

'Kettle?' She sniffed and reached down to her handbag for her handkerchief. 'What are you on about? I shan't stay, if you're talking nonsense. There is nothing wrong with my kettle, and if there was, I would go out and buy myself another one! I'll leave right now, and get my bus.'

And then she was gone. He should have known better.

Not so long ago, Harry thought in the aftermath of Evelyn's departure, a broken shaver would have been such an easy thing to fix, almost a pleasure. He'd have gone out and bought himself another one, or, more likely, the replacement part. He'd have nipped into town, parked outside the new shopping centre, stood at the counter in Boots and chatted to the girl there. He'd have complained about the price, compared it with the cost of new, then paid using banknotes crisp from the newfangled cash machine at the entrance to the shopping centre. He would have enjoyed the half hour spent installing it almost as much as the shave itself . . . But that was then. And why the hell all this damn hair? You couldn't wait for it to come, and then you had to deal with it forever after.

'Your father is *rambling*!' Evelyn told her eldest, Lillian, who was on the verge of retirement herself. Evelyn had to shout because of a hissing sound on the line. 'Going on about my kettle breaking when it's absolutely fine! Rang me up to complain that the girl was cutting him to bits when she shaved him, so I rushed over, and there wasn't a mark on him! He's managed to break that shaver we gave him. It's all about what the carer wants, but what are they paid for? They haven't been cleaning it. So I bought him disposables.'

'Mum, you can get self-cleaning shavers now,' Lillian said. 'And I don't think the staff are paid a huge – '

The line was terrible, so Evelyn hung up, explained it all over again to Valerie, who turned out to be just as dense about the matter of the shaver as Lillian had been – and then, as a last resort and *knowing* it was a mistake because nothing had ever been simple with her and teaching philosophy in a university hadn't helped one bit – she called Louise.

' . . . Valerie said he'll always be running out and wanting me to bring him another packet,' she concluded, 'but I dare say it won't matter if he waits. It wasn't worth replacing.'

'Worth in what sense?' Louise asked.

'What do you mean?' Louise launched into a complicated speech about how important shaving was.

'Of course!' Evelyn interrupted. 'No one wants to look at a stubbly old man!'

'I mean, shaving is part of their sense of themselves *as men.*' Louise's voice was irritatingly calm. 'So, if Dad wants – ' Wants? What about what *she* wanted? A river cruise down the Rhine, for example. Someone to carry her bag, take her on drives if the sun ever came out. A man who did not drive her crazy. A husband who could walk and fix things, who didn't wet himself, or need help with his buttons, blow his breath out between his teeth, or insist that things had not happened the way she perfectly well remembered them happening. What about that?

Who would have thought things would end up like this! That a person could change this much, without her being able to stop it. What difference could any kind of *razor* possibly make?

'It's a *waste*,' she told Louise, her voice heavy with rage.

'I'm so sorry, Mum. Look. Suppose I just send him one and say it's from you?'

'Do what you damn well please!' Evelyn told her, her eyes filling with tears. 'I should have known better than to tell you anything!' She was sick and tired of the whole damned razor thing and of Harry and of her daughters – who argued with her, were too sentimental, too intellectual, and far too young to understand.

'I'm not quite sure how I ended up with a new shaving kit, but thank you all the same, dear,' Harry told Evelyn when next she appeared in the chair opposite his. 'I do like your outfit,' he added. 'It's very elegant.' But mention of the shaver, combined with the sight of him wearing his pyjamas at ten, had upset her, and she stared past him at the wall, her jaw set. Evelyn was tiny now; she wore glasses with thick lenses, her hair was thin, she tried and failed to cover up the age spots on her face . . . He could see all that. Yet at the same time, the woman who had lain beneath him on the grass, her firm breasts filling his hands, existed in her still.

Who was that poet – *be not coy, but use your time*? Rosebuds. Herrick? Whoever the man was, he had it right, Harry thought – but he did not take things far enough. Being young himself, perhaps he did not realise that what he said was *always* true, even in the very worst of times.

He adjusted the blanket on his lap, looked up.

'If you send a message to let me know when you are going to visit, I'll make sure to be properly dressed,' he told her. Still, she said nothing. 'This is what we have, now, dear,' he said, and Evelyn's mouth trembled, but she kept her gaze on the wall, and would not reach out and take his hand. *Hell,* Harry thought. Struggling against the pain in his hips, he pushed himself half out of the chair so he could reach her. Her hand in his, half the size. Evelyn's hand. He felt her resist, but pulled it to him. Rubbing her palm on his freshly shaved cheek, he told her, his voice urgent, 'Feel me.'

Harry had a persistent feeling that something was missing.

He surveyed the room from the armchair with its new foam cushions. His back was to the party wall, the windows to his right, a small bookshelf and then the door to the left. It was a commanding position, from which he could see Evelyn's picture above the other bookcase near the bathroom door, the bed, newly made, the table next to it with the buzzer and the radio he never used and the glass of water he never drank. A picture of a ship hung on the long wall above the bed. The bathroom door was ajar – nothing of interest in there. What he was look- ing for was probably on or in one of the bookcases, or else it could be between him and the bed, on top of the TV – various papers and magazines and a book or two had piled up there, capped with the TV remote . . . It definitely wasn't the remote he was looking for, damn stupid thing. Or the magnifying glass. The walker was out of reach, parked near the bathroom. He bent forwards, pushed down hard on the arms of the chair and tried to stand. Nothing happened.

Then there was a woman in sunglasses wishing him a good morning.

'Daddy,' she told him, 'it's Louise.' She pushed the sunglasses up into her hair, and yes, it was her. But it startled him, some- times, to see what his children had become. She, the last of

279

three, the most trouble of all, now in her fifties and wearing sensible shoes.

'Do you remember? We're going to the square to see the tree. It's flowering.' Perhaps someone had said something about a tree, connected in some way to Evelyn. The manageress was always keen for him to take part in trips of one kind or another and a flowering tree was more his sort of thing than the donkey rescue centre excursion she and Krista had tried to involve him in a few days ago. So he told Louise yes, and forgot whatever it was he was looking for in the preparations for departure.

He and Louise shared a ride in the care-home minibus, which was first delivering a woman whose name he could not recall to the hospital (he'd been there, more than once after falls. Once, he'd split his head open and had to have stitches; he knew that much). The streets lurched and tore past, familiar, yet alien at the same time. It was like being in a film, and perhaps not a particularly good one: 'I'm a hundred and two,' the woman kept saying – shouting, really – to Louise, 'I'm a hundred and two and I can't hear a thing you say, not a damn thing!' Louise, because of the wheelchair arrangement, was sitting in front of him and next to the woman. She smiled and shook hands, and the woman began all over again: *I'm a hundred and two* . . . Before long, his own lips were mouthing her words, and he found he was half enjoying it: 'Not a damn thing! A hundred and two!'

It seemed very quiet once they had stopped at the hospital and handed her over. Harry fell asleep, woke only as the chair jerked into its tracks, then eased down the ramp at the back of the van. It was very bright outside.

Forty minutes, the driver said. The square looked rather familiar, and Louise, wearing sunglasses again, informed him that he and Evelyn used to live nearby.

That was before he moved to The Beeches.

She and Lillian had been sorting out the house, she said, and had found all sorts of odds and ends. Evelyn would not like that, he thought. She hated interference.

'Jottings. A lot of notes about Edward Thomas. Would you like to look at them when we get back? I could read them to you.'

'No,' he told her, 'I know I'm looking for something, but that's not it.'

She pushed him slowly up a path beside a deep green laurel hedge; to their right, mature silver birch trees were just bursting into leaf, and beyond them, across the road, stood well-tended Georgian terraces, cream-painted, almost but not quite uniform. The pavement was very uneven but Louise did her best to smooth out the bumps and he did his best to ignore the shooting pains they provoked in his back, as well as the unpleasant tingling in his feet. The breeze was light, the sky a heart-aching blue.

They passed through a wrought-iron gate into the garden, where the path was suddenly smooth, and the hedges made the space sheltered, noticeably calm. They had entered an all green, many-hued world. The grass to either side was luxuriant and dotted with daisies and daffodils. In the centre of the garden was a huge, dark-leaved evergreen oak, *Quercus ilex*, if he was not mistaken. To their left and right a Japanese maple, an aspen. A horse chestnut, a lime, and there in the shade, banks of glossy rhododendrons. All the trees were huge, except one, a whippy sapling with tender leaves, covered with white blossoms. They moved steadily towards it.

About three feet away from it, the chair stopped. Louise appeared and crouched down next to him. She pushed the sunglasses back into her hair and cupped her hand over his.

She told him it was called *Pyrus calleryana Chanticleer* – named for the Victorian missionary who discovered it and, because of the brightness of its autumn leaves, after a clear-singing bird. The blossom trembled as a breeze blew through it.

'Lovely. I'm sure she approves,' Harry said. Evelyn was away, he knew, though he couldn't remember exactly where.

'No, thank you,' he told Louise when she offered him a handkerchief.

'Do you hear the birds?' she asked, as they moved on slowly between other shrubs and trees.

'I do,' he told her. What was it about birds?

Casting the body's vest aside,
My soul into the boughs does glide . . .

For a moment, he saw his old teacher, Whitehorse, standing before the class in the dusty-bright light of the schoolroom. Heard his strong, clear voice:

There like a bird it sits and sings,
Then whets, and combs its silver wings.

The old words flowed through him as they moved on and round, and the garden, step by step from different angles, gradually revealed more of itself. He felt a kind of blessed emptiness. The sun warmed his face and the backs of his hands; he let his eyes close and slept again.

He and Evelyn were on holiday, in Devon in the summertime. They walked arm in arm on a path that took them past mounded rhododendrons and azaleas, past stately trees and broad lawns. On the hill behind them stood a sandstone manor house covered with purple wisteria, ahead of them an oak wood which shimmered with bluebells. Evelyn wore a light, sleeveless summer dress and a white cardigan, and big, film-star sunglasses. As they entered the wood she removed them, breathed deeply, turned to Harry, smiled.

'A good sleep?' Louise asked. She'd made daisy chains while he slept, and he let her put one round his neck.

There were three bales of garden peat in the back of the van, along with a coiled hosepipe wrapped in plastic, and a tray of small geranium plants, but the hundred-and-two-year-old woman was not there. The driver turned the radio on, some awful, jangling thing, and Harry woke from his next nap with a headache.

Did he want to sign up for an excursion to the duck ponds at Boughton tomorrow? No, thank you, he told the ghostly looking woman with huge glasses who was asking him. There was a cream tea afterwards, she said. But he did not feel like eating a cream tea tomorrow. And equally, he did not feel like eating today's lunch downstairs, or like eating whatever it was they brought up on a tray, and no, he did not want to be hauled out of the wheelchair or go to the bathroom and no, he didn't want to be read to . . . Thank goodness Louise got the message and left him to it. Because what he wanted to do was to read Evelyn's letter again. He must have put it somewhere on the nearby bookshelves. He twisted himself as far around as possible, examined the contents of the top shelf, then ran his fingers along the tops of the books so far as he could reach. Nothing.

She had not warned him she was going away, probably because she knew he'd worry. But then she had written to him, from France – that was it, France! – using six sheets of the hotel paper. He remembered clearly how Krista (or was it Samantha?) had brought the letter with his tea and three Jaffa Cakes, a wonderful surprise, and a huge relief to know why he had not seen Evelyn for so long. The envelope was well glued and his hands were useless, but he had not wanted to ask for help and eventually he'd slit it open using the nail file from his drawer. He had quite recently lost his glasses, so it was fortunate that Evelyn's writing was always so bold and clear.

Dear Harry,

I was not going to write since we are only here a week and I didn't want to confuse you, but Lillian insists a letter will reach home before we return. I am on a little holiday with her and Rosemary from the gardening club. As you can see from the paper, we are at the Hotel Paris, France. I'm writing from the hotel lounge – comfortable, if dark. Anything would seem dark after yesterday's visit to Versailles! I remember that when you and I visited the city we decided against the trip because of it being a tourist trap. We were right to be wary, but even so, I am very glad to have seen it now.

After an early breakfast coffee and baguette – still warm – we took the metro almost to the door, and queued about ten minutes to get in. It's vast. Everything is painted or gilded and bristling with statues. Marble, marble everywhere. The wallpapers! All handmade. Gold leaf and velour. In the Hall of Mirrors, the light comes at you from all sides, and it somehow makes you want to prance and sing. Of course, it's full of tracksuited hordes clutching their phones and cameras, but you can still feel what it would be like to walk though it watched by admiring courtiers. Though according to Lillian, back then they wandered through such magnificence pressing scented handkerchiefs to their noses against the smell of their own body odour and the chamber pots they kept everywhere. They had no toilets or proper plumbing! I'm glad Lillian only told us about this on our way out.

It seems that the physical side of life was very unpleasant back then. I know I do always complain about having to go to the hairdresser, but having a tower of hair stuck together with rotting ox fat would be far worse. Lillian, Rosemary and I all feel that another disadvantage of the royal life would be the lack of privacy. Waking up to a gilded ceiling would be insufficient compensation for having an audience gawping while you rub your eyes and prepare for the day. Of course, they were eventually executed. All in all, I feel content with my lot in comparison.

The shower in the hotel is feeble and hard to adjust. I still prefer a proper bath. I am very glad of the en suite at home and look forward to returning to it, though not to the long evenings. The next event is Louise's visit. I'm not sure how much of the family will come this time. After that, Valerie is planning something big to celebrate both of our birthdays. I love a celebration, but I'd prefer to ignore the reason for it, if it's to do with getting even older. As you'll agree, there's nothing to recommend it, especially if it involves a lingering decline. I do hope you are making the effort to get out and about.

Lillian fusses rather but deals with all practicalities, just as you always did. She doesn't seem to mind shepherding two old ladies, waiting for us to get ready. Yesterday she went shopping for a couple of hours and bought herself a very expensive blouse. Her French is still excellent after all these years. I commented on it, and she said she was glad her education had come in useful at last! She suggested we go past where you and I stayed in the Place de la République, but I thought it best not. I remember the boat trip we took on the Seine, the cathedral at Notre Dame, and the cabaret we attended the second night, and the perfect weather that day we took the train to Giverny. I have good memories of other trips too, including those early family holidays in bed and breakfasts in Devon and Cornwall, before we even had our own car. Happy times. I must say you were a good father to all the girls, burying them in the sand and such while I fell asleep in the sun. Louise was the lucky one in that we were able to take her abroad: do you remember her playing with those Spanish children and picking up the words she needed? But I'm wary of reminiscing. Rosemary agrees. The thing is to keep going forward for as long as you can, and not look back.

At home, I find the house very quiet these days, and the evenings long, so it has been a tonic to have company. It must be different for you, with the other inmates around you all the time, not that I imagine they are very entertaining. And it's a shame that you missed Versailles, but there was an enormous amount of walking. They have wheelchairs but the cobblestones looked very uncomfortable to be wheeled on. Even Lillian is exhausted! After all, as she pointed out, she is nearly seventy. I still remember the ward in Reading and you coming in to see us in your uniform, how she sicked up on it.

We return Monday. Lillian will fly home to Ed two days later. She left him all his meals in the freezer. He's never done a thing.

I will visit you when I have settled after all this travelling.

Love,

Evelyn

He had read the letter several times and he kept it within reach, in its envelope, with the French stamp, on top of the bookshelves. But now it was gone. Perhaps he had slipped it inside one of his books? He levered a few out and shook them: it was not in not the *Collected Poems of Edward Thomas*, or *The Nation's Favourite Poems*, or *Whyte's Treasury of Verse* . . . Someone had tidied it away or lost it, and he wanted it back . . . Because it had been lovely to think of Evelyn sitting in the hotel lounge and writing to him. Of Lillian taking her and her friend to Paris. And the bit about the plumbing and the hairdos – how she loved her comforts. Also it was very touching that Evelyn had acknowledged how well he used to organise their travel arrangements. And as well as that, she had mentioned the emptiness of the house, which was tantamount to admitting that she missed him . . .

He disagreed about too much reminiscing being a bad thing. He wanted to explain to her when she came next (soon, soon!) that reminiscence was one of the better uses of time when your movements were limited, though hers weren't yet, of course. She'd been to Versailles! What a thing. She was so very energetic, so full of life! He wanted the letter back. It wasn't in any of his books, or on the floor. It wasn't on the nearby bookcase, though of course it might have slipped down the back of it: that could well be what had happened. He gritted his teeth, twisted, got hold of a corner, and pulled it forwards. A small avalanche of books hit the floor and one of them knocked the waste bin over, but he still couldn't see right down behind the bookcase, which must be where Evelyn's letter was, since he'd looked absolutely everywhere else. He pushed again and the whole damn thing – top-loaded for convenience – fell over and then he tried to get his feet on the floor and get up and couldn't because they were strapped in and there was nothing to do but to press the red button.

'I want to speak to the manageress, and I want my letter back,' he told a girl with black hair dyed blue at the ends.

But it wasn't there, and the room was a real mess.

They wheeled him into the shady part of the garden while they tidied up. A tall woman lowered herself into a striped canvas chair opposite him.

'Harry,' she said, 'we've been over this several times before.' It was Sandra, he realised, when she removed her sunglasses and tucked them into her cleavage. She was awfully sorry, she said, they all were, and they had looked everywhere. She had nothing new to offer. Perhaps the letter had slipped from his lap onto the floor or even into the waste-paper basket, and then been accidentally thrown out? 'Whatever happened, Harry, it was an accident. Of course no one would knowingly do such a thing. But after all this time, I honestly don't think the letter is going to turn up . . . I know it is very upsetting.'

He had to accept that they didn't mean to lose it. And he could remember a great deal of it. But he still wanted it back, to have it in his hand.

'And the thing is, she wrote in it that she was visiting soon. But I don't think she has,' he told Sandra. There was something wrong with his voice. 'Has she? I'm worried about her. Could you please phone one of my daughters for me?'

Sandra squatted down on the grass in front of his wheelchair, held both of his hands in hers, and looked up into his face.

'Harry, you might have forgotten that there was some very sad news about Evelyn. She passed away almost two months ago, not long after she got back from her holiday.'

'That's impossible!' he told her.

'Valerie gave you the news,' Sandra said. 'It was a heart attack, and then her kidneys failed. She was very brave, and didn't suffer. Everyone agrees it was the way she would have wanted to go . . . '

Impossible! *The way she would have wanted to go*? Evelyn would never want any way of going. Sandra kept on looking up at him.

'Valerie was with her. The other two flew over right away. You were too frail to go to the memorial, but Louise just took you to see the tree they planted in her memory. And of course we can call her or Valerie or Lillian if you'd like.'

She was still holding his hands, and looking up into his face.

And for a moment it seemed as if Valerie might have told him about a phone call from the hospital in the middle of the night. That Evelyn had been *comfortable*, and still able to talk. And then – but if – surely there would have been a message for him?

No, it was impossible. Dear Evelyn – always so very ener-getic, full of life. Only this afternoon, she had kissed him in the bluebell woods, the air honey-sweet. She had just been to Paris. She remembered all their holidays.

He wanted his letter back.

support from the Access Copyright Foundation who assisted with research expenses, and from Vancouver Island University and the British Columbia Arts Council which enabled me to set aside the time to finish drafting it. As for emotional support, I am not sure where I would be or whether I would write at all without my husband Richard and my two children whose love, belief in me, and forgiveness of my absences make the whole enterprise possible.

Many people helped me research and then write *Dear Evelyn*. Heartfelt thanks are due to my friend Carole Miles who accompanied me on UK research trips, wearing out at least one pair of shoes while documenting land- and cityscapes with far better photographs than I would take; to Tony Jones, archivist at Emanuel School; to Colin Thornton of the Edward Thomas Fellowship for fielding my many questions about the poet and his life; to historians Simon Fowler and Colin Taylor for helping me understand and visualise the messy end of the Desert War; to the British Library for its wonderful maps, and to Battersea Public Library for its local archives; to Alison Harvey, SCOLAR archivist at the Cardiff University library; to Kate Fisher for her fascinating book *Birth Control, Sex, and Marriage in Britain 1918–1960*; to the late Alan Moorehead for his classic account, *The Desert War*, from which I borrowed the image of surrendering troops as butterflies, and to Edna Longley for her notes in *The Collected Poems of Edward Thomas*.

Several writer friends read various versions of the manuscript and supplied me with both encouragement and excellent advice, some of which I did not act upon, but all of which I appreciated: many thanks to Vicky Grut, Gillian Campbell, Lynne Van Luven, and Margaret Thompson, and also to those who answered an important question: Adina Hildebrant, Shirley Graham, Peter Levitt, and Maggie Zeigler. I'm grateful to Pamela Mulloy, editor at *The New Quarterly*, which published versions of four segments of the book while I wrestled with others.

I have been lucky with editors. John Metcalf from Biblioasis – acute, brilliant and tireless as ever – saw what I was really trying to do with this story and pushed me hard when necessary; without him and his faith in the project, *Dear Evelyn* would not exist. Likewise, Tara Tobler at And Other Stories always appreciated the essence of the book, while at the same time understanding – and passionately advocating for – what it needed in order to come to its final form. My final thanks go to everyone at And Other Stories and at Biblioasis for their dedication to imagination, language, story, and the ways they connect us and enrich our lives.

Dear readers,

As well as relying on bookshop sales, And Other Stories relies on subscriptions from people like you for many of our books, whose stories other publishers often consider too risky to take on.

Our subscribers don't just make the books physically happen. They also help us approach booksellers, because we can demonstrate that our books already have readers and fans. And they give us the security to publish in line with our values, which are collaborative, imaginative and 'shamelessly literary'.

All of our subscribers:

- receive a first-edition copy of each of the books they subscribe to
- are thanked by name at the end of our subscriber-supported books
- receive little extras from us by way of thank you, for example: postcards created by our authors

BECOME A SUBSCRIBER, OR GIVE A SUBSCRIPTION TO A FRIEND

Visit andotherstories.org/subscriptions to help make our books happen. You can subscribe to books we're in the process of making. To purchase books we have already published, we urge you to support your local or favourite bookshop and order directly from them – the often unsung heroes of publishing.

OTHER WAYS TO GET INVOLVED

If you'd like to know about upcoming events and reading groups (our foreign-language reading groups help us choose books to publish, for example) you can:

- join our mailing list at: andotherstories.org
- follow us on Twitter: @andothertweets
- join us on Facebook: facebook.com/AndOtherStoriesBooks
- admire our books on Instagram: @andotherpics
- follow our blog for news: andotherstories.org/ampersand/

Current & Upcoming Books